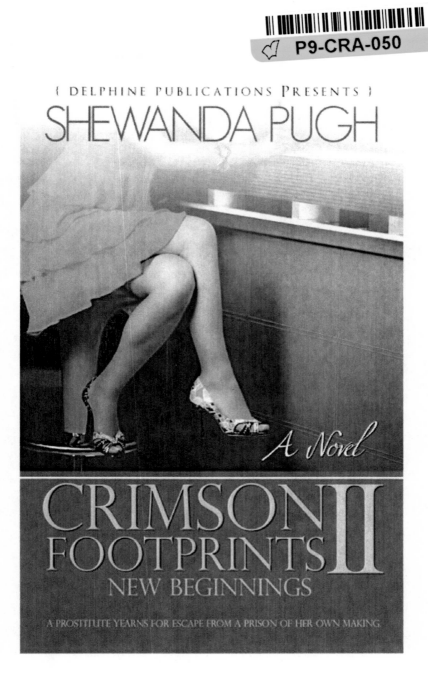

P9-CRA-050

{ DELPHINE PUBLICATIONS PRESENTS }

SHEWANDA PUGH

A Novel

CRIMSON II
FOOTPRINTS
NEW BEGINNINGS

A PROSTITUTE YEARNS FOR ESCAPE FROM A PRISON OF HER OWN MAKING

Crimson Footprints II: New Beginnings

Delphine Publications focuses on bringing a reality check to the genre urban literature. All stories are a work of fiction from the authors and are not meant to depict, portray, or represent any particular person Names, characters, places, and incidents are either the product of the author's imagination or are used fictitiously, and any resemblances to an actual person living or dead are entirely coincidental.

Crimson Footprints II: New Beginnings

© 2013 Shewanda Pugh

All rights reserved. No part of this publication may be reproduced, stored in or introduced into a retrieval system, or transmitted, in any form, or by any means (electronic, mechanical, photocopying, recording, or otherwise), without the prior written permission of both the copyright owner and the above publisher of this book.

ISBN: 13 - 978-0988709324

Published by: Delphine Publications

www.DelphinePublications.com

Layout: Write On Promotions
Cover Design: Odd Ball Designs
Editor: Alanna Boutin

Dedication

To Mom, who taught me one bit of Shakespearean truth: *It is not in the stars to hold our destiny but in ourselves.* And to my grandmother, who taught me another: *Hell is empty and all the devils are here.* Forward I venture, boldly.

ACKNOWLEDGEMENTS

For the initial creation of Tak, Deena, and all those of the *Crimson Footprints* world, I owe a lot of thanks. First, to Dr. Christine Jackson of Nova Southeastern University, whose encouragement and guidance proved invaluable in the early days.

To my Nova classmates, Stephanie Fleming, Lyndsay Dustan Prasad, Nichole Coombs, Racquel Fagon, Jenny Boyar, Tara Spiecker, Michael Bergbauer, Raymond Levy and more, whose voices and encouragement I still hear when writing.

For *Crimson Footprints II,* special thanks goes to Dr. Allison Brimmer and my twin sister from another mother, Shantrelle Pugh; both of whom helped me trudge through the mud on this one. Special thanks to my husband, Pierre, who suffers through and adores my idiosyncrasies in equal measure. Finally, and most of all, thanks to you, dear reader.

CHAPTER ONE

The distance between Milwaukee and Miami was just under fifteen hundred miles—1,469 to be exact. Tony knew it because he'd asked the trucker with the GPS on the dash. He had beef arms and a chest like a bull, but when he smiled, the trucker lit up like Christmas on the Commons.

Once, Tony had heard someone say, "Christmas on the Commons," but had no idea where the Commons was, though he assumed it festive. In any case, it sounded good to him, so he kept it, jotting down the phrase on a napkin and shoving it in his pocket for later. As of yet, there'd been no opportunity to use it aloud, but when it did arise, you better believe he'd have it.

In the first hour of their journey together, Tony learned his name—Michael—his wife's name—Chelsea—and that Chelsea couldn't have any kids. Michael was originally from Minnesota though he lived in Milwaukee, so he dragged out his *o*'s in that ugly way Minnesotans did. After twenty minutes of it, Tony felt ready to paw the ears from his head, so annoyed was he with the accent. But he was a good faker. Five years in a Bismarck group home had given him more *o*'s and "don't cha knows" from the Minnesota bullying twins Donovan and Bruce than he could stomach.

Than he could stomach.

He'd heard Miss Chester use that once, his English teacher back in Dickinson, and he'd jotted it down instantly. Tony used it when he could.

Mike the Trucker had been pretty nice to him so far, nicer than anyone since Mrs. Crabtree, his fourth-grade teacher, who had liked him enough to bring him a slice of cake from her son's graduation party. "Going to Northwestern," she'd said proudly, "on scholarship."

Tony did his best to feign interest in Mike the Trucker's stories—and there were lots, so he nodded or sighed when it seemed the right thing to do. But as time unraveled in the selfishly absentminded way it tended to, Tony grew anxious. It was taking far too long to get to Miami, and Miami was where he needed to be.

Mike the Trucker hadn't wanted to pick him up and had

threatened to call the police at the sight of such a young kid on the side of the interstate. But one go of Tony's well-rehearsed story, complete with measured sobs sprinkled in—and the genius part about running away and just wanting to get home—had Mike the Trucker's eyes watering in response.

And just as Tony hoisted himself up into the cabin of the self-proclaimed Thurmond & Co. 18-wheeler, he gave what would be his only warning.

"I won't stay if you call the police," Tony said. "I'll run. I just—I wanna get home to my mom, OK?"

He'd measured the pause just right. Mike nodded solemnly before offering a pinky to seal the deal. Tony raised a brow. He'd seen a pinky swear once in a Japanese anime cartoon Joe Rooks had smuggled in. But there'd been tits in there as well. Quickly, Tony hooked pinkies, sealing the deal.

Before flagging down Mike, Tony had practiced a few stories— one where his dad was a dirty cop, another where he hopped in and threatened to kill himself if he wasn't taken promptly to his destination. In the end, he rejected them all for being stupid in an obvious way.

Michael the Trucker was going as far as Atlanta—at least three-fourths of the way, and promised to take Tony there.

"We'll call your mother. Maybe she can meet us," Mike had suggested at the start of the trip.

Tony nodded. Every few hours he would go so far as to fake dialing his mother from a payphone. When he did, Michael stood near his 18-wheeler and waited eagerly for the news.

"She'll meet us," Tony announced, after attempting a collect call to Domino's Pizza. "She was crying and everything. So happy."

"But she didn't want to talk to me?" Michael asked incredulously.

Damn. He hadn't accounted for that.

"She was just so excited. I don't think it occurred to her. She

2

said she had lots of phone calls to make, people to tell."

Michael nodded slowly, as if trying to understand. "I can't imagine," he admitted. "How long ago did you run away?"

By the time he asked, Tony was already heading back to the passenger side of the truck. He swung himself up, using the footing for leverage, and climbed in. When Michael joined him, Tony answered.

"Been gone a long time. Three months."

Lies were best laced with truth, and three months was how long he'd been on the streets.

Michael nodded. "Well, let's get you home, kiddo. I know your mom must be anxious."

Despite that, he laced the next leg of the trip with questions; so many as to make Tony gnaw on his nails. He wanted to know everything about him—his age, his grade, why he'd run away. Lies poured from him like shit from an ass.

Shit from an ass.

That was another phrase he'd picked up somewhere. But as he thought about it, he realized it was none too reliable. Diarrhea, difficult bowel movements, and normal ones, all seemed different. So, he'd remove that expression from the rotation.

It occurred to Tony that most everything diminished from lack of usage. Truth telling was no exception. For him, lies came easier than anything—easier than food, water, or a decent place to sleep. Lies were the currency of his livelihood, and in that regard, he was rich beyond measure and had been since his mother's death.

Tony fingered the crumpled clipping in his pocket. Once again, lies would get him what he needed.

He peered out of the passenger window, marveling at the sight before him. He'd never been so far from the Midwest, had never been much of anywhere, in fact. Now that he was on the move, he found the thick way that people clustered together fascinating. Milwaukee, Chicago, Indianapolis. Great cities formed near bodies of water. Early settlements

3

required it; later ones liked it. He remembered that from school and could see why. As they drove along I-94, Lake Michigan shimmered at their side. Though Tony was sleepy he found his eyes couldn't close, so immersed was he in that Great Lake. Second largest by volume, third by surface area, it was the only Great Lake entirely in the United States. A ratty copy of *National Geographic* that had served as his pillow for three weeks taught him that.

Tony brought a hand to Michael's grubby window, cool to the touch, and imagined that he floated along, oblivious to time, in one of those great white yachts that dotted the waters. He stood in a pair of those shoes without laces, wooden deck damp beneath his feet. He supposed they wore white slacks and a Polo shirt of some sort, too, so that was what he'd wear. Most importantly, he'd stand at the wheel and feel the wind batter his neck as he looked outward to a limitless horizon and a sun rising instead of setting. He closed his eyes, and for a moment, it was real.

In Indianapolis they passed a river, unimpressive after the lake. Michael pulled into a roadside diner named Junie's, in Taylorsville, just south of the city, to stretch, gas up, and grab grub. When he offered Tony dinner, he tried his damnedest to be indifferent.

"Come on, kid. When's the last time you ate?"

Suddenly, there were no lies available. His last meal had been half a Big Mac, trashed outside a McDonald's in St. Paul. It didn't even have pickles. That was two days ago. His stomach cramped with the memory.

"Come on. They've got a meatloaf sandwich here that's to die for."

To die for. He'd heard the phrase before, but refused to claim it. He'd had death in his family, real death, and knew there wasn't much worth dying over.

Michael grinned wide enough to show gaps where two incisors should've been. He placed a hand on Tony's back and led him inside.

The meatloaf sandwich might've been good, but Tony would never know. A short lady with a shovel head and thick red lips brought it out on a plate so hot it scalded his fingers. Tony engulfed the thick and

4

meaty sandwich, made sopping with grayish gravy. He licked his fingers and asked for a second glass of water, hoping to fill the void left with the finish of the meal.

"You want some bread to sop up that gravy?" the woman asked, eyes on his scraped clean plate.

"Yes, please," Tony said, unable to believe his luck.

She brought three big white slices, and he used them to "sop up" the juices. She stood there as he ate, causing him to slow with the realization that he had an audience.

"Big appetite, huh?" she said, turning an eye on Mike.

He nodded, burger and fries on his plate untouched.

After gassing up and thumping tires with a baseball bat to check tire pressure, Michael jumped back behind the wheel of the truck. On a tight deadline, he had a cargo hold full of beef and grocery stores expecting him by the next afternoon. They would drive straight for Atlanta, stopping only for gas thereon out. So, with his stomach relatively settled, Tony snuggled into the door for a nap. Mike kept the cabin chilly and his radio squeaky, but sleep came easy for the boy who'd made due with sidewalks. When he did wake, night had turned to an uneven promise of daylight and Mike was shaking him up.

Nashville.

"Call your mother," he said. "Tell her we're close."

In Nashville, Tony told him there was no answer. But when he said it, Michael fidgeted and hesitated and asked him to try again. Worried that he might be prone to action, Tony ran through the ruse again and pretended to catch her on the second try, going so far as to gush joy and promise the dial tone that he'd see her soon.

Four and a half hours later, they pulled into a Waffle House in Marietta, a suburb of metro Atlanta. There, they would meet Tony's dead mother.

"Do you see her?" Mike demanded, following him into the tiny diner.

Tony scanned the sparse crowd. An old white couple idling over coffee, three fat women, all black and pressed into a booth, and a single middle-aged man, balding and broad-bellied in his Georgia Tech tee. No one looked like a proper substitute for a long lost mom.

"No," Tony said. "I'll wait here, though. You go on. She'll be in soon." Tony grinned in what he hoped was a disarming fashion. "She's late for everything, you know."

Michael scowled. "How 'bout we check the bathroom?"

He was a tall man with combat boots and a wide stride; Tony hadn't noticed how tall until just then. Mike barreled through the restaurant more than walked.

"Can I help you, sir?" a big-bottomed waitress called, rushing after.

Mike burst into the women's restroom.

"What's her name?" he demanded.

Tony floundered.

"Meh—Meagan," he stammered. He'd never known a Meagan, but he liked the name anyway.

"Meagan!" Mike yelled. "Meagan, are you here?"

Tony shot a pained look at the thin crowd, their attention now on them.

"Mike, I told you! She'll be here soon."

He shot Tony a look. "Meagan! Meagan!"

With a snort of impatience, he pushed past and back out to the parking lot, where he, no doubt, resumed screaming again. Tony rushed after.

"Meagan! Are you here?"

He turned to Tony. "How old are you?"

6

"Twelve."

Michael's eyes narrowed. "Before you said you were thirteen."

"I—I will be. My birthday's in a few days."

"Meagan!" Mike shouted wildly at the parked cars. "Your twelve-year-old boy is here! He's alone! Come all the way from Minneapolis by himself! How could you be late?"

A family climbing out of a nearby station wagon gaped openly. Tony's face burned with shame.

"Please stop," he begged. "She'll be here. Soon. I just—she'll be here soon."

Mike stared down at him, blond and snow-white bristles of a moustache twitching ever so slightly.

"You understand that I can't leave a twelve-year-old boy in the middle of Georgia," he said. "It ain't right."

Tony's heart pounded. He hadn't calculated for a sense of decency.

"Okay. Here," Tony said, heading for the payphone. "I'll call her. I'll call and see where she is. Just—wait."

Tony left the man looming in the sunny parking lot as he made his way to a defaced set of antiquated phones. He dialed a bunch of random numbers and faked his way through a conversation. Then he returned.

"See? She's on her way."

But Michael only glared, face near-black in the shadows of an overhead tree.

"There is no mother. At least not one you're willing to call."

Tony went cold.

"What?" he managed.

7

"You didn't dial enough numbers." Mike headed for the diner again, strides quick, purposeful.

"What are you doing?" Tony cried, running after him.

"What I should've done in Milwaukee! Calling the police!"

The police.

Tony bolted.

Across the parking lot and four lanes of honking cars, through a thicket of oaks, he flew. A shopping center emerged quick on the other side. Tony slipped in, breathless, and smoothed out his wild, two-toned brown hair. Only then did he wheeze in relief.

CHAPTER TWO

It took Tony a week to get from Atlanta to Miami. Whole days of walking at a time, interspersed with a few rides. Walking first, then the old man with a lisp who took him from Smyrna to Macon, before letting him know he expected something in return. What he got was a shiner and a pair of busted nuts, free of charge, thank you very much.

After spilling from the old man's Camaro, Tony footed it all night. Along 75 he went, low and in the brush, too afraid to try another ride, too afraid to sleep. At sunrise he started on the shoulder, a wary eye on the lookout for cops. From there it'd been a series of short hops—Perry to Valdosta with a wannabe rocker, Valdosta to Gainesville on foot, Gainesville to Miami in a car. The last one had been sheer luck. A rowdy group of frat boys from New York had pulled over, half drunk and chanting on their way to a Marlins-Yankee game.

They asked Tony tons of questions and gaped at him as if they might poke him with a stick out of horrified fascination. His age, his ethnicity, whether he'd ever had sex. He'd been honest with them about his age—eleven—which impressed them and made him want to tell more. He admitted he was black and white, that his parents were dead and that the closest he'd ever come to sex was the tits he once saw in anime fashion.

They had a bucket of KFC extra crispy that they passed around, letting Tony get his fill from it and the case of Bud Light wedged between his legs. Pretty soon, his lips were loose, causing him to mouth off all sorts of truths—that he'd run away from a group home in Bismarck, that he was in search of a woman he was convinced was his aunt, and that he had no other prospects should it turn out not to be true. At their prompting, he pulled a newspaper clipping from his pocket and passed it around, yelping when one of them grabbed it harshly.

"Definitely looks like you," one slurred. "Except the tits. Excellent tits." The words sloshed roughly.

"I have to find her," Tony said, ignoring his irritation as he tucked the picture away. "She's the only family I have. And I know she's my family."

"You got an address?" the driver said, a Bud in his grasp as he drove.

"Sure. From the Internet."

The driver glanced up, unmistakably impressed. "Well, then, little guy, let's burn it to Miami."

"To Miami!" one shouted.

"To Miami!" they echoed.

Tony settled in, did a tug on his seat belt, and made up his mind to close his eyes. Gainesville to Miami was three hundred and thirty-eight miles, five hours according to the GPS. Five hours to a house, hope, and the absence of hunger. Five hours more and Tony Hammond would have a home.

CHAPTER THREE

Takumi Tanaka grabbed a bag of butter-laden popcorn from the microwave, shut the door, and dumped the contents in a bowl before dousing it in hot sauce. He took it, the salsa and chips he'd uncovered in the cabinet, and carried it all to the coffee table. Absentmindedly, he shoved aside the pristine vegetable platter his wife had made and arranged his findings in their place. Afterward, he moved on to the bar, made himself a rum and Coke—heavy on the rum—and settled down at the flat screen for the game. The Miami Marlins and New York Yankees met momentarily in what he hoped would be a massacre. After all, New Yorkers could be damned annoying.

It was Saturday morning, which meant the girls were gone. After dropping their daughter Mia off at ballet practice, his wife, Deena, usually headed to work for a few hours before picking her up later. Today, the girls had plans for an afternoon of shoe shopping and a trip to the pet store for a replacement goldfish after Pokie, his daughter's old one, went belly-up a week ago. The game, a few drinks, and an afternoon of food his wife would have a conniption about if she knew he was eating it, were all within sight.

But seconds into the first inning the doorbell rang.

He decided to ignore it.

It rang twice more, the quick and obnoxious ring of a person who's lost patience, and Tak leaped to his feet with a groan. By the time he crossed the living room and foyer to open the broad double doors, he was muttering to himself about time and the point of having gates.

Tak threw open the door and glared at nothing. After a blink of confusion, he looked down to find a boy, short and golden, with gold-flecked eyes and the thickest brown hair unencumbered in a wavy, shoulder-length afro.

"I don't want cookies, and I gave to the Boys and Girls Club last week," Tak blurted.

The boy stared.

"I . . . uh, don't . . . have anything to sell you."

It sounded like an apology.

"Oh."

"I'm looking for Deena Hammond."

Tak raised a brow. "Why? What do you want with my wife?"

The boy's eyes widened. Tak somehow encouraged the kid at a moment when his aim had been the opposite. A shout rang out from the next room, and Tak strained to hear vestiges of the game.

"So, she's your wife?" the boy whispered eagerly.

"Uh, yeah," Tak said, eyes keen on seeing whether the Yankees would use Villanova or Rousseau as their starting pitcher. He couldn't tell from where he stood.

"Her, right?"

The sound of crumpled paper caught Tak's attention. The kid fumbled in his pocket before coming away with a stack of clippings that shook in his hand. He turned them to face Tak, holding it just below his eyes.

He held an old picture of Tak's wife from an issue of *Architecture Digest*, her grinning as she held up a plaque. He remembered it from a ceremony in Phoenix where she was honored with the Young Architect of the Year Award. They'd done a full bio spread on her, making a fuss of her difficult upbringing. As his father's protégé and the principal architect of the single most desirable address in South Florida, the sordid details of Deena's life—worthy of a full seven pages—and her shy smile on the cover—helped create what would become *Architecture Digest's* best-selling issue in recent history.

"Yeah, that's her," Tak said.

The boy swallowed visibly. "Good."

He folded the pages neatly and placed them in his pocket.

"Then you must be my uncle." Tony extended a hand. "I'm Anthony Hammond Jr. Maybe you knew my father."

CHAPTER FOUR

Tak opened the cupboard and frowned at the selection of canned goods. He closed it and opened another, filled with his wife's Raisin Bran, his daughter's Saturday morning Cocoa Puffs, and the Wheaties he ate by the shovel full. Mrs. Jimenez, his maid since childhood, was out for the weekend, so really, there were few other options.

"Anything's okay," the boy mumbled from the table.

But Tak frowned at the loose way fabric hung from limbs on the kid. Nephew or not, he wasn't feeding a starving child a bowl of cereal.

Remembering the lasagna from the night before, three thick layers of tangy sauce, ground sirloin and blended cheeses, he pulled it out. Tak microwaved a palm-sized square and placed it before Anthony Jr. with a glass of milk before taking a seat across from him.

"Eat as much as you want, OK? The whole pan if you like."

Tony nodded, cheeks already stuffed with food.

"Thanks," he said, bits spewing.

Tak glanced at his watch, then the door. Thankfully, his wife wasn't coming home straightaway. The boy ate in silence, unperturbed by the audience. A lifetime away, an announcer shouted enthusiasm for a wholly inconsequential game.

When Tony finished his plate, he rose and grabbed more from the glass pan on the counter. He warmed it, brought it to the table, and found his seat again.

"Where do you live?" Tak said.

The boy licked sauce from his fingers. "I don't live anywhere. Used to live in a group home."

The sound of fork-scrapping-plate filled the silence. He took his milk in big gulps, as if afraid Tak might change his mind and take it.

"So," Tak chewed on his lip, "you caught the bus over?"

Tony shook his head. "Hitchhiked."

Tak stared. "You . . . *hitchhiked?*"

"Yeah. From Bismarck." He smacked his lips in appreciation.

"Bismarck . . ." Tak trailed stupidly.

"North Dakota," he said. "That's where my group home was."

Tak squeezed his eyes shut. A dull throb started at his temples and radiated outward.

"I don't understand. I thought you said you were from here." He massaged his temple vigorously.

"Not me. My dad. I've never seen the place. Beautiful though. I can see why people make such a fuss about it."

The boy was twelve, tops, but talked as though he were forty. Lived as though he were forty, too, judging by the offhanded way he'd just hitchhiked from Bismarck.

"So . . . did you grow up in Bismarck?" Tak ventured.

"Yeah. Well, in the Dakotas for a while. I lived in Rapid City, Sioux Falls, and Bismarck for a good long while."

"But where's your family?" Tak insisted.

"*You're* my family."

The boy scraped up the last of his lasagna and returned to the pan for thirds. Tak followed him with his eyes, unable to keep the skepticism from his voice.

"Besides us. Where's your mother, for instance?"

"Dead. Died in a three-car pileup when I was seven."

14

Something like panic surged in Tak. Not just from the kid's confidence, but from his appearance—especially his appearance. Bronzed skin, wild brown locks wavy and streaked with auburn—and the molten brown eyes, far too close to his wife's for comfort. All of that was in addition to the unequivocal evidence that was his name, the same as his wife's dead brother.

"Where's your mother's family, Tony? Here? In Miami?"

Tony shoved his plate in the microwave and faced him. "Mom was a foster kid, like me. Didn't have family."

Tak pinched the bridge of his nose and sighed. It was then that Tony looked past him and into the hall just beyond the kitchen. There were pictures there, and he ventured toward them, wide-eyed, enamored. Tak followed him and together, they stared at a family portrait. Deena on the left, Tak on the right, baby Mia in the middle, gurgling between the two.

Tony brought a hand to the picture and touched Deena's face, eyes unblinking, entranced.

What was he thinking? Feeling? Wanting? Whatever it was, did they have it to give?

A jingle of keys at the door interrupted Tak's thoughts. The sound made him freeze, breath stolen as he waited.

His daughter Mia spilled in first, dashing at the sight of him, a tangle of jet-black mane at her back. Behind her, Deena fumbled, fussing with the lock, a Macy's bag in one hand, a fish bowl in the other.

"Hey, let me help you with that," Tak said, rushing to her side.

It was his hope to cut off her view, prep her for what was to come, but as it turned out, he never got the chance.

"Oh, Mommy, look! There's a boy in the hall!"

Deena lifted her head, confused, before her gaze settled on Tony. Her lips parted, a myriad of emotions overwhelming her face, before the fishbowl ended up crashing to the floor.

15

CHAPTER FIVE

"Have you eaten, yet?" Deena whispered, hands clasped beneath the kitchen table. She clenched them to stave off the shaking and reminded herself periodically to breathe.

"Yeah. Your husband gave me some leftover lasagna. It was really good. Thanks."

They were alone, Deena and Tony, as Tak had put on a cup of coffee, flushed another in a long line of dead goldfish, and whisked Mia away next door.

Tony went silent for a moment, gaze lowered thoughtfully before returning to her face. "Did you make it?" he asked conversationally. "The lasagna?"

"What? Oh. Yeah." Deena shifted.

"Then you're a good cook."

He stood, unfolded really, his long narrow frame like that of the brother she once had.

"You want me to make you a cup of coffee?" he asked.

"Make what?" she said, certain she'd misheard.

"Coffee. Do you want me to pour you a cup of coffee?" He nodded toward the already-filled pot. "Seems like you need it."

Deena sat up straighter. She was used to taking extra precautions with Mia, a boisterous and inquisitive kindergartner, and would've never let her pour coffee. But he was no five-year-old.

"How old *are* you?" Deena whispered.

He was opening cabinets now in search of cups. "Eleven," he said. "Eleven and a half, really."

She did the math quickly. Her brother had been dead for ten years, nearly ten and a half. She couldn't imagine him having a child and not telling her, even if he had been a child himself.

"My brother never had a baby," she announced. "He would have said so."

Tony looked at her, staring with eyes that were hers—wide and bronze and tapering up like a smile.

"He didn't want me," he said and turned back to the cupboard. "You can understand that. Too young to be a dad."

Deena sputtered at his obscene maturity.

"Want you or not, he would've said something! He wouldn't have—left you."

Deena and her siblings had been raised without parents and knew the heartache of it. They could never do that to another.

Right?

Tony pulled a white coffee cup from the cabinet and filled it with dark brew.

"Try not to be angry," he said. "He didn't know the whole story. Mom was a foster kid, living with a foster family. But they kicked her out once they found out she was pregnant—bad influence on the other children or something. Anyway, she went from home to home, getting kicked out or running away, or whatever was going on, you know? And all the while waiting on public assistance, an apartment, all that. When Housing gave her a place, she started looking for my dad again, so she could tell him about me. But by then, this was the only trace of him."

He set the mug before Deena and dug in his pockets, coming away with a sheet of newspaper. She took it, unraveling with shaking fingers, not wanting to see, but wanting.

Her brother, sixteen and smiling in a picture taken months before death. Above him was the headline seared to her memories with grief: *Liberty City Teen Found Slain*. Beneath him were the details of his murder and discovery atop a heap of garbage.

"Why do you keep this?" Deena whispered.

17

"It's the only picture I have of him."

Sniffling, Deena smoothed out the clip purposefully, set it on the table, and rose. She hesitated only a moment before grabbing her purse and keys and brushing past Tak on the way out. She hadn't noticed when he'd returned.

"Dee? Where're you going?"

She turned on him, their space in the hall narrow as they stared at each other. "There's only one person I can think of who would know whether this is true or not. One person still alive, anyway."

He glanced past her to the kitchen where Tony sat.

"Let me go with you," he said.

Deena started for the door again.

"Stay with Tony. I'll be back."

CHAPTER SIX

The drive from tree-lined Coral Gables to seedy Overtown was twenty minutes long, a short romp up I-95, as the sun made a hasty retreat from the sky. It took Deena thirty-five, with the stop at McDonalds, before she reached her destination.

The streets narrowed with her arrival in Overtown. If Liberty City was the bowels of Miami, then Overtown was the back end, split like an ass by dodgy old railroad tracks in the place once known as Colored Town. Deena could feel eyes on her, the eyes of the city, wide and threatening, as she crept down the streets, searching for one of their own. An outsider now, no longer poor, not really disadvantaged. She supposed they could smell her; smell her money, her fear and what she risked, just by coming among them.

She used to live in a place like this. Back then, poverty embraced her, as the scent of death and rank were as much her home as the house she held keys to. She knew them intimately, though they couldn't tell it now. Without money, without chance, without anything except fear and pain, both gifts given to them in abundance.

Deena drove at a crawl's pace; the narrow, brightly colored shacks with tattered fences lining either side of her. Dark eyes stared, dark eyes with black faces, waiting, promising.

A man of forty or fifty, shirt tattered, shorts frayed, both yellowed and smeared in dirt, began to walk alongside the car, keeping pace with her window. He kept an even gait, gaze unblinking, expectant.

Deena turned down a side street, then another, before he stopped, content to stand in the road and watch her. On porches, black teens sat or stood, drinking from containers in paper bags, hunched over dice games, or peering, hand poised above a pocket as they watched her pass. A regular Wild West in the heart of Miami.

Up ahead, two brunettes walked, one in a black bra, red mini, and fishnet stockings, the other in knee-high black boots, silver panties with "Hustler" scrawled across the ass, and a plain white tee, torn short and baring the bottom half of too big tits. Deena pulled up alongside them driving at the pace they walked.

The women glanced at her. One smiled; the other frowned.

"Hey, cutie," said the one in fishnet. "You looking for someone to play with? You and your man, maybe?"

Deena looked past her, to the one outside in her panties.

"I need to talk to you. Get in the car."

She rolled her eyes. "Working, Deena. And talking to me costs. Just like with all the other tricks."

Deena sighed. "Even about Anthony?"

Deena's sister froze, eyes narrowed.

"What about Anthony?"

Deena shot a distrustful look at the girl in fishnet before turning back to Lizzie. "Get in the car and I'll tell you."

Lizzie shot her friend a reluctant look. "I'll just be a sec."

"Hurry up," the girl warned. "You know how he is."

Deena unlocked the door, and Lizzie jumped in, tugging on the shirt that exposed her bottom cleavage.

"What?" Lizzie demanded.

"What do you know about Anthony having a kid? Is that something you've heard before?"

Lizzie stared.

"Maybe," she finally admitted. "Why?"

"Because there's a boy at my house claiming he's his son. So I need to know when you first heard this."

"I dunno. Long time ago."

Deena shook her head. "Do better than that."

"Well, I really don't know! And you're holding me up," Lizzie snapped.

"Dammit, Lizzie!" Deena's palm slammed into the steering wheel. "Do you think I'd even be in this shit hole if . . ."

Her words trailed just as she contemplated tattooing her sister in the eye with a fist.

"All right, all right," Lizzie said. "Anthony was still alive, okay? And dating this girl. She had a stupid boy name, like Reggie or something. And when she *supposedly* came to him and said she was pregnant, he was pissed. End of story."

"Supposedly? What's the hell's that mean?"

"Just what I said. I didn't hear it from him. It's what people on the street said. Anyway, nobody believed it was his. She was into Anthony, but," Lizzie grinned, "no girl with any sense would get serious about him."

When Deena didn't share her smile it quickly faded.

Lizzie glanced pointedly at the clock on the dash. "We done yet?"

"I think he's Anthony's son. He looks like Anthony."

"Well, God help him if he's one of us."

With a laugh like a snort, Deena reached for the burger in the backseat and handed it to her sister. She took it, tore the paper open, and swallowed it in four bites.

"Tell Mia, Auntie says 'hi.'"

"Yeah, okay."

Lizzie dropped the trash where she sat and opened the passenger-side door.

"Take care of yourself," Deena called. "And be careful!"

21

Crimson Footprints II: New Beginnings

Lizzie slammed the door behind her without answering.

CHAPTER SEVEN

With Tony parked in front of the TV marveling at the high definition and broad selection of channels, Tak rounded the block with his cousin John's new wife, Allison. Tak's daughter, Mia, was back at the newlywed's home, contentedly roughhousing with the chocolate lab they'd adopted the month before. Tak had the sneaking suspicion that the dog was John's temporary fix for a wife who'd increasingly hinted at the immediacy of her biological clock.

"How old is this kid?" Allison asked, heels clicking on cement.

"Eleven."

"And what state did he come from?"

"North Dakota."

"How long has he been at your house?"

Tak shrugged. "Two hours is my guess."

"Okay. Well, in twenty-two more you can be prosecuted for harboring a runaway."

"Well, shit."

"Shit's right."

On either side of them, massive, gleaming, two- and three-story Italian Mediterranean mansions with lush gardens, grand porticoes, red-tiled roofs, all stood pretentious alongside adjacent pools, tennis courts, private docks, more. In fact, the street where Deena chose to design their masterpiece of a home rested on a single strip of land, giving each residence exclusive access to the bay it jutted into—a bay which, incidentally, spilled into the Atlantic Ocean. Usually, at least one family vacation a year consisted of sailings to the Caribbean with a departure from the Tanaka backyard. Tak needn't any more reminders beyond that to show him how fortunate he'd been in this lifetime. The wife, daughter, and a multitude of zeros in his bank statement provided ample evidence, as well.

Eh, well. He supposed he was due for another round of misfortune sooner or later. His old car accident was but a flicker of a memory.

"Tell me," Allison said, "your estimate before we get back in front of the wife. Is it possible that he's her nephew?"

They stopped just before the Tanaka home, a sleek white domicile modeled after Frank Lloyd Wright's *Fallingwater*. Before them were a series of cantilevers—jutting, curved floors cascading like spiral stairs—segmented by waterfalls that only appeared to run through the house. All of it nestled deep into a painstaking two-acre re-creation of tropical nature. It was his wife's great masterpiece, heralded on the cover of *Design Today*, prompting her to earn the unofficial title of Wright's heir, which she quickly shied away from.

"Crazy as it sounds," Tak said, "I think he might be her nephew. I don't see how, but it looks that way."

Allison glanced at him, brown eyes tinged with worry. "Listen. I know you're a good guy, better than most. But kids like this—broken kids—they lie. A lot. So just guard yourself against the possibility that what he's saying might be a carefully constructed fairy tale."

She followed him up the walkway, red Prada heels loud on brick, and waited for Tak to unlock the door. But before he could, she placed a hand over his.

"You have to call the police. There's no two ways about it. He's a runaway. If you harbor him, they'll charge you."

Tak sighed, the weight of possible outcomes heavy like a burden on his shoulders.

"She'll never forgive me," he said, "if I call the police, and they haul him back across the country."

Allison gave him a smile, small and sad. "But you have to. There's no other way."

~*~

Despite the lateness of the hour, when Deena returned from

24

driving aimlessly, both Tak and Allison waited on the couch.

"Where's Tony?" Deena said, dropping her purse on the coffee table, a molten sterling silver capital "T" of her own design.

"He's sleeping in the guest room." Tak stood and cast a wary glance back at Allison.

"Listen. I called Allison to, uh, give us some perspective on this. Some legal advice."

Deena stared at him, level. "Good. Because Lizzie verified what Tony told me. That his mother was pregnant and dating Anthony."

Allison stood, too.

"Deena, sweetheart, you need to call the police. You can't just have him here, living. He's a runaway. Unaccounted for."

Deena whirled on her. "And when I call? What will they do?"

Allison froze. "Well—it depends. They—"

"What will they do?" Deena demanded.

Allison dropped her gaze. "Take him to a juvenile detention center and hold him till extradition."

"Lock him up?" Deena cried. "He's not a criminal! He's a boy! A little boy!"

"Dee—"

She turned on Tak. "You think I'm gonna let them arrest him? You think this is a good idea?"

"Dee, let's just get all the facts, okay? Just . . . let her talk."

Tak placed a hand on her arm. It felt foreign, cool on suddenly hot skin.

Allison rushed to fill the silence. "We can file charges," she said.

"Have the order stayed. We can file a petition for temporary custody, but we have to cooperate with law enforcement. And you have to prove you have legal standing. Not a hunch."

"Which means what?" Tak said.

"A DNA test. But first you have to report his appearance here. Then we work on a stay of extradition, keeping him in Florida. We can beat the judge to a DNA test and, should it come back the way we're expecting it to, get to work on temporary custody. How's that sound?"

Allison pushed the blonde hair from her face, skin paler than usual. Tak squeezed Deena's limp hand and pushed on when it became clear that she wouldn't speak.

"It sounds good. Real good. And, as always, thanks for the help."

He released Deena and ushered Allison to the door.

"No problem. We'll keep Mia tonight and longer if needed."

Once out of earshot, Allison turned to him in the shadows of the hall. "This is a lot, Tak, I know. What you're doing for Deena is tremendous."

"I'm wrapping my mind around it still. But if it were my brother's kid or John's . . ."

"I know." She placed a hand on the doorknob.

"How is he, anyway?" Tak asked.

Allison pulled a face. "John's still John," she said, which he took to mean that they were still at odds over her sudden want to have a baby. The shadow across her face confirmed as much.

"Take her to Traced," Allison said sharply. "It's a DNA testing lab on Eighth and Biscayne. They'll look closed but just bang on the door. Ask for Chuck and tell him I sent you. Tell him you need results by noon tomorrow. They do the processing on site, so it's possible. He'll bitch, but just stand there and wait, and eventually he'll change his mind. Remind him if you have to that he owes me. Keep in mind that in twenty-four hours we're all aiding and abetting."

CHAPTER EIGHT

Lizzie thundered up the stairs, white boots clanking, hand yanking on an electric blue mini in wet latex. Hall lights flickered with the sizzle of old wiring as grimy, peeling, yellow and narrow walls threatened to brush her on either side. The air sat thick and funky, a putrid mangle of piss, vomit, smoke, and cheap booze. Three landings up, Lizzie found her door, unlocked a series of intricate bolts that would prove ineffective with a strong kick, and stepped into her apartment.

She hated her roommate.

The thought occurred to her every time she opened the door. Old blankets met her like a welcome mat. Empty Gulp cups, Big Mac wrappers, panties, towels, DVDs, boots, pumps, sandals, and condom wrappers layered the floor in an uneven carpet. On the single bed they shared, always unmade, the assortment of clothes she'd gone through and dismissed lay heaped in mounds, alongside a pile of battered circulars, a sippy cup, and a baby doll. Kit's three-year-old must've been visiting again.

Lizzie yanked off her go-go boots at the door, using the frame for balance, and tiptoed to the bed, cursing all the while. She didn't know how Kit managed to bring tricks to the apartment when there was hardly space to fit 'em. Knowing her roommate, she probably sucked 'em off in the hall and left a cum-filled condom for Mr. Parks, the super.

Lizzie waded over to the radio mounted on a precariously balanced plastic shelf and turned on Hot 105 for the Sunday afternoon funk fest. From there she took a steaming shower, melting as much as washing off the scent of her work, before heading for the lone room of the flat to start in on the cleaning. It was slow and tedious work. She couldn't understand why someone would choose housekeeping over taking a few blasts in the ass and calling it an afternoon. In fact, Lizzie knew a Guatemalan whore who worked under the bridge, thirty-five and looking sixty. She used to clean houses over in Brickell till her boyfriend turned her to tricking. "Twenty-five hundred a day" she claimed, versus the two hundred and fifty under the table she made a week scrubbing toilets. But one look at that pit-faced junkie told Lizzie that if her pimp had twenty-five hundred in his pocket, no more than a quarter had come from the Guatemalan whore living on her back.

Lizzie bagged trash, tossed dishes in the sink, and stopped every so often to shake her ass to music. When she uncovered a wad of weed in a fuchsia pump, she headed straight for the apartment's lone closet and yanked open a door that immediately swung off its hinge. A roach scurried out, and she stomped it before lifting a stack of folded dresses for the Black & Mild cigars underneath. Armed with the tobacco and a teaspoon-size portion of leaves, she hopped and hurdled to the yellowed kitchen counter left of the front door, laid out a cigar, pulled a knife from the kitchen counter, cut it open, and emptied out the cigar in a miniature basin. She then lined the marijuana in a neat little row, resealed the cigar with saliva, lit it on the pilot, and rushed to the opposite side of the room. With her blunt balanced on the sill, Lizzie yanked open the grimy window for a view of the littered and narrowed alleyway beneath. A deep tote followed.

Years ago in the very same alley, she'd fucked tricks on a shadowy wall, traded needles filled with smack, and slept on a stretch of tarp when she couldn't find a bed for the night. She'd met her roommate Kit in that same alleyway and bonded in addiction.

Lizzie tapped off the ashes from her miniscule blunt and rubbed a life-worn face. Twenty-six. Twenty-six fucking years old and all she had was a body fingered more than a grand piano at Berkeley, a garbage bag full of badly cleaned clothes, and track marks that looked like a tiger mauling. In contrast, she only needed to walk outside to see what her sister had managed by twenty-six; it blinded in sunlight and gleamed at night, like a second sun they were all compelled to rotate. *Skylife*. The gem of Miami's skyline.

Lizzie flicked off more ashes. Inadvertently, her gaze fell to a stark white card underneath her foot. She retrieved it and snorted with an incredulity that would never waiver. A wedding invitation on behalf of one Keisha Hammond and Steven "Snowman" Evans. His dumb ass had even gone so far as to put his nickname on the invite. Lizzie tossed it; no doubt she'd tease him about it when he stopped by that night, like usual. She'd never heard of a pimp who neglected to collect from his hoes.

The door behind her opened. Lizzie jumped and stumped out the blunt on her cousin's wedding invitation. A sigh of relief escaped her at the sight of Snow instead of Kit, whose weed she'd stolen.

"What the fuck I tell y'all about keeping this place together?" Snow cried, six feet tall, dark and filling the doorway.

He kicked a mountain of clothes, catapulting dirty panties and plastic cups, before stepping in and slamming the door behind him.

"It's Kit. I keep telling you. Just look around. Whose shit you see?"

Lizzie retrieved the stumped nub of a blunt and crossed the room to relight it.

"Tell that dirty-ass hoe to handle this shit before I come give her some encouragement."

"Get a fucking canary," Lizzie said and burned fingertips on the stovetop, so short was her blunt. She cursed.

"It's a parakeet, you fucking idiot."

Snow rounded the corner to join her, bald no longer by choice but necessity, brows, moustache, and beard still sharp and looking penciled in. He took the blunt from her and lit it.

"And if you read half as good as you sucked a fat one you'd know that."

Blunt sparked, he tucked it between his lips, pinched in his fingertips.

"Speaking of which," already his hands pulled at the button of his jeans. "Go head and choke on it."

He sucked on the blunt until nothing remained. Four big totes turned it to ash. Lizzie scowled before frowning down at the fat and ashen lump he pulled from jeans and plaid boxers. He shook the wad at her, dick and balls all in one hand, and her lips curled inadvertently. Still, she dropped to her knees, as compelled as she'd been fifteen years ago, at the age of eleven.

Eleven.

Lips around Snow's cock, her mind drifted to her dead brother, who once tried to kill him. She then thought of the child Anthony might or might not have. Did he look like him? Any kid of Anthony's would have that stupid silly grin. It would be nice to see that again.

Shewanda Pugh

"Hell, yeah. Suck that. Shit, yeah," Snow grunted.

She imagined him with bronzed hair, wild as a summer storm, and brown eyes bright and flecked with gold. She imagined him a replica of the brother who'd loved her and would've killed to protect her. And suddenly, she had to know for herself if he existed.

Snow gripped her ponytail, a wad of limp brown hair, and thrust furiously into her open mouth. He snapped her head back with a yank, pumping deep with the intention of making her choke. Lizzie wouldn't give him the satisfaction. Instead, she concentrated on breathing, mind floating, resisting, until reflexes refused her and she gagged, body rejecting him even when her mind wouldn't.

~*~

With the door locked behind Snow, Lizzie peeled off a set of crumpled ones from a wad inside the hollowed out Bible on her shelf. Kit thought it disrespectful that she hid her savings in the Lord's Word, but Lizzie thought it more like burying demons in it and praying for a way out.

And there were plenty of demons.

She couldn't blame Snow for the drugs—she'd smoked weed for the first time with Anthony while Deena was away at MIT. He hadn't let her try alcohol though—arguing that the weed was virtually harmless, but she got her hands on some just the same that year. From there, it was X, coke, and heroin, all compliments of Snow. Her first time snorting coke had been bullshit, a numbing effect, a little shaking, poor quality all around. But her first time trying heroin—*goodness,* that was something. Syringe in her arm, head slumped back, and bliss—bliss like the heavens swallowing her whole. She'd gone back the next day for more.

They made a habit of it quick, Lizzie and Snow, who already handled it regularly. He dealt in heroin some, though crack was his main line of business back then, so usually there was one or the other on hand. But when it or the money for it ran low, Snow always had a couple of cocks lined up for her with the promise of drugs at the end. And back then, Lizzie thought herself lucky.

When she went missing, as she often did as a teenager, it was usually because a wad of money had come her way. A trick or two who

31

paid more for a weird assortment of tastes would give way to all the coke, crack, alcohol, and heroin she could stand—at least for a day. Nothing was too much for the happiness at the end, not getting choked and fucked at the same time, not even get beat up for a room full of men. No, for the high she got at the end, she would've taken that, and worse. Back then, she'd wig out on the cheap shit Snow brought her, no doubt skimping on quality to pocket a profit. There were times when Lizzie would black out, one time waking with the needle still in her arm. She'd return to her grandmother's house shit-faced and attempting to sleep it off, only to have the old woman scream or chuck a Bible at her, and worse, call Deena.

Lizzie's sister enrolled her in rehab—once, twice, a dozen times, maybe. But she never stayed clean, no matter how nice, or expensive, or far away they chose to send her. More often than not, Snow was there to greet her when she returned.

Once, Snow had called her a junkie whore, and she flung herself at him, intent on killing him with her bare fingernails. One month clean. Two months clean. A year, it made no difference. She was as much a whore and junkie as she was black and white, female and twenty-six. As it turned out, no amount of praying changed any of it. He'd known something at the time that she hadn't.

Lizzie tucked her Bible away with the seventy-two dollars in it. Back when she was young and firm and without the track marks, the drugs flowed free. When Snow began to charge her for them, she had no way of knowing. Not until she settled her drug debt with him would she be free, free of their world forever.

Some might've suggested that she ask her sister, who sat so rich that she smiled on the cover of magazines and had a fucking river running through her house. But asking Deena was asking for a lecture, for humiliation, for a reminder of all the wrongs she'd done. She would never believe Lizzie wanted to get clean, and more importantly, she never *should* believe it.

More than once, Lizzie had gone to her older sister, faking a tale of remorse. In doing so, she had money poured on her, sympathy, hugs. But of the three, there was only one that she wanted. Every few months, Lizzie would return to her sister and brother-in-law, ready to get clean and off the streets, only needing a bit of cash to tide her over. Always, they were willing—sure as the earth turning round the sun. Tak and Deena

Tanaka had sponsored crack parties and coke parties and even a trip to the ER, the last of which came hours after a visit to their home, a visit which resulted in a pocket full of volunteered cash and a few lifted trinkets. It was then, however, when Lizzie was hospitalized for an accidental overdose that the money dried up.

She never got a cent again, no matter how hard she tried.

CHAPTER NINE

Tak took Deena and Tony to the place on Eighth and Biscayne and spoke with Chuck, who yelled as Allison predicted. But when Tak waited him out with a bored expression, and then reminded him of the favor he owed her, Chuck gave in with a dramatic sigh.

Sunday morning, Deena rose and went to work on breakfast. She took eggs, bacon, and sweet maple sausages from the fridge, dug out onion, bell pepper, and fresh mushrooms, and began to whip the eggs for scrambling. At the edges of her mind was the conversation she'd been forced to have with Tony before bed, the one where she told him that she'd have to call the police to come get him, that he couldn't stay; that he'd have to go. Worst of all was the stoic expression with which he absorbed it all, leaving her to flee in tears as though she were the child.

Deena slid back the lid on a wooden box and pulled out the raisin bread for toast. She made oatmeal, and grabbed blueberries and brown sugar for it, because she didn't know which, if either, Tony would like. The bacon sizzled on the stove in the same pan as the sausage, while Deena chopped onions and mushrooms. There was cheddar in the fridge, shredded, and she added that to her egg omelet mixture. She remembered the lone box of blueberry muffin mix in the cabinet and dug it out, never needing the instructions for Mia's oft-requested favorite.

Bacon, sausage, toast, oatmeal, and muffins done, Deena scanned her spread with a critical eye. French-toast-or-pancakes, French-toast-or-pancakes, it felt monumental. She stood back, hands clasped at her mouth, eyes watering with indecision, when Tak slipped a hand on her shoulder.

"Baby, you have to call them," he said to her ear.

Deena turned.

"Pancakes or French toast, Tak?"

"You'll see him again, Dee. I promise."

She turned back to the breakfast. "I want him to have a decent meal before he goes. He's so thin. And I don't know . . . when he'll get another."

He turned her, forcing her to face him. "If he's ours, we'll get him back. I promise."

Deena nodded and closed her eyes, more tears threatening to spill.

Tak kissed her forehead with a smack. "Make the French toast. I'll wake him," he said and disappeared.

Deena made the French toast and the pancakes, placing a stack of both on the table with her other offerings. When Tony made his way into the kitchen, he was freshly scrubbed and in Tak's T-shirt, the golden UCLA one with the purple collar. His hair sat fat and damp, pulled into a ponytail with a single office rubber band.

"Wow. You cooked a lot," he said, pulling out the chair Mia usually sat in.

Deena stood over him. "I didn't know what you liked. And I wanted you to—to have a good meal, before—before—"

He stared at her, waiting, patient, daring her to admit that she was calling the police on him. But Deena couldn't so much as meet those eyes, let alone say it, so she turned and headed back to the kitchen. Hands busy, working without her, desperate for something to do. She wiped a clean counter and stove, swept the floor, and emptied out the fridge as Tak and Tony ate in silence. Despite all the food, she couldn't possibly think of eating it, couldn't think of much but Tony and the phone call she had to make.

Breakfast done, Tak appeared at her side and placed a hand on her elbow. "How about I call?" he said. "You and Tony could just chat."

Deena shot him a grateful look.

"Tell him about the fun things we'll be doing in a few days. And afterward, when we adopt him."

Deena shrieked, a surprise to both of them, and nearly toppled him with the force of her hug. She hadn't known. They hadn't talked about more children. In fact, he'd complained that life as a husband and father had somehow changed his art. Deena shook her head. So many years later, and still, Tak was her biggest blessing.

CHAPTER TEN

The police removed Anthony Hammond Jr. from the Tanaka home at eight twenty in the morning. A courier arrived at a quarter to ten with a plain manila envelope, sealed and addressed to Deena. She tore it open for the crisp, single sheet of paper inside; and on it, what she'd known all along.

PROBABILITY OF RELATIONSHIP: ANTHONY HAMMOND JR. TO DEENA TANAKA > 99%.

Deena stared, even as the paper slipped from her hand, even as Tak stood behind her, asking what it was, even as Tak grabbed the fallen sheet and read it for himself, even as Deena stood, door still slightly ajar.

Even with the gold-flecked eyes and frizzy brown hair, she'd doubted, just a little. But with this, there was no doubt left. None.

Tak returned, though she hadn't seen him leave.

"I just talked to Allison," he said. "She got her copy twenty minutes ago and is already on her way to file for temporary guardianship. We're supposed to meet her at the courthouse."

~*~

They dressed in subdued suits, Deena a charcoal and tailor-made skirt, Tak in a black Armani once forgotten in the back of his closet. He chose a red tie because he read once that politicians use them to give an air of command and control.

They were in court on a Sunday morning after some pleading and posturing on Allison's behalf. In hand were copies of their bank statements, two character statements—one from Allison's husband John, the other from Tak's father, Daichi. Allison had gathered them without either Tak or Deena's knowledge. She'd also made contact with Tony's court-appointed advocate in Bismarck, who, after extensive talks, was now in favor of the proceedings.

The judge was a salt-and-pepper haired Cuban man with deep creases in his face and a permanent scowl, made harsh by hanging jowls. He turned watery eyes on Deena and surveyed her frankly, as if trying to uncover the hidden lie in her posture.

"You knew nothing of this boy until he showed up at your house?" he demanded.

"That's right, Your Honor," she insisted.

The judge turned on Tony, seated on a side bench next to a pitch-black woman with a small, sheen-laden afro.

"That true? You've never spoke to these people before?"

"Never, sir."

The judge leaned forward on elbows, attention on the papers before him. Silence stretched on, interrupted only occasionally by the turning of a page.

"I can see from your bank statement that you have ample means to support him. But what are your plans for him? For his overall well-being?"

Deena opened her mouth to speak, only to have Tak place a hand over hers.

"As soon as we have the proper paperwork we're going to enroll him in a private school. Edinburgh Academy, where our daughter Mia already attends. We want to make sure he has all the resources he needs, in case there's some catching up to do. We'll take him to the family doctor and dentist to make sure everything's up-to-date and as soon as we're settled in, we'll do some family counseling to ensure that the four of us bond."

The judge gave a muted, small smile of approval. "Sounds good, Mr. Tanaka. I see no reason why we can't proceed in that direction."

Deena gasped.

"Is that really all there is to it?" Tak looked from Allison to the judge, waiting, waiting for the "more," whatever that was.

"I see no reason to keep a family apart. So, yes, that's all." The judge grinned. "Oh, and before I forget, could you please remind your father, Daichi, that he owes me a round of golf?"

37

Tak grinned, still grinning as the judge disappeared into his chambers. The sheen-laden social worker approached them. Huddled together, she and Allison began to bombard them with information, requests for documents, and various forms they needed to fill out and have notarized.

CHAPTER ELEVEN

Tony ran a hand over butter-cream leather and inhaled what could only be that new-car smell. He had his own cup holder, and there, in the back, was a television in the headrest. It wasn't on, and though he wanted to check it out, he didn't know how to ask. So, he rode in silence.

In the trunk were more pairs of pants and shoes, shirts and pajamas than he'd ever seen outside a store. And they were all for him. At first, when they stood inside Nordstrom's, Tony didn't move when Deena told him to pick what he wanted. Then, when Tak nudged him, he grabbed a shirt—a black graphic tee with a skater, midflip, on the front. He held it out to Tak, who laughed, and asked him if he planned on making it part of a uniform. Tak tossed it in the cart and waited.

Tony had seen the cost of that shirt—thirty-seven dollars—and felt sure he could have nothing else from the store. Secretly, he wondered if a city like Miami wouldn't have a Walmart. Why go to a place that charged thirty-seven for a thin tee? Despite the absurdity of it all, Deena picked up a pair of blue jeans, faded in all the right places, and asked Tony if he liked them. He nodded. She verified his size, which he wasn't altogether sure of, and threw them in the cart, too.

"Fill it up, Tony. That's your job." She poked a finger in the empty basket. "Don't look at the tags. Just get what you like."

She'd said it as if wasting money gave her joy, so, Tony shrugged and went at it. Starting first with jeans in every shade, from the darkest rinse to the palest blue, torn and untorn, he threw them in the cart and waited. When he looked at Tak and Deena and saw that they were still unsatisfied, he moved on to khakis and repeated the process. Cargo. Army fatigue. Something weathered-looking. After a while he stopped examining the designs and just focused on finding his size, otherwise they'd never leave the joint. Anyway, he was certain they'd be putting some stuff back once they made it to the counter, like his mom always had to do.

"You need shirts," Deena announced and disappeared, only to return with an armful. By the time they left, he had twenty-five pairs of pants, forty-seven shirts, thirteen pairs of pajamas, and seven pairs of shoes. He counted at the counter, unwilling to look at the digital readout of the register. Still, the cashier saw fit to announce it: $4,779. Tony's tummy grumbled in response. And Tak, not even slowing the flow of conversation, pulled out a slim black card and handed it over, all the while describing a massive roller coaster at Disney to Tony. Afterward, they'd piled everything into the trunk of a pearl white Benz with butter-cream interior.

Eyes on the back of Tak's glossy black hair, Tony blinked with a latent realization. "So, are you guys, like, rich?"

Tak glanced at him in the rearview mirror. "We're doing okay."

His mother used to say that when she worried about money. "We're doing okay, Tony." Somehow, someway, someone was getting it wrong.

Deena made a list with the pencil and pad from her purse as Tak drove. They would need paperwork from the Bismarck school system, new furniture for the spare room that would become Tony's, and a record of all his shots. Monday, she would put in calls to Mia's dentist and doctor to see if each could squeeze Tony in ASAP. No doubt, his nutrition was poor. She would call Allison and be sure they were okay with keeping their goddaughter until school on Monday.

She needed a list of known allergies, but could probably get that from him. He seemed old enough. And they should've measured him before rushing out and buying all those clothes. They would probably have to take them back. And as for—

"Hey. Here's an idea. How about we head to Disney World?" Tak said.

"Disney World!" Tony cried.

"Disney World?" Deena echoed uncertainly, gaze skimming her list.

"Yeah. Disney World. We could grab Mia, pack a few things, and hit the road. Three hours in the car."

"Disney World!" Tony exclaimed.

Tak grinned at him in the rearview mirror. "Heard of it, huh?"

Just as he pulled up to a red light amid four lanes of traffic,

Deena scowled at him. He was always doing this. Up and running, with nary a thought about what he'd shirked with his impulsivity.

"There are things we need to do. A million of them," she said.

"All of which can wait."

He straightened his rearview mirror.

"We need to get him in school. Get him caught up if he's behind."

Tak glanced at Tony in the mirror.

"You promise to work hard when you're back in school? Do your homework, brush your teeth, eat your broccoli?"

Tony grinned. "Yeah, I promise."

Tak looked at Deena. "See? He promised."

She rolled her eyes.

"We'll get him a tutor if he needs it. Or two or three. But for now, let's have fun. Or better yet, let him decide. Disney or school, kiddo?"

"Disney World!" Tony cried. "You guys are awesome!"

Tak looked at Deena. "See? We're awesome." He followed it with a squeeze of her knee.

"You're bribing him," Deena said.

Tak grinned. "Worked on you," he said and let the top down on his Benz.

Tony hooted in approval, fists reaching for the heavens as they sped down the interstate.

CHAPTER TWELVE

When Kenji Tanaka entered the Tanaka firm Monday morning, he waved to Carlos the security guard and headed for the elevator. It was kind of late, he guessed, and his sister-in-law Deena would probably be mad. It was his hope that the arrival of Tony over the weekend had held her up, though he doubted anything could make her late.

Kenji decided to skip the morning visit to her office and head straight for his own instead. That way, when she did turn up looking for him, he could at least pretend he'd been there for hours.

Kenji's office was on the seventh floor, same as Deena's, implying a seniority he didn't have. He rode the gold-toned elevator up while whistling a catchy hook from a Wild Thugz concert the night before. Best hip-hop band, hands-down.

The elevator stopped with a jerk and Kenji peeked out before stepping off. Right, then left, and no sign of Deena. He stepped off and dug in his pocket for keys as he walked. Not only would she hammer him for being late, if discovered, but she'd hardly approve of the absence of a briefcase, as well. No briefcase meant no work over the weekend, and for Deena Tanaka, the thought was obscene. Kenji rolled his eyes at his sister-in-law and self-appointed mentor.

He stopped at the last door on the right, hardwood, gold plaque, brass knob. His father had put his name on the door the day he passed his ARE, or Architect Registration Exam, so happy was he to have another architect in the family. With a sigh, Kenji stepped inside.

He had a base salary, small but bigger than most around there, and a commission, like all the other architects, though it wasn't enough money to notice. His trust fund was more than most guys there made in a lifetime, and he was content to never design anything, if left alone. Still, every once in a while, he made noise upstairs and told them to send something his way, just to keep the old man happy. Every once in a while he did that, but not too often.

Kenji dug his briefcase out of the closet, set it on his desk, and powered on the PC. Last night he'd been at the concert, so that meant missing the Dolphins game. Time to log onto ESPN for highlights.

A final score of 27–0 ensured Kenji that he'd made the right decision in going to the Wild Thugz concert with the pretty accountant downstairs. He ignored the internal memos, checked his e-mails, and only answered the one from Brandon Sweets, his best bud since high school. He wanted a recap of the concert. Kenji happily obliged. Afterward, he staked out his favorite message boards. Miami fans were the craziest, and he could count on them to get him laughing in the A.M. DolphinManJamiaca976 said that he knew a blind golfer back in Montego Bay who had a better arm than the Dolphins QB. BallerBoyMIA said that it would take two dozen first-draft picks, a new coaching staff, and all the voodoo of a priestess in Little Haiti to fix their beloved Dolphins. Kenji snickered. It looked like a good day, so far. He'd make himself a cup of coffee and settle in, maybe check out a movie on Netflix, too.

Kenji went to the sixth-floor break room and saw they only had decaf. A visit to the second-floor one turned up no coffee at all. Time for the Starbucks on South Miami, he figured.

It took an hour to get that cup of coffee, an hour made up of a short chat with Carlos the security guard, a walk two blocks, and another especially long chat with a sassy black barista with almond eyes. He was getting into black girls lately, especially their curves, but hadn't worked up the nerve to get one's number. So, he left this one alone.

Kenji headed back for the gleaming monument that was the Tanaka firm, wedged between towering banks and hotels. He stopped for a talk with the old black man they paid seven dollars an hour to park cars whose drivers got charged fifty for valet. It turned out the old guy played lotto seven days a week and was getting the hell out of there the second his numbers came in. Kenji gave him a dollar and told him to play for him, too. The old man laughed and tucked the bill in his front shirt pocket.

"Boy, ain't that your name at the top of that building?" he pointed one crooked finger at the gold letters bearing the Tanaka logo.

Kenji smiled. "Something like that."

Back in the building, he stopped again to see what Carlos was doing. One of the many tabloid talk shows was on, and this time, a too-skinny white girl with greasy brown hair didn't know who in the hell her baby daddy was. Kenji leaned against the counter for a better view. Carlos insisted it was the guy who worked part-time at the gas station, so naturally, Kenji went the other way, with the black guy who said he'd never even slept with her. Both Kenji and Carlos put a dollar on the counter to seal the deal.

"We should double this," Kenji said, staring in disbelief as a third girl stepped out with as many teeth in her mouth as he had in his pocket at the moment. "I smell victory."

"What you smell, my friend, is—"

Carlos looked up, froze, and blinked once.

Kenji turned to see Deena, if she were ten years younger and a whore. He cursed and peeled the jacket from his suit, hurrying to throw it over his near-naked sister-in-law.

"What the fuck?" he hissed and threw a glance over his shoulder. While doing so, he caught the eye of Carlos, who was grinning.

"This your friend, Kenji?" Carlos said, consonants disappearing the way of his thick accent.

"No! I mean," he turned back to Lizzie. "What are you doing here?"

And didn't she know better than to show up at someone's job looking like a whore? Sequin mini, gold, glittering, and doing little to cover her ass. She'd paired it with a tube top of the same fabric, fabric that could hardly be expected to keep breasts so big in check.

"Deena," Lizzie said. She looked past Kenji to the elevator. "Which office is hers again?"

"She not in, Mami," Carlos said, eyeing Lizzie with distinct interest. He leaned over on the counter. "Eh . . . How old are you, anyway?"

Lizzie popped bubble gum and eyed the middle-aged Latino man with boredom. She leaned in, so close that they could've kissed without shifting. "As old as you need me to be."

Next to Carlos, the television screamed with news of a verdict. One man leapt and cartwheeled, while the other thrust his hips emphatically. Carlos didn't notice.

44

Kenji yanked Lizzie to him by the arm and buttoned up the tan Calvin Klein jacket he'd draped over her torso, ignoring the roll of her eyes. Naked legs the color of butter peeked out from underneath the coat.

"Deena in?" Kenji asked, glancing surreptitiously around the lobby.

"Didn't show today," Carlos said. "Listen, Mami, I've got fifteen minutes and a twenty in my pocket."

Kenji snatched Lizzie by the wrist and swept her to the elevator. Grateful when it opened immediately, he yanked her inside and held his breath till it swallowed them whole.

~*~

"Why would you show up dressed like that?" Kenji shouted as the door to his office closed behind them.

Lizzie shrugged and plopped into the plush armchair facing his desk. Her eyes locked with his as he lowered himself into his chair, scowling.

"What happened with the kid?" she said. "Did they tell you?"

"Why don't you call and ask?"

"Don't play games, Kenji. You know damned well Deena can't stand to see or talk to me."

"Well, I can see you came here today to make a strong argument against that."

"One more time. What happened with the kid, *Kanji?*"

He waited.

"*Kenji.* Please. Can you tell me whether he's my nephew or not?"

"He is. Ninety-nine percent certainty."

She stared, eyes growing wide, and then suddenly damp. He looked away. He shouldn't have been the one to tell her.

45

Lizzie cleared her throat. "So, what you do here?" she said loudly.

When he didn't answer, she sauntered around his desk, catching him by surprise. "Other than read about sports?"

Kenji's cheeks flashed hot. He hurriedly punched off the monitor. "It's a slow day. That's all."

"Mhm, I bet." She returned to her seat with a smile. "Bet my sister never has slow days."

"Yeah. You'd, uh, win that bet."

She smiled, folded her arms. "But you . . . Rich daddy. Nice office. Nicer bank account. You have a lot of 'em is my guess."

Lizzie shoved aside Kenji's briefcase, a black leather Prada that hit the floor with a thud. "I bet you pretty much do whatever you want around here."

She let his jacket fall away, revealing a body too naked for Kenji's comfort. He got up and went to the window.

"You'd bet wrong," he said, the darkness of shade engulfing his room as he closed the blinds.

That wasn't good either.

Lizzie's eyes followed him.

"When my sister went to work for your daddy she didn't have shit. He stuck her in a cubicle with a bunch of other nobodies on the first floor. She was here seven years before she got a window. By then, she was fucking your brother, which probably helped."

She had most of that right, except the implication that Deena's relationship with Tak had somehow helped her early on. He could remember at least some of those seven years, but was surprised she knew anything about them. Back then, Lizzie was a strung-out teenager intent on selling her body and snorting coke. Now, she was a strung-out woman intent on selling her body and snorting coke.

46

"I didn't think you kept up with Deena like that," Kenji said, back pressed to the window.

Lizzie eyed him suspiciously. "I don't."

Deftly, Kenji returned to his seat. He managed to turn on his monitor for the sole purpose of looking busy.

She went back to hovering over his desk, shifting thighs so that soft smooth flesh would catch his attention, breasts perked like an avalanche waiting to happen. Finally, Kenji met her gaze.

"You can stop now. Nothing's gonna come from it."

"Well, shit." She stomped over to her chair with exaggerated frustration and collapsed. When she caught him staring wide-eyed, she dissolved into laughter. "You're really not interested, are you?"

"Nope."

"You don't like me? You don't think I'm sexy at all?"

Kenji searched for a shred of work on his desk. There was none. Finally, he looked up. "I think you're beautiful," he said. "I'm just not into paying money for sex."

"Yeah, right."

"Yeah, right, what?"

"Yeah, right, you. On your high and mighty. You don't pay money for sex. All guys pay money for sex."

Kenji sighed. "You're misinformed, Lizzie."

"Am I? Aren't you paying for sex every time you take a girl out for dinner and a movie or some other bullshit? Aren't you just waiting for the goods at the end of the night?"

Kenji chuckled. "The goods?"

"Oh, don't play! You guys are all alike. There's one thing on your mind, all the time, even now."

Kenji returned to his monitor. An internal memo appeared, something about signing a congratulations card in Human Resources for the new addition to Deena's family. He dismissed it like the others.

"You think too highly of yourself," he said. "You think that because you show everything you're the sexiest girl in the place. Some guys like a surprise, you know. And even more, like to know that everyone else hasn't had a sample first."

Lizzie's gaze narrowed. "You just think that's what you want. But I promise you, when it's going down, you won't be thinking of that."

"Well, you won't have to worry about it 'going down.'"

He turned to his computer, a Fandango ad brandishing the screen. Having given up the guise of finding work, Kenji bit his lip with a thought.

"There's a new *Spiderman* out. Have you seen it?"

Lizzie raised a brow. "What?"

"*Spiderman*." He looked up in impatience. "You've heard of him, haven't you?"

Lizzie sputtered. "Of course, I've heard of him."

"Well, do you wanna go or what? It's supposed to be good."

She blinked her confusion.

Kenji clicked the advertisement.

"Say 'no' if you want. We can see something else, if that's not your thing. I don't do chick flicks, though."

"You—want me to go to a movie with you?"

"Sure, why not?" He scrolled down for times. "There's one at seven. That should be fun." He shot her a look. "I'm not paying you, by the way."

"Seven tonight?"

"That's what I said."

"But I thought you didn't want to—"

"Do you not know how to be a normal person? People go to the movies together. They pay admission, sit down, enjoy the show. That's all I'm talking about. You in or not?" He swiveled away from his desk, stood, and stretched. Ten minutes in an office left him with a caged-in feeling.

"You could meet me here and we'll go down to the theatre on Lincoln in South Beach. Maybe get something to eat, too," he suggested.

"Why?"

"'Cause I thought it'd be fun. But fuck it, if you're gonna act like that."

"No, I—" she reached for him, and then drew back. "Seven? Meet you here?"

"The movie's at seven. Meet me here at six. In the lobby." Kenji eyed her for a moment. "And wear some pants."

CHAPTER THIRTEEN

Kenji stood in the lobby of the firm, a hand in his pocket as he waited. The Prada briefcase he pretended to tote around was back up on the seventh floor, stored in his closet for another night. It turned out Deena was gone for the week, so he could do away with the pretenses. *Yippee.*

Lizzie showed up ten minutes late, in skinny blue jeans, shiny black pumps, and a fitted red halter with a V so deep and wide it barely held her jiggling breasts in check with three strips of rhinestones. They sparkled as she walked.

Kenji lifted his gaze. "You're late," he said. "Let's move."

Lizzie nodded. Her wavy brown hair, pulled high into a messy ponytail, shifted with the movement. Two oversized hoop earrings, silver with rhinestones, also shook. She panted only slightly.

"Where'd you walk from?" he asked, suddenly remembering she didn't have a car. That'd been a little inconsiderate of him.

"The bus stop. Where else?"

Kenji rolled his eyes.

"Oh, I don't know. The People Mover, the passenger side of a moving car . . . Never can tell with you."

Lizzie scowled, honey brown eyes darkening, before breaking with a giggle. "That's true," she finally said.

Kenji snorted. "Come on, Looney Tunes. The garage is this way." He looked down at her feet. "If you can make it in those heels."

Kenji's car was on the second floor, a candy red Audi with a drop top. It was his father's gift to him for passing the AREs, replacing the Mustang he drove in college. Lizzie plopped down on a leather gray bucket seat, causing Kenji to have to reach underneath her for the access card he needed to exit the mammoth garage.

"I usually charge for stuff like that," she said as he slipped the card out from beneath her.

His cheeks went hot, and he turned away, starting the car as she laughed.

The drive from Brickell to South Beach was about ten minutes. Even for a distance that short, she wanted him to put the top down on the car. He obliged before turning on the Wild Thugz and cranking it up.

"What do *you* know about Wild Thugz?" Lizzie demanded, laughing.

Kenji glanced at her in seriousness. "All I know is that a 'niggaz claim to fame—'"

"—is when a bitch's calling his name!" Lizzie shouted, finishing the infamous line.

But then she scowled. "I don't think you can say 'nigga.'"

She thumped him in the head with two fingers, walloping him right. Kenji batted distractedly, missing without the benefit of looking, insufficiently protected when she did it a second time.

Kenji laughed. "Would you quit? I'm driving! Besides, I can say it! My niece is black. Sort of."

"Barely!"

"Barely counts."

At six thirty, Kenji pulled up in front of a South Beach high-rise. Lizzie looked at him and raised a brow.

"I'm just changing real quick. Stay in the car. I'll be back."

"What? I can't come in?"

"Course not. I like my possessions."

Kenji slammed the door behind him, leaving Lizzie with folded arms and a running engine.

A seventeenth-floor condo, yet another gift from Dad, was what waited for him upstairs. Kenji rode the elevator, unlocked the front door, and dashed for the bedroom. The night before, when he'd returned from the concert, he'd peeled off his jeans and Polo shirt, dropped them where he stood, and climbed into bed. He stepped over those now and went to the closet, hoping for something that wasn't too wrinkled. He found a navy Polo and dark jeans, close fit, and paired them with some canvas dock shoes that were checkered white and blue.

Ten minutes. *Not bad,* he thought, when he made it back to the car. But Lizzie was scowling at him.

"God, you really couldn't invite me up? Offer me a cup of water or some shit? I thought you people had class."

Kenji smirked. "You people? Would that be Asians?"

Lizzie rolled her eyes. "That only works when you're black."

He pulled on his seat belt. "Well, as I've already explained to you, my niece is black." He shifted into drive and took off from the parallel parking space labeled "Tanaka."

~*~

The umpteenth *Spiderman* remake rocked, so much so that Kenji didn't mind explaining near everything to Lizzie. She needed to be briefed on basic stuff that even his grandmother knew, like why Peter Parker was a spider to begin with, or what was up with him and the girl. Then again, his grandmother probably just knew that stuff because he'd told her, so apt was he to go off on a comic book tangent.

Movie done, Kenji and Lizzie walked over to Senorita's, a Cuban restaurant on Ocean Drive, for dinner.

Their waitress was a short and wrinkled woman, though she couldn't have been more than forty-five. Frail but animated, she interrupted herself with suggestions for the suggestions she was making, always with the arms flapping. A brittle-looking blonde with hair swept in a ponytail, she had emphatic crow's feet and watery lumps for brown eyes.

Kenji looked down at his menu. He hated when he saw people like that, older and in hard professions—stocking shelves, serving burgers, sweeping floors. They embarrassed him and reminded him of an inescapable truth: that all he'd done for the things he had was be born into the right family. He glanced at Lizzie, found her attention on him, and looked away.

"Rum and Coke," Kenji said, muttering the first drink that came to mind. It was his brother's preference, not his own.

Lizzie scrutinized the drink menu. She turned it over, frowning. "There's so many things I haven't tried. I don't know what to pick."

"Try a Chocotini. It's chock full of chocolate," the waitress said. "Oh, but instead, you should have the Godiva Chocolate Liqueur. That's good, but it's only served on Valentine's Day. You could think about it, you know, if you ever come back then. Otherwise, I'd recommend the Chocolate Mint Martini, Chocolate Cake Martini, the Espresso Martini, or the Triple Chocolate Dip Trip. You did say you liked chocolate, right?"

"No," Kenji blurted.

Lizzie laughed.

"Oh. Well, in that case—"

"I'll have the Chocotini," Lizzie said.

"It's speed," Lizzie explained the moment the waitress disappeared. "She's on speed. Guess you can see how it got its name."

Kenji shot a look at the waitress and near ducked when her gaze swept toward him. Heaven forbid she start in on the entrée selections.

"The movie," he said when he saw he had Lizzie's attention. "How'd you like the movie?"

She shrugged. "It was cool. You're really into that comic book stuff, huh?"

"How'd you know?"

"Well, when I asked you where Peter Parker's parents were, you gave me a pretty good bio."

53

Kenji shrugged. "I thought you wanted an answer."

"I did. Just not the long one." She flipped over her menu. "It's cool though."

Kenji stared at her, trying to catch a glimpse of her eyes without being obvious. Earlier he'd thought them honey, but a moment ago, they seemed closer to bronze. He really wanted to know.

"This is probably gonna sound crazy," Lizzie said, "but, I've never done this before."

He blinked. "Done what?"

She looked up.

Bronze. A deeply hued brown tinged in gold.

"Movies, dinner with a guy. This is new."

Kenji grinned, all ready for the punch line. But when it didn't come, his smile faded.

"You've never had a boyfriend take you out before?"

Her elbow rested on the table, chin on her hand, and slowly, she shook her head at him. "No boyfriends. Ever."

He began to smile again. Truly, she was teasing him. After all, all things equal, the girl was gorgeous. Plenty of guys existed who were chumps for a pretty face.

"Come on, Lizzie. Guys pay to be with you. Certainly someone has—"

But again, she shook her head. "The closest I ever came to a date," she said eyes on a napkin she fingered, "was this guy once in high school."

"And what? He cheated?"

"He asked me to his house for a party. I came over, saw a room full of guys, and realized I was the party."

"Shit."

She shrugged. "I already had a name for myself, even if I didn't know it. I was easy, so, they did to me what you do to an easy girl."

The moment stretched on between them.

"And?" he said eventually. "After that?"

"After that, I decided that no one else would take from me without paying. After that, I hooked up with Snow."

"Snow?"

The waitress placed a Chocotini in front of Lizzie; and a rum and Coke Kenji didn't want in front of him.

"Ready to order?" she prompted.

Kenji glanced at his menu.

"Pick something for me," Lizzie whispered.

He glanced at her, then back at the menu. *"Bistec a la plancha* for me and the *Ensalada de mariscos* for her."

The waitress bounded off with the order.

"Tell me about Snow," he said.

Lizzie stared at him.

"He was my first. The first time I got fucked, did crack, coke, X, heroin. It all came from Snow."

"And this is a guy . . . from high school?"

"He went to high school with Deena and my cousin Keisha. He's the father of Keisha's kid, her fiancé, and my pimp."

Kenji took a long gulp of the rum. The words reached him slow, delayed.

55

"Wait. He went to high school with *Deena?*"

Lizzie sipped her chocolate. It painted her lips, glistening them like gloss. "That's right. I was a kid the first time I had sex with him. He was twenty. Maybe twenty-one."

"Then he should be in prison. Why isn't he in prison?"

She looked away. "For what? I was already a slut. Eleven and giving blow jobs for stupid shit, that was me. A Whopper, a CD, makeup, a purse. And anyway, it was me who went looking for him. I went right up to him and just started sucking."

"Why?"

"'Cause I was mad at my cousin. She was always calling me a slut. So, I went after her boyfriend figuring I'd show her what a slut was."

Kenji took another long gulp, hardly tasting the drink he loathed, and suddenly wishing it was stronger.

"It's hardly his fault," Lizzie went on. "I mean, think about it. I went up to him, unzipped his pants, and put him in my mouth. What man could resist that?"

"From a kid?" Kenji blurted. "All of them! Or nearly all of them."

He went back to his drink, swigging it in a go. "And by the way, there's nothing erotic about a child who's obviously been abused acting out. It's just gross."

She lowered her gaze.

"And who even—"

"Never mind. I don't want to talk anymore."

"Lizzie, if you think—"

"I SAID I DON'T WANNA TALK ANYMORE!"

"Okay. Yeah. Of course. I'll just . . . enjoy my drink," he said reaching for the glass. He scowled into emptiness.

"So," Lizzie said loudly, suddenly preoccupied with her drink, "have you seen him?"

"Seen who?"

"My nephew. Have you seen him, yet?"

"No. They're at Disney just now. Took Mia out of school for a few days and everything."

More silence.

"He'll have a good life with Deena and your brother. They've got money. All his problems are over."

"Money doesn't solve all your problems, Lizzie."

"No," she agreed. "Just the ones that count." She smiled. "So, Mr. Tanaka, we talked about my first time. What about yours?"

"What?"

"Your first time. Tell me about it."

Kenji waited. She couldn't possibly expect him to . . .

She did.

He could ignore her, he supposed. But at the same time, he felt the burden of what she'd told him, the guilt of suddenly wanting to be impersonal when he had no qualms about trampling through her history a second ago.

"There's . . . nothing really to tell," he said.

She continued to stare.

Kenji sighed.

"Okay. I was in high school. I dated a girl, off and on from the end of junior year till the end of senior. We'd talk about doing it sometimes." He blushed with the memory of begging. "And eventually we did."

"And?"

"And she said she loved me. It kind of weirded me out. So, I broke up with her."

"You broke up with her because she loved you?"

"I broke up with her because it wasn't mutual."

Dinner arrived.

"God in hell, what is this?" Lizzie demanded as the waiter set a plate before her.

"Seafood salad," Kenji said. "There's shrimp, clams, oysters, mussels, scallops, calamari, chunks of crab, and lobster." He hesitated. "You don't have a shellfish allergy, do you?"

Why hadn't he thought to ask that? He was always screwing up, not thinking things through and—

She looked up. "How would I know?"

"Because you'd die." He shook off the odd question. "You have had seafood before, right?"

"There was shrimp at Deena's wedding, remember? Oh, and I've had catfish. But that's it."

He didn't feel like explaining why catfish wasn't shellfish. Instead, he pushed her plate closer. "Eat. I think you'll like it."

She stabbed a shrimp and dumped it in her mouth.

"Spicy," she said, chewing.

"Order something else if you don't like it."

"No, it's good. Real good. I'm surprised."

"You know," Kenji said as he prodded his steak, "if you think about it, you're pretty inexperienced in a way."

Lizzie laughed. "Oh, I doubt that."

"Well, I don't know. Let's see. Have you ever had a man say he loved you? Make love to you? Say he felt lacking, incomplete without you?"

Lizzie's smile faded.

"That's stupid. Fake. Something for TV."

"How would you know?"

"Have you ever felt that way?" she demanded. "About a girl?"

"Nope."

"Then how can you know it's real?"

"Because I've seen it before, that's how."

It was she who looked away first.

"Whenever I bring Mia here," he said, "she always gets a hamburger, even though there are a thousand things on the menu." He sawed at his own steak in irritation. "Maybe I should have, too."

"I wish I could see her," Lizzie said softly. "But they don't let me. They say I'm a bad influence."

"You are."

He bit the steak. Regretted it.

Halfheartedly, Lizzie stuck her fork in fleshy white calamari and swigged it in pepper sauce.

"I wouldn't—"

The calamari dislodged from her fork and her face pinched in frustration.

"I wouldn't show her that part of me."

"Which part? The drugs or the dangerous men that pay you for sex part?"

"I would keep her away—"

"Away from what?" he cried." The guy you answer to? The pimp who's a known rapist of children? The guy who taught you that?" He jabbed his fork in the direction of furious black lines snaking her arm, only thinly veiled in foundation. "What's it take for you to break? For you to promise your soul and hers? A line of coke? An eightball?" He shook his head vehemently, cooked to a sizzle with fury. "God only knows what you'd do should you get desperate enough for a high."

He hadn't meant to make her cry, had no idea when she'd started, but it was only with the faint acknowledgment of streaming tears that his anger abated.

She bolted from the table, upending her chair and another at her back, before fleeing from the covered portico out into the street. He couldn't say what compelled him to talk that way to her, when he could scarcely remember having occasion to raise his voice to anyone, ever, let alone to purposely hurt them. Yet he got a grim satisfaction in hurting the girl who'd hurt Tak and Deena, and inadvertently hurt him, it seemed. And still, he needed to go after her.

Kenji dug in his pocket, threw a fifty on the table, started off and returned with a wad of ones. Lizzie was halfway across the street, too slow in too-tall heels. She halted near a bus stop, scowling and purposely looking through him. There was no bench or shading, so she would have to stand, holding on to a pole for relief. When he got close enough to directly block her line of sight, she folded her arms and made a point of looking the other way. Kenji stopped before her.

"Look. I'm not sorry," he said. "So, if it's an apology you want, you can forget it."

She turned on him with the rage of a tsunami. "I would never hurt Mia! I would never let this happen to her! I'd kill myself first if that's

60

what it took!"

Kenji took in the whole of her wrath. She trembled, fists balled, tears threatening once again.

"Lizzie—"

"You can call me a whore. You can me worthless. A junkie. All that's true. But what you can't say is that I don't love my niece." She turned away from him.

"Lizzie—"

"Go away."

"Lizzie, come on. You're not worthless. You just . . ."

"Just what?"

Just spent the last decade of your life being victimized by a pedophile and rapist, he wanted to say. But he knew he'd gone far enough for one night. Kenji shot a look behind him, where Ocean Drive unraveled to a series of all-night, waterfront nightclubs. Already, the pulse of the club beats wafted out to him.

"You just can't dance, I'll bet," he said.

She shot him a suspicious look.

"What?"

"You heard me. You can't dance."

She folded her arms.

"And you can?"

"Better than you. Especially in those shoes."

Lizzie scowled at the challenge, brows furrowing as she looked him over. "Well, there's one way to see."

Kenji started off, certain she'd follow.

As they moved together later, oblivious to night becoming dawn just outside club doors, it turned out she was a better dancer than him, though she'd never been to a nightclub before.

CHAPTER FOURTEEN

After Tak helped Tony pack for the trip, he gave him a proper tour of his new home while they waited on the girls.

There were more trees in front of the house than Tony had ever seen outside a forest. For some reason, the Tanakas seemed intent on keeping their house hidden, like the slight of eye magicians like to use. Jutting and not jutting, their house split down the middle with a waterfall, wasting water all the day long. Tak assured him the water was reused over and over in some sort of natural process, but Tony's mind began to wander with the explanation. He hadn't a care in the world for the water itself, except, he thought it looked pretty cool. He could imagine what his mother would've said about the water bill, though.

Tak and Deena were another species from her altogether it turned out. Tony's mom would always worry that someone could see in the house, but the Tanakas, hell, they hoped for it. There were windows everywhere, floor to ceiling on the bottom landing; sunroofs on the top. There were places where glass wrapped the house in big sheets, exposing them where the trees didn't block. Funny, Tony thought, how poor people tried to hide the little stuff they had and the rich put theirs on display.

The Tanaka backyard, as impressive as a football field, stood lush with greenery. It dropped off to a dock, where a shiny white yacht treaded in water, *Darling* painted on the side. Even as the backyard unraveled before him in some fanciful rendition of a child's fairy tale, complete with brightly colored foliage, a mountainous swimming pool and slide, and an outdoor juice bar, there was only one item that could hold Tony's attention. He looked from it to Tak in disbelief. He remembered the yachts teetering in Lake Michigan and how he'd thought of freedom, of sailing on a lake for hours on end. But as Tony took in the length and height of the *Darling,* an ultra-elegant and white polished beauty, his gaze turned to the bay spilling out into the Atlantic. He could only think one thing: those people didn't know shit about being a Tanaka.

"Boat got your eye, huh?" Tak said, placing a hand on his shoulder.

"It's beautiful," Tony said.

"Good," Tak said. "We'll go sailing, real soon."

Something in Tony's belly did a pivot. This was what his mom used to call a "shit steak"; when a surge of bad luck turned to good, when shit turned to sirloin right before you.

"And when you're older, I'll show you how to sail, like my dad did me."

Sirloin? It was filet mignon with a fat piece of bacon wrapped around it, just like on TV.

~*~

Tak and Deena had a vacation home at the resort, a three-bedroom waterfront cottage at Disney's Boardwalk Villa. During the drive up, Deena bought the Florida resident tickets over the phone and arranged with Human Resources to be out of work for the week. She knew Kenji would be relieved.

Despite Mia and Tony's insistence that they visit the Magic Kingdom the night of their arrival, Deena ordered pizza and a movie and made them settle instead. They would rise early and start out for the park, but that evening they would just enjoy each other's company.

Tony's lack of fussiness bothered Deena. When they bought clothes, whatever she and Tak picked up was just right for him. When they ordered pizza, whatever toppings they chose were just right for him. And the next day, as they planned their route at the park, whatever rides they wanted to try were just fine by him.

Tak told her not to push it, that it was a matter of him getting comfortable. Once he did, he reasoned, they would know what he really wanted and didn't want. Until then, they'd just have to guess. But since Deena was so worried that Tony might not enjoy himself, Tak insisted they try all the rides.

They spent Monday in the Magic Kingdom, reining Mia in as she tried to dominate all choices as the once supreme and only child. She wanted Snow White's Scary Adventures, a Mad Teacup ride, a view of the parade, and a visit to the Bibbidi Bobbidi Boutique, all at once. Deena fussed at her, but Tak was always of the mind to give her whatever she wanted.

Partway through the day, when Deena took Mia for her

customary princess makeover, Tak dragged the severely grown-up Tony down to The Pirates League, where they both returned made over as swashbucklers. While Tak wasn't the type to usually get into costume, it had been a must to persuade Tony that as an eleven-year-old, he was not too old for the treat. All in all, a breakfast of eggs, bacon, and Mickey Mouse pancakes at the Contemporary Resort, four hours of rides, a hurried lunch of hamburgers and chicken fingers, and five more hours of rides, meant that they returned to their room with a whining, fussy, and disheveled Mia and the rest near-dead.

Deena made sure the kids showered as Tak ordered takeout. Junk again, she noted in dismay. This night the kids ate in silence, never bothering with a movie, before collapsing into bed at ten thirty. Tak tucked Mia in, while Deena stood by impotently, trying to make sure Tony had everything he needed. Eventually, she found the courage to come closer.

He smiled up at her as she pulled back the covers and allowed him to slip in. Golden eyes weighty, he watched as she pulled the red quilt up high on his shoulders and smoothed it out with a hand.

"You're tucking me in," he said, eyes droopy, still smiling. "I thought that only happened on TV."

"Not exclusively," she murmured and bit back a smile. Gingerly, she sat on the edge of the bed.

"No 'good night'?" he said.

"I'm not ready to leave you, just yet."

He was so Anthony, she thought, right down to the smile, and she had to stop herself from needing to touch his face, endlessly.

"You look so much like him," she whispered.

"I know," Tony said, eyes fluttering closed.

"Thank you," Deena said.

He snored in response.

CHAPTER FIFTEEN

Lizzie ambled from the drop-top Audi, heels in her hands and sunrise at her back, aware of the stares that followed. Mike, who sold shit-quality crack on her block, eyed her with a smirk. Pooch, the wig-skewed drag queen who camped out nightly on Lizzie's stoop, shifted to one side, allowing her a wide enough berth to cross.

"Don't forget to give Snow his cut," Pooch jeered and jabbed the cigarette in her mouth.

"Fuck you," Lizzie said and ventured into the hall.

Up three stories and through a series of locks she went. She found Kit at home and working.

A massive, muscle-laden and tattooed guy had her knees pinned to her shoulders and fucked like he could've drilled a hole in the floor with only a little extra effort.

Lizzie ventured into the kitchenette, turned on the faucet, and waited for the water to run clear as she searched for a cup. Big Gulp in hand, she filled it and took her drink to the windowsill. There was only one other place to sit and that was the bed.

The black guy put Kit on all fours, like Lizzie knew he would. He was an obvious ex-con with a shitload of tattoos sheathing him like a shirt. They ran dark and near black, others faded to extinction. She could make out the mark of her brother's old gang among them.

Kit began to scream, ringing like some ragged old church bell striking noon in the day. She shot peals through Lizzie's head, shrieks of false ecstasy meant to bolster his ego and make for a quick finish. They were thumping, insistent, agonizing, and discordant, causing her to heave open the lone window and hang her head out in relief.

How many times she'd sat by and busied herself as Kit worked she didn't know. In turn, her roommate had done the same, sitting by as the need required. But as Lizzie looked out on a strewn-laden alley, with a tire, cigarette butts, and needles below, a dirt-ridden, limping, and pale black man slumped over to a far wall, curled up, and slipped something in his mouth. Lizzie turned away.

It rang cruel that she should come back, back to the seedy existence of a whore, with the taste of salted butter and lobster on her tongue and her hair still windswept from dancing. Foremost in her mind was an image of Kenji, catcalling and howling at her slightest careen, beating off imaginary suitors on the dance floor, and professing her to be the very source of rhythm.

It was all a tease, she knew. After all, a man with money, style, and a smile both broad and bottomless, could have his choice of women, or a stable should he choose. And in choosing, she would wager that there would be no high school dropouts or heroin-addicted whores to blush at the smiles of Kenji Tanaka.

For the first time, Lizzie felt poor, inept; inadequate as a woman. She didn't know what was expected of her, or how to deliver it. Suddenly, she wanted more than the knowledge of how to please a man physically. She wanted to know how best to amuse him, indulge him, intrigue him, make him smile. But she didn't know any of those things.

And it bothered her.

A lot.

CHAPTER SIXTEEN

Kenji stared out at the blue waters of Biscayne Bay, hating the feel of being holed up in an office. He couldn't understand how people like Deena made work their life, when things like baseball and sailing, television and sex existed. Work didn't even come close to making a list like that.

An overcast sky threatened rain as Kenji turned away from the window. He went back to his desk, weary of the message boards, done with the social networking, having read all the news and still wondering what he could do.

He pulled a magazine from his desk, *Brickell Today*. It was one of those high-end glosses that catered to local rich people. He flipped through it, though for what, he had no idea. He couldn't even remember picking it up, yet he must've, because he'd found it in his desk.

There was a knock at his door and he looked up, surprised. He rarely got visitors.

Kenji got up, opened it, and smiled at the sight of the accountant from downstairs. A delicate beauty with silky black hair, saucer brown eyes, and a little ski-jump of a nose, thin with slight curves, Kenji knew she jogged seven days a week and read poetry in her spare time.

"Hi," she said softly. Her lashes were long and thick, blinking as she spoke.

"Paige."

Even her name sounded good. He leaned against the door jamb in an effort to look cool. "How are you? Great, by the looks of you," he said.

Too much, Kenji thought; *tone it down.*

She smiled.

"I was just nearby and wanted to say hi. So, 'hi.'"

"Hi."

Had his voice gone off pitch? God, he hoped not.

"I liked the concert," she said.

She didn't like the concert. He knew that by the way she kept wincing when they cursed. But she was hot, and he hadn't been laid in six months, so he went along with the lie.

"Great. We should go out again. Maybe you could pick this time."

Her eyes brightened with the dangled treat. "There's an art showing downtown. A week from Thursday, I think. Seems like I remember reading that your brother's work would be on display. We could do that."

Yeah, they wouldn't be doing that.

"What else did you have in mind?"

Paige shrugged. "Theatre, maybe? A poetry reading?"

Jesus.

"Gavin Hurst is reading at the Barnes & Nobles by my house tonight. We could do that, and go back to my place afterward for drinks."

"Gavin . . . Hurst, you say?"

"Yeah. You've heard of him?"

"Maybe." *Absolutely not.* "Let's make it a date."

Paige smiled. "Awesome. See you tonight."

Kenji gave a short nod and watched her ass on departure.

~*~

Gavin Hurst was a short and big-bellied man who forced Kenji to look away each time he licked his lips, usually in vigorous fashion and about every moment or so. Black hair draped his arms right down to the

69

knuckles, and he wore a red cable knit despite the full seventy-five degrees outside. As he stood at a podium in the café section of Barnes & Nobles, he thumbed through a tiny green hardback in search of something to read. Only women were in attendance; women and Kenji, that is—the latter of which sat in blue jeans and a sports coat that belonged to his brother and looked decidedly better on him.

Kenji and Paige were on a chocolate leather couch at the back. He had an arm around her, though she seemed not to notice, so engrossed was she in this hairy and ultra-gay poet. Her pale hands clasped as if in prayer at her lips, her eyes never left Mr. Hurst.

Gavin took a sip of water, paused, and then chimed into the silence like thunder. "Volcano. Volcanoes erupt like the soul. Inward. Upward. Quaking."

Kenji stared at the guy. He bet he drank. Beer. Scotch. Whiskey. Wild Irish Rose on tough nights. He bet he drank too much and pissed himself. He bet he gambled all his money away and owed a guy named Big Larry way more than he could pay. He bet he wrote about love yet been divorced three times. He bet the guy was full of shit.

Gavin read three poems. The first one about volcanoes and his soul, the second about the illusion of completion, and the third, well, hell, Kenji didn't know what he was talking about there. He exhaled audibly when the crowd leaped to their feet in applause, signifying the end of his ordeal.

"You didn't enjoy it," Paige accused, arms folded as they walked the three blocks to her condo. After leaving his Audi in her parking lot, they'd hiked to the bookstore.

"I pick the next outing," Kenji reminded her, and was met with a giggle.

It was dark out, but downtown, the part of town that housed the American Airlines arena, the docks for the cruise ships, and a varying assortment of tourist traps, action never quite died out.

They were coming up on her building, a five-story white stucco just ahead on the left.

"Next outing? Are you asking me out again, Kenji Tanaka?"

He smiled—but not much, though—because he knew his gums would show.

"Something like that."

Her apartment was small compared to Kenji's, a series of white walls compacted with a suede red couch, 27-inch tube, and a massive bookshelf in the living room. He could see the kitchen and hall from where he stood.

On entering, Paige locked the door and gestured to the couch. Kenji sat gingerly and on edge, the way people did when sticking around wasn't a given.

"What do you feel like drinking?"

"I don't know. Whatever you have."

Paige headed for the kitchen. "There's a bottle of Pinot Grigio. Probably not as nice as what you're used to."

Of course. Because Tanakas took Dom Pérignon daily with their breakfast.

"Pinot's fine," Kenji said.

When Paige returned, she had the bottle of refrigerator-chilled wine and two glasses. She poured and set one before Kenji on the coffee table.

He took a sip. Sweet, dry, went down easy.

She sat down with him, and they launched into awkward talks about working for his dad, architecture, Gavin Hurst, when Kenji grew desperate. She took long swallows from her glass, going back for seconds.

They sat that way, talking and not really talking, with her going for seconds, thirds, and a portion of a fourth. When the last stood close to empty, Kenji's temples began to dampen with the urgency of a man failing to conjure nerve.

"So, are you going to come on to me or what?" she demanded.

"I, uh—is that what you want?"

What a stupid-ass question. He thought to replace it with another.

"So, is this, uh . . . something you like to do often?"

Stupider. What the hell was wrong with him?

"Do you like me or do you just want to sleep with me?" she asked, wine sloshed her words.

Kenji's gaze fell to her neck. He could kiss her there he supposed, and she would know what he wanted. But his heart was beating too hard.

"Both," he admitted.

She looked at him, eyes wet and laughing. Even her laughs rang thick. "You're not supposed to tell me. You're just supposed to try."

She threw back the last of her wine emphatically.

"You're not drinking," she accused.

He looked down at his glass, still holding half of the first contents.

"Drink more," Paige said. "I can't get drunk alone."

Kenji threw it back and instantly, his belly warmed with wine.

"That's better," she said.

Paige finished the Pinot Grigio, and they started in on a half-emptied bottle of vodka. A few sips in and Kenji's head began to whir. Once he was significantly sloshed, he scooted over, close to Paige. He kissed her cheek first, as a friend would, and when she didn't resist, he set his glass down and kissed her mouth. She tasted like booze and onions, and it distracted him, causing him to try to recall when she would've had time to eat onions. She wrapped arms around his neck and leaned back, inviting him to climb atop her on the couch.

72

He was hard in an instant, hands falling to hips and simultaneously wishing there was more there to grab. He pushed the thought from his mind.

"I've never been with a Japanese guy," she murmured.

"Me neither." Kenji nipped at her neck.

But she didn't get the joke, or didn't notice, and suddenly, she was pulling off her top and therefore pushing that thought from his mind.

It occurred to him that there wasn't much between them; that she was an ambitious accountant who spent meals and casual conversations engaged in what she only thought was a casual assessment of his wealth. In the few dates he'd had with Paige, they'd discussed his stake in the firm, his trust fund, the vacations he took, and what he stood to inherit on his father's death. Still, here they were, because here was where he was dying to be.

Her breasts were disappointing, oblong instead of round, and too far apart. But he'd never been especially picky before and couldn't understand his sudden fussiness. Kenji pushed it from his mind and reached for the button of her jeans.

It was like pulling pants from a pole, so bone straight and thin was she. Nothing to grab, nothing to hold, but her mouth felt good on his neck, then his chest ,and even lower. She started sucking him—and it was incredible—warm and wet and tight and perfect. Rigid friction, damp and gliding. And in his mind, another woman's lips were suddenly upon him, a woman with S-curves, wild brown hair, gold-flecked eyes, and honeyed skin.

He leaped to his feet with a start, dumping Paige onto the floor and upturning the last of her vodka. Clear liquor gushed emphatically, plummeting to the carpet, darkening and spreading by the second. Still, his brain worked; worked around the image he'd birthed at the worst moment, wrestling it from his mind.

Lizzie.

"I—I have to go," Kenji blurted, only vaguely aware of the instantaneous death of his erection at the moment when cognizance put a name to the image. "I can't—"

He shook his head, grabbed the car keys, and burst out the door.

"Send me the bill for the carpet," were his last words to Paige.

~*~

When Lizzie rang Kenji's phone the next morning, he answered with the resonating pitch of a guilty man. One glance at his clock alluded to the reasons why. One, he was late for work, and two, he could remember little of his dream, except the voice he now heard.

"I wanted to know if you were doing anything later," she said softly.

Kenji sat up, sluggish and groggy from alcohol.

"Later?" he echoed stupidly.

"Yeah," Lizzie said in an uncharacteristically softened voice.

Kenji sat up.

"Why? What's happened? What do you need?"

"I call you so I need something? What the hell is that?"

Kenji snorted. "You've never called before."

"And you've never called me! Ass-wipe."

"Fine. Bye."

"Bye," Lizzie spat.

Still, neither hung up the phone and the seconds ticked toward infinity.

"So," Kenji said finally, "what are you doing? Picking your nose?"

"Being mad at you," Lizzie snapped, though the edge had seeped from her voice.

"Want to be mad over here?" he asked.

She paused. "What do you mean?"

"I mean that I'm about to order a shitload of hot wings and watch a few a movies on rental."

"You're not going to work?"

Kenji glanced at his clock. "No. Don't think I'll bother."

So, she agreed to be ready in an hour.

Two hours later, Kenji and Lizzie were in a battle over who could down the most Lava-Scorched Hot Wings from Bass Charlie's. Kenji won with seventeen to Lizzie's measly ten. They ate them and watched a slew of old films, getting into it each time she complained about the picture quality.

A week later, Kenji happened on a pair of tickets to the Maddox-Princely fight and figured Lizzie would be better company than Paige. A week after that, it was a hip-hop concert with Young Benjamins, backstage passes included. On Sunday, she trekked with him to the batting cages, a weekend ritual of which he'd never included another.

Eventually, they went to the zoo. The zoo at twilight had been her weird idea of a good outing, but one that paid off for him the moment she cooed over pandas in surprising fashion. He could almost see her as a mother that day, fussing over a newborn, saddling up a toddler in snow boots and a wool cap the way crazy Miamians did when it dropped down to 60 degrees. Still, days lapsed between one moment when they saw each other and the next, days in which his mind taunted him with the absurdity of the thought and of his time with her. After all, she was still Lizzie.

CHAPTER SEVENTEEN

Deena, Tak, Tony, and Mia stood in a tight room at the back of the Guest Relations office at Epcot. Low ceilings, baby blue walls, and a single oversized desk were the whole of their surroundings. Behind the desk, Mickey cupped a hand to one ridiculously large mouse ear and declared that he wanted to hear their thoughts. Nonetheless, Deena got the distinct feeling as she sat on the glossy, hard-backed red bench, with a bastion of hospitality out there and an even glare on her in there, that no one wanted to hear her thoughts. Red-faced, she looked from the officer who stood over them to Tak, imploring someone to see reason.

"I'm telling you, what you're saying is impossible. He was with me the entire time." Deena looked at Tak. "Tell him that Tony was with me."

Tak rubbed his face in fatigue. Still, he said nothing. Deena turned on Tony.

"Tell this man you were with me."

Tony looked him straight in the eye.

"I was with her."

She shot him a look of satisfaction. "There," she said.

"The truth is simple enough to get at," the officer said, tall and imposing despite the powder blue cast member uniform. He bent low so that his face fell even with Tony's.

"Turn out your pockets," he said.

Tony's eyes went wide. "No. I won't do it." He turned to Deena. "This man's a racist."

"What?" She shot the officer an apologetic look.

"He's racist," Tony insisted. "Outside. I heard him use the 'n' word."

Tak sighed. "Empty out your pockets, so we can pay the man

already."

Tony turned on Tak, his gaze wild. "You can't believe him! I wouldn't do that! I wouldn't—"

Tak got up.

"I'll be outside," he said and shouldered past the officer.

"Deena—" Tony started.

She massaged her temples with trembling fingers. "Please, Tony, just take everything out of your pockets. I'm very tired."

Mia looked from new brother to mother, back stiff, eyes bulging.

Slowly, Tony reached in his pocket. A wad of tissue emerged, and beneath it, a silver Mickey Mouse spoon.

Deena gasped, disbelieving gaze on Tony.

The officer took the spoon.

"How—how much do I owe you?" she managed.

Though she stared at Tony, he carefully avoided her gaze.

"Nothing," the officer said. "We've recovered the property. But you'll have to leave the park. And forfeit your tickets."

Mia burst into tears.

The ride from Orlando was stoic. Mia, in the back, sniffling the whole way; Deena in the front, doing the same. Tak drove at hypersonic speed down the turnpike, jaw clenched, eyes keen on the road.

"Half a dozen shirts from Disney," Tak said. "Three key chains, six snapshot pictures, two water bottles, mouse ears—"

"Tak—"

"A lanyard, a pin collection kit, a watch, sunglasses, a Pirates of the Caribbean hat—"

"Tak, *stop*."

"A pirate makeover, a jacket, a friggin' knapsack—"

"Would you stop?" Deena cried. "What are you doing? Keeping score?" She shot a wounded look at Tony in the backseat. "If we only knew why he did it!"

"We know why! Because he's a thief or greedy or both!" Tak said.

"Calm down," Deena said. "Don't let your temper—"

"Too late," Tak snapped.

Face pinched, she careened around for a better view of Tony, hoping for an inkling of understanding and found him face-passive, eyes on the pavement. And when Deena turned back to Tak helplessly, he fed her a withering glare before accelerating headlong into a traffic ticket.

CHAPTER EIGHTEEN

Tak opened the front door wide enough to let Deena and the children in. Tony eked past, head lowered, not having uttered a word since the revelation of his thievery.

"Get back here," Tak said.

"Tak, maybe you should calm down before—"

He shot Deena a single, acrimonious look and her mouth clamped shut.

Tony, halfway down the hall and toward the safety of his room, stood with his back to Tak, waiting.

"I'm pretty sure I told you to get back here."

With a dramatic sigh, Tony returned to the middle of the hall, technically listening to Tak but managed to stay safely out of arm's reach.

"You're gonna find that I don't have a lot of patience for nonsense," Tak said. "The way this works is that I'm the adult and you're the child, meaning I tell you what to do, and you do it. Got it?"

"Yeah, I got it."

"Good. Now tell me why you stole a spoon when we have plenty in the house."

Tony's eyes remained on the floor. "But, I didn't even—"

"Room. Now," Tak spat.

He watched his nephew slump away, lips thinned to nothing in anger.

"Tak—"

He started for the kitchen, convinced that he didn't want to hear a thing from Deena.

She followed him.

"Tak—"

He opened cabinets and slammed them until he found the Wheaties he needed. Another handful of cabinets later and he had a porcelain bowl in one hand, a silver spoon in the other.

A spoon.

It occurred to him that they knew nothing about this kid, family or otherwise. Only that he was the son of a confessed murderer, and to his own credit, a thief. In Tak's overzealous effort to make his wife happy, he'd neglected to consider reality.

Gingerly, Deena placed a hand on his arm. Tak glanced at her, fully intent on railing about the slack hand she had with Tony and the excuses she'd made from Disney to doorstep, but the look on her face stopped him. He knew it well, had seen it often back when Lizzie would go missing and they'd have to go searching. Back then, she looked half hopeful, mostly fearful, and wholly convinced that he'd get some sense and get the hell away.

As if he ever could.

Tak set his cereal aside and embraced her with a weighty exhale. She held him—clung to him, and they stood that way for a long time.

Four hours of ESPN highlights later, Tak peeked into Tony's room. He found the kid on top of a made bed, fully dressed, including the new Jordans he got so excited about. The moment he'd shown interest in them, Deena insisted that he have not one pair, but three. As Tak took inventory of the new console, sneakers, video games, sports equipment, and clothes, their error was made plain.

In an eagerness to earn his love, Tak and Deena had been unwise in an obvious way. Jordans, video games, the basketball hoop getting installed on Monday—what was it all for? It would bring them no closer to knowing him, or understanding.

Tak stepped into the room and leaned against beadboard wood paneling. Before Tony, the room had been fluffed and preened for guests. It still bore the distinct mark of impersonal hotel accommodations. They would have to do something different.

"You haven't eaten today," Tak said. "You'll worry Deena if you don't."

Tony met his gaze evenly. "Most everything still has the tags on it. I was careful not to mess your stuff up. I'll—be outta your way by morning."

Tak crossed the room, but Tony sat up quick, scrambling back like a spider—tense, guarded.

Tak froze. *Jesus*, he thought, *what has this kid been through?*

He held out a hand to him.

"I'm just going to sit down, okay? Just . . ." he gestured to the portion of mattress furthest from Tony, "just here."

Only when Tony nodded did he ease down onto it.

Tak waited, judging words and turning them over, conscious of the unfamiliar realm he sought to conquer. He thought back to Tony's comment and decided to start there.

"Tell me, kiddo, is that how things worked at the foster homes? Someone takes care of you a little while, you screw up and get shipped out?"

Tony glared at him, as if seeking to suddenly intimidate by sheer determination alone. Apparently he'd already forgotten the way he'd scrambled like a hunted animal.

"Nobody gets rid of me," he said. "I'm no trash recycled from one family to the next. *I* go when I've decided I've had enough. *I* go when it's time for me to move on." He jutted a thumb at his chest proudly. "I take care of myself just fine."

Slight, hair blooming, ponytail like a peacock's fan, Tony dared him to contradict, to insist that he needed others.

Tak's lips curled ruefully. "First truth you've told all day," he said.

81

Tony smiled reluctantly. He was tough. Tough as his father, it seemed.

"I'm gonna tell you something," Tak said. "And it's something you can't figure by looking at our house, clothes, or boat in the backyard."

Tony raised a brow in skepticism.

"We argue sometimes," Tak said. "We get angry, say stuff we don't mean, make mistakes. But you know what?"

Tony shook his head

"There's only one thing around here that isn't okay, and that's giving up on ourselves and each other. You do something wrong, you work to make it right. Especially when it comes to family. What you don't do is walk out. You don't ever walk out on your family, you got it?"

Tony lowered his gaze and said nothing.

"Now listen to me," Tak said. "You're eleven. Halfway to being a man."

Tony sat up straighter with the admission.

"And what a man would do is make this right," Tak said.

"But how?" he whispered. "We got kicked out of the park and everything! Mia kept crying. And Deena, too."

"You begin by apologizing to your aunt and cousin. Then you wash up for dinner, sit down, and eat everything she puts in front of you. And you compliment it constantly."

Tony smiled despite himself. "I don't think—"

"I mean it. I'm teaching you about women here, too, so you need to listen. She's making salmon tonight, which doesn't taste that good. But you're gonna act like it's a mountain of Snickers on Easter Sunday. Got it?"

Tony giggled. "Yeah. I got it."

Shewanda Pugh

"And afterward, you're going to clear the table and load the dishwasher. While you're working, you don't want or need Deena's help. And when that's done, you're going to read Mia all the stories she wants to hear, enthusiastically. You okay with reading?"

"Yeah," Tony sulked. "I read baby books okay."

"Good. Then you're going to read to your baby cousin until it's time for bed. You then shower and tuck it at the same time. Not a peep of complaint. Tomorrow, you get up and write a letter of apology to the Disney company and ask your aunt to mail it. And it's your own idea, not mine."

"All that for a spoon?" Tony cried.

"You prefer jail?"

"No."

"Good. Then go clean up. Dinner'll be ready soon."

83

CHAPTER NINETEEN

Tony stood before the man with tiny square eyeglasses and blinked when he blinked, unable to help himself. For reasons beyond him, the man squinted and peered as if he'd never seen a boy before, despite his school being full of them. Briefly, Tony wondered if it was the hair, and regretted rejecting Deena's offer to braid it the night before.

"Edinburgh Academy, as I'm sure your uncle has told you, offers a rigorous liberal arts curriculum and a small yet distinguished faculty. You will find more foreign language courses here than in any private school outside of New York. Students begin laboratory sciences as early as fifth grade, and by the time they're ready for upper-level courses, why, the selection is substantial."

He sounded like a butler to Tony. A butler in a big white house, maybe the White House. It occurred to Tony then that he now lived in a big white house.

"So tell me, young Mr. Hammond, how does robotics sound to you?"

Tony looked from the man to Tak. Certainly, they meant to teach him more than how to use remote control toys?

"Sounds okay," he murmured when they both seemed intent on hearing his answer.

Butler Jeeves smiled. His cheeks were massive and red, giving the appearance that they'd been scrubbed to swelling. Jeeves came around his desk and sat on the edge. In his hand was a slim manila envelope.

"I see you're from Bismarck." He flipped a page. "And a few other places."

Jeeves scanned the contents, flipped forward, then back, before finally settling on a scowl.

"There's a gap here. Three months, in fact. Is another file coming?"

Tak and Tony exchanged a look.

"There is no other file," Tak said. "He was out of school that long."

Jeeves's scowl look set to scar. "Illness?" he guessed.

Tak shifted in his seat. "No. He, uh, stopped going. And lived on the streets for a few months."

Jeeves tossed the file on his desk, papers scattering and floating to the floor. He hardly seemed grieved by the mess.

"Edinburgh Academy is known for its excellence, Mr.—"

"Tanaka," Tak supplied.

"Mr. *Tanaka*. We offer courses in biomedical sciences, engineering, architecture, and law. Our students go on to Ivy League schools regularly."

"Yes, I know. My daughter's here," Tak said.

He looked around, as if searching for the help Tony knew wouldn't come. In fact, Tony knew it didn't even exist.

"He's had a rough start," Tak said.

"This is not an alternative education program."

"Yeah, sure. What were those subjects you specialize in again?"

"We offer biomedical sciences, law—"

"And architecture, right?"

"Our architecture program is the most innovative—"

"Hall, please."

Tak leaped from his seat and out of the dean's office, leaving Jeeves to stare after. The old man glanced at Tony briefly, declaring with his eyes that this was most irregular.

Most irregular.

Hadn't he heard a Jeeves say that on TV once? White gloves, polished silver, back perched like a telephone poll. *"This is most irregular!"* He hoped to use that one out loud one day.

Jeeves slipped outside. Tony sat in the chair facing his desk, black leather and high backed, as he stared at the paintings. The stuff on the wall was Cubism, like Pablo Picasso. He'd seen it once in a crumpled *Design & Style* magazine at Dr. Wayneworth's office in Bismarck. There'd been few times in his life he'd had cause to see a doctor, and because of that, he wasn't apt to forget any of them.

Tak and the dean returned.

"Anthony? Mrs. Henderson, down the hall will work with you in designing your schedule. Your father tells me you're ready to begin."

"Father?" Was that what the hell he was? He wasn't calling him that.

"Let's get moving, Tony," Tak said evenly.

"Now?"

"Yeah, buddy. *Now.* We talked about starting today, remember?"

Tak clapped him on the back, like a friend. Tony had had grown-ups for friends before. Friends who thought him only good for the state money that came attached or for their own gross satisfaction. But he'd never let one of *them* get the better of him.

Yeah. He'd had grown-ups as friends before.

Shiny.

Tony's first impression of Edinburgh Academy had conjured a single word, and that had been it. As he stood in the hall, recalling gold letters embossed against red brick at the front, he figured the moniker alone must've been spit polished each day. Inside was no different. The floors were a dazzling bronze, the walls a deep wood. Centered in the main hall were trophy cases stuffed with rich kids' awards, accolades for robotics, chess, golf, debate. Somehow, he couldn't fathom where a kid who'd gratefully eaten half a Big Mac out of a Dumpster would fit in.

"How about I come with you?" Tak suggested.

What did he think? After a few square meals, a handful of clothes, and a bit of fatherly advice, he was suddenly a man Tony couldn't do without? Had he realized how long he'd survived on wit alone, on sheer grit alone, when wind and ice and hunger were the only realities in abundance?

"I don't need you," Tony said.

He waited for the burst of anger, righteousness, of outrage at the very least. But nothing came. So Tony rose slowly, certain of nothing except his own uncertainty.

"I'll be there in a sec," Tak said as he headed for the door.

Tony shot him a look of impatience. Hadn't he said him he could manage? Hadn't he proved as much? Try as he might, he couldn't affix a stamp to Takumi Tanaka. Time, Tony supposed, would help him with that. Tony plucked open the door and slipped out, but not before overhearing the dean.

"Mr. Tanaka, how soon before your father can address the student body?"

He slammed the door on Tak's response.

Tony's new shoes squeaked with each step he took. Jordans. Vintage limited edition. Still, he couldn't believe it. Bobby and the other guys back at the Bismarck group home would've never thought it possible, either. He knew the advice they'd give him; it was the advice he pressed himself to take: "Self before else." In a house with more rooms than he had years on the planet, there was but one thing to do. Grab all the cash he could, all the valuables he could manage, and work over the Tanakas before the opportunity dissipated. He'd drifted in on a fairy tale, believing food and a better family would somehow make him less of a liar or a thief. Hadn't he committed himself to the notion that there would be no more reasons to lie once he found the things he needed most? But of course, there were reasons to lie, reasons to cheat, to steal. And always, he could count on himself to find them. What else from the son of a drug-dealing murderer and an addict? What else but deviance?

Tony threw open the door to Enrollment Services. An ancient woman shot up from her seat like a rocket, white haired and trembling, tight-mouthed in her outrage.

"Exit and enter properly!" she shrieked.

Tony inched out, knocked, eyes frozen midroll as he waited for her invitation. When it came, he stepped inside.

"Here, at Edinburgh Academy, there is excellence in all that we do!" she drawled.

Tony blinked. More startling than the haughty English accent was the Little House on the Prairie blouse she insisted on wearing, buttoned up as if to check her turkey-gobble neck. He imagined her as a pod for an alien of some sort, with angry popping eyes and skin like crepe paper. Should her shirt ever have occasion to tear open, something monstrous would surely spring forth.

"Anthony Hammond?" she shrilled.

"Tony Hammond. I—"

"*Anthony* Hammond," she corrected as if she'd known him longer than he had. "Now take a seat. I am Edith Eberdine Mueller, head of enrollment."

She pointed a crooked finger at an old man's leather chair, and he dropped into it. Without preamble, a glossy blue book was dropped on the desk just before him. A handful of smiling kids, all white and locked arm to arm, stood before Edinburgh Academy.

"You'll find course descriptions for the sixth-grade offerings on page forty-two." She flipped to the appropriate pages as if she could hardly be bothered to wait for him. "While math, literature—"

She pistoned off "literature" with an emphasis on each syllable, making Tony giggle until one hot look straightened him out. Mueller cleared her throat.

"Math, lit-tra-chure, general science, English, and geography are *required*. In addition, you have a choice of two electives."

Tak slipped in without knocking. Tony sat up straighter, eager for the Mueller rebuttal, but scowled when none came.

"Mr. Tanaka, so glad you could join us. Please, have a seat."

He lowered himself into the chair next to Tony.

"See anything good?"

Tony shrugged. "Not really."

Tak took the brochure from him. He ran a finger down the print, frowning as he read. "There's lots of great stuff here, Tony."

"Like what?"

"There's art, music—"

"I don't know how to play anything."

"Well, they teach you. That's the whole point of school."

Tony lowered his head. "I don't want to look dumb."

Tak snorted. "As if they could. Bismarck to Miami? I guarantee you the dean couldn't pull that one off."

Mrs. Mueller stood up straighter, eyes widening at the jab. But Tony grinned. Maybe this Tak guy was decent after all.

"You could take up the drums," Tak said. "I could help. I've got a pair at home that've been catching dust for a while."

"You play drums?" Tony heard the wonder in his voice and immediately regretted it. Being impressed with a person put you at a distinct disadvantage.

"Sure," Tak said. "Drums. Keyboard. Guitar's my baby, though. So, how about we get you on one? Music's a balm for the soul, you know."

Tony looked at the floor. He'd never heard that before. Probably because the closest he'd ever come to a music lesson was Mrs. Peabody's kindergarten sing-alongs in Louisville.

"Drums sound pretty cool," he said softly.

Tak beamed. "So, music and what else?"

Mueller cleared her throat. "If I may, I'd like to suggest a start on upper-level coursework. Advanced mathematics or—"

"Art," Tony said.

"Art," Tak sat back as if done.

"Sir, it might be advantageous, if I may, if you'd allow me to—"

"You may not," Tak said evenly. "He picked art and music. Now print out his schedule. He's eager to start."

Tony shot him a look. He was, of course, not eager to start—but admired the old guy's panache in setting Mueller straight.

At eleven fifteen, Tony received a printout of his schedule. According to it, he was supposed to be in literature, second floor, Room 238. So, he slumped out of Enrollment Services, climbed the gilded staircase, and tapped on the appropriate door.

A man answered, which was his first surprise. He had dry, curly hair, his second. Though he'd never actually seen a live reference, Tony suddenly knew what people meant by Jew-fro. He touched his own hair, wondering if he had a Jew-fro too. After all, the texture between his hair and the lit-tra-chure teacher's wasn't all that different, both wild and full of volume. But was having a Jew-fro predicated on being Jewish? He couldn't be sure. It irked him not to know.

The teacher before him had a widow's peak, sunburned scalp, and a big mouth of a smile. He stuck a hand out and hesitantly, Tony shook it. When a few from the class snickered, he realized the teacher expected his schedule.

"Anthony Hammond?" he confirmed.

Tony nodded.

"Excellent. Introduce yourself to the class."

Tony sighed. Fourteen schools and this part never got easier.

He stepped into the classroom, moved close to the dark wood desk up front, and opened his mouth. What came out sounded like a croak. He tried again.

"I'm Anthony Hammond from Bismarck, North Dakota."

"And what brings you to Miami, Mr. Hammond?"

Reflex.

"My dad got a new job," he said.

"Wonderful!" he exclaimed. "And what does your father do?"

Jesus, he should've said mom. What the hell did Tak do? Nothing so far as he could tell.

"He's an architect. Real important, you know."

In having made lying a pastime, Tony knew that deviating little from the truth helped hold it together.

"Wonderful," the lit-tra-chure teacher said. "You may find that you have much in common with Brian Swallows. His grandmother is an architect, too." He cast an indulgent smile on a pasty pale boy in a sweater vest and button-up, blond hair separated down the middle by a severe part.

"In any case, we are glad to welcome you to Edinburgh Academy. Please take a seat. Any seat will do."

Tony surveyed the crowd. Usually classes were the same. Good kids in the front, bad or dumb in the back. But he couldn't read this group. Third from the rear was a boy in black wire frames and a button-up. Had to be a braniac. Last row on the right, a black kid, fat and too engrossed in his textbook to even look up. Jesus Christ, was he reading ahead? And up front, a girl with thick black hair and the slightest hint of a wave. When she looked up, Tony met velvet brown eyes and lips tinted with sparkling pink. He took the seat behind her.

91

The lit teacher went into a closet at the back of the room and returned with four books, all pristine. The first had a tan kid, mostly obstructed by shadows on the cover, holding what Tony could only guess was some all-important scroll. Up above it was the title: *Panoply's Sonnet*. The book beneath it was a glossy paperback of lime and burgundy with a girl lounging in bed, titled *Jill Norris and the Dog Catcher*.

"We're an eager class and have already begun *Tower in the City*. I'm afraid you'll have to catch up a tad," the teacher said.

Tony shuffled to that one. A sorry-looking white kid—boy or a girl he wasn't sure—stared back at him.

He glossed over the description. Nazis. A death camp. Jews. Sweden.

"Are you familiar with these?"

Tony looked up. Back at his school, when he was going, at least, they read short stories from graffiti-covered books. For him, finding "Wendy takes it up the ass" tattooed across the page was far more interesting than Jill Norris trying to catch a few dogs. And why catch 'em when you could go to the pound and get one anyway? Unless you wanted a Rottweiler or pit. Plus strays walked the street readily enough. There'd be plenty of opportunity to catch one there. No cause to write a book about it though, or to make him read it. Tony flipped through the pages with a sigh. There'd be no Wendys taking it up the ass in this one.

CHAPTER TWENTY

Kenji was loathed to admit that time with Lizzie was fast becoming an addiction. Already, he had plans for what they could do that night, and another, should she decide to keep him company again. *Company.* He supposed that was one way to put it, even as he pushed aside incendiary thoughts of what her nights without him entailed.

"Friends," he said firmly and dialed her number.

He took her to a tapas bar in Little Havana with standing room only. The bar stood a rich tapestry of overlapping browns with plank wood floors, mahogany paneling, and Spanish chocolate marble for the countertops. Only a handful of patrons mingled at the counter, including a pudgy-face man who plucked slivers of ham and olives from a dish. Lizzie's gaze swept a room rendered dim by a single overhead light and shot a glance backward at Kenji quizzically. It could've been the absence of chairs that caught her eye or the planks of ham that hung behind the counter. Then again, Kenji wagered that the stout bartender grinning and greeting them at the door in a bow tie might've been enough to baffle.

He placed a hand at the small of her back and surveyed the offerings on display. Rich oils, salted meats, and a plethora of cheeses looked back at him. A chalkboard menu hung low behind the bartender, but even that made no difference. Eyeing the display of Spanish appetizers was the only way to truly know any choices.

He ordered her chopitos, battered, and tiny squid, aceitunas or olives with anchovies, and sliced jamón ibérico, a smooth, rich-textured ham from the rare black-footed pig that ran one hundred twenty-five dollars for a pound. He did it all knowing she would squeal at the squid, shriek at the anchovies, and sniff the jamón before tasting. Half of him enjoyed introducing her to new things because the reaction was always spectacular. The other half of him just enjoyed it.

She surprised him that night, nibbling on a quarter pound of jamón, taking seconds on the chopitos, and daring to try the pulpo a la gallega, or octopus in olive oil.

"It's not good," she admitted. "And yet I can't stop eating it."

Kenji plopped a sliver of ham in his mouth and chased it with sangria. "It's because you're greedy," he noted. "Among other things."

Her eyes lit at the barb. "Like?" The tease in her voice unmistakable.

What he'd planned was an insult, a quip that she'd trade, one for another and so forth. But she'd smiled at him, and her hair hung free; loose coffee curls that framed an exquisite face and emphasized full, pink-painted and upturned lips. Kenji sensed that his mouth planned a mutiny.

Lizzie leaned forward, as if knowing, as if suddenly in tune with the very stirring of his heart. Drawn, he did the same.

"Say it," she said.

"Say what?" he said, the words taking effort.

Only with reluctance did his gaze lift from her lips. The room shrank, bar to table to Kenji and Lizzie.

Friends, he thought. They weren't just friends, and yet, these weren't just dates. Dinner, wine, mundane conversation, mediocre sex: *those* were the ingredients of dates. But this, even calling it "different" somehow did it disservice. More than friends and less than more, they balanced in a precarious limbo of trust where she could admit to drug addiction and prostitution, but not to whatever was happening between them. But Kenji fared no better. He, in turn, could readily talk about the gap between his dreams and reality, of abandoning baseball for the residue of his father's legacy, but dared not breach the chasm between them. Wrong. There was *nothing* between them, nothing before him but an addict bent on self-destruction. Nothing between them but life's realities. And yet, there was more; as he couldn't deny the bitterness he felt when nightfall came and the truth of how she made her living nudged at him, unwilling to give him rest.

He pushed the thought from his mind.

Kenji's gaze fell to the daffodils potted on the counter. He plucked a few, arranged them in her hair, and stood back to survey his work. He had expected the flowers to enhance her, but he'd not expected this—her blushing at up at him, gingerly thumbing the flowers, enhancing them instead of vice versa.

Lizzie caressed the daffodils of her hair with fingertips. What did a girl do when a man gave her flowers? What did she say? What did it mean?

Marveling at the effortless way Kenji made her feel both adequate and lacking, both certain and unsure, Lizzie knew herself to be a woman who earned wages by pleasing men, and because of that, found herself ensnared. Kenji didn't want the obvious, and yet, what he did want was less than obvious. She heated at the thought of what she possibly could give.

Stupid.

She was stupid for thinking herself a woman useful for more than a man's lust; stupid for thinking a man might want her for more; and stupid for believing they could ever be anything but sister and brother-in-law, ever.

But the feel of his fingers brushing her face in the moment he withdrew from planting flowers in her hair lingered still. She thought nothing more tender than that touch and her lashes fluttered with the memory. He was close enough for her to bask in faint traces of his scent: cool lavender and spice; she pulsed in response. So infrequent was her desire, a real desire for another, that it nearly mystified her. There'd been so many false coins, so many counterfeit transactions that she could hardly stand to desire a man. It didn't help that she couldn't understand what the flower in her hair meant, or his touch, or the darkening of his gaze, even. But she turned away nonetheless, fearful he might look at her and understand too much.

CHAPTER TWENTY-ONE

Lizzie climbed the stairs of her building in slow and indulgent fashion, still fingering the daffodils in her hair. A self-conscious smile crept to her lips, the mark of thorough embarrassment. Who knew the sway an unwavering gaze and a few cheap flowers could have on her! Pulse pounding childishly, she suspected her cheeks were the dull color of salmon. Before Kenji, she hadn't thought blushing as the prerogative of a whore. But neither were flowers or the company of a single man, night after night. Five evenings he'd claimed from her exclusively; five nights too many, she supposed. And yet she'd grown reckless, unable to stave it. Still smiling, Lizzie noted a petal as it wafted from her hair to the stairs. So reluctant was she to part with the perfection of the evening that she thought to retrieve it and tuck it anywhere in her hair. When Lizzie bent to get it, she rose to the sight of Snow in her doorway.

"Have a good time?"

Her mouth worked furiously.

"Get your stupid ass in here."

"I was just out for a walk. I was just—"

He sledgehammered her with a palm, blasting so that her head slammed into the side wall. She lost her footing and tumbled back—sliding, plummeting backward down concrete stairs.

A long time ago, Lizzie had thought them equal partners, with Snow sending her clients and content with only keeping a cut. He was a consultant, a protector, a sound voice, and practical friend. But that façade had ended almost as soon as it begun.

"Get up, you worthless bitch!"

When her grandmother threw a teenaged Lizzie out, Lizzie fled to Snow, frightened and desperate not to be homeless. He took her in, dolled her up, and splurged for a week on coke. She slept in his bed, cooked for him, pleased him on command, and thought herself his girlfriend, in both name and deed despite the age difference.

Snow snatched Lizzie by the wad of her mane and heaved her upward, forcing her to scramble so that scalp and hair would not part. He dragged her that way, feet tangling on stairs, hands groping at air, till he heaved her through the front door of her apartment. It was clean.

"For a week you inconsistent on my streets!" Snow screamed. "For a week I'm looking for my money! Tell me what that cost! Tell me what that cost me!"

He blasted her in the abdomen, smashed her in the temple, and righted her when she crumpled on the way down. She could find no air, only spots, black spots, widening, closing in from every direction.

He would kill her. It would be an accident, she knew, but just the same she would die. Maybe it'd be better that way, to wither at his hands, quick, to finally succumb to the life she'd led. Pain would only be fleeting, then death, and maybe death would be like the high she chased.

Lizzie's mouth began to close in on itself.

A week after the she'd moved in with Snow as a teenager, he began to complain about the money they'd spent. She'd snorted all of it, and she needed to replace it. Lizzie figured they'd do it the old way, the tried way that worked in high school, where he'd direct a few older guys to her bed, guys who were halfway to hard at the thought of a teenager already. But Snow wanted more.

"On the stroll," he'd said. "You could make two, three grand a week with a body like yours."

On the stroll. She'd been leery of standing on a corner and waiting for a stranger, unwilling to take the final leap to what she thought of as real prostitution. But when she actually said as much, he grew dark.

"You sit in my house and suck any dick come through that door. You do it for a line of coke, a nickel bag of weed, for a beer sometimes. You already a trash hoe. What's the difference?"

She opened her mouth to tell him the difference, to tell him the dangers of the street. But a slap halted her words. A slap halted them back then. A beating halted them now.

"Answer me, bitch!"

The bitter metallic of blood filled her mouth. "I don't know," she moaned. "I don't know."

"What a fuck cost, Lizzie?"

She lowered her gaze. "Seventy-five dollars."

"And where you better be if I can't find you?"

"With a john."

"So, where the fuck's my money for the last week?"

She had nothing, of course, but the dollars in her Bible, seventy-two that she'd manage to smuggle.

He gave her a murderous look. "You got a baller coming around here every day. You must be pocketing my money!"

"No!"

"Then you stupid enough to fuck for free! What? You think he gonna wife you?"

"No, Snow, please. I—"

He hit her.

And hit her.

And hit her.

CHAPTER TWENTY-TWO

Kenji stared at the buttons of his cell, pissed with how expectantly they stared back at him. He wouldn't call. He refused to call.

Three thousand variations on emotion and not a postcard from her. Hadn't she enjoyed the movies, dinner, the zoo, his one hundred twenty-five dollar jamón ibérico? What kind of woman disappeared anyway, without the slightest inclination that she'd do so?

Kenji cursed and tossed his phone onto the desk. He watched it clatter and skitter precariously before returning to the view of the bay from his office.

But as fury settled, he recalled the track marks he pointedly ignored and stories of humiliation she routinely suffered for a few crumpled dollars. Lizzie Hammond could be anywhere—sleeping off a near-lethal dose of cocaine or dumped facedown in a ditch.

Kenji turned back to his phone. Eyed it as if it were a sneaky enemy.

Still, he wouldn't call.

~*~

Lizzie kept ice on her face till night, when she dressed in a pink fishnet mini that sculpted ass and tits, paired it with patent leather pumps, and stepped out, huge hair fanning her face to hide the bruising.

Her ribs ached, and she could take only shallow breaths, but pain was the least of her worries. Eating away at her core like a double-mouthed monster was her true master, the one she'd tried to ignore. Tonight, however, he would get his due.

A suffocating night greeted Lizzie, air thick with humidity and smog. She nudged by the drag queen asleep on her stoop and veered right, the start of her stroll. Even in her deteriorated condition, she didn't have long to wait. In fact, Lizzie rarely ever did. A silver Sentra pulled up alongside her.

She bent low to peek as the passenger-side window skated down, fingers in her hair and twirling to mask the bruising of her cheek.

"What you feeling like?" Lizzie said.

Well-rounded and black, he pressed the edges of the interior as if trying to expand it. Scalp protruded from a mass of uneven and unkempt hair; a few pieces of lint waded in it precariously.

"Whoa! Who did that to you?" he said and leaned forward for a better view of her face.

A cold sort of meanness ate her insides, making her want to slash and claw at his thick frame, clear to the promise of bone. Had he known what she felt, what she imagined, he would haul ass outta there. No cocaine, no crack, no heroin. She was empty, restless, nothing.

"You want to fuck or not?" she blurted.

The trick recoiled. "Yeah. I . . . I've never done this before. I don't know if you just get in, or, you know . . ."

He waited for her instruction even as she blinked blankly. Eyes wide, even so as not to betray anything and yet betraying everything, in that moment, he reminded her of Kenji.

"Fifty dollars," she said softly.

He dug into his wallet and handed her the money through the passenger-side window. After stuffing it in her shoe, she jumped in the car.

"There's an alley up ahead on the right. Park there," she instructed.

He pulled off. They went two blocks before veering off in a lane so narrow a car's doors could barely open in it. He killed the engine and turned back to her.

For a guy who'd never had a hooker, he warmed to the idea quick. The moment after removing his keys from the car he reached under Lizzie's seat and yanked on a handle, zipping her back to the hilt. His door flew open and thudded against the wall of an abandoned tenement before he squeezed out into the alley and dropped his pants. Comically, Lizzie's john shuffled round the Sentra, legs bound at the ankles by his pants and frosted white despite his darkness. He threw open

Shewanda Pugh

Lizzie's door.

She leaned back, legs open to make room for him and waited for him to pull on a condom. He looked around quickly—why he hadn't done so before dropping his pants was beyond her—and then climbed in, back brushing the windshield with his stature.

He ambled atop her, heavy breathing like a wind tunnel in her ear. With two hands he gripped the headrest and heaved. In her, he twitched and pulsed on pause, cock like a fattened and stirring Vienna sausage.

Lizzie closed her eyes, as the starkness of withdrawal cramped her insides and dried her mouth. A mountain of a man thrust into her, violating her, forging deep and simultaneously repulsing her. Stinking of musk and manhood and perspiration, he heaved and ho'ed and grinded with theatrical laboring, but paused intermittently to whisper appreciation for her body. He was but a gross miscalculation of affection, a falsehood for the girl who'd had flowers in her hair and a kiss on her forehead.

Lizzie turned away, hiding the tears in her eyes.

She touched him, a single hand on his hip with the realization that she'd been neglectful, and he moaned uproariously. He took to humping her, hips curling, car bouncing with each hopping stroke. He would go and go and go, pay her, and at the end, there she would find her prize: the high. Already, Lizzie could feel bliss tromping through her veins, stamping out pain, stamping out all. Eyes rolling, she arched her back at the pleasures that waited. He could beat her, bruise her, drill her in the dirt and leave, so long as at the end, happiness waited.

And yet, even as she craved it, as her stomach knotted for it, Lizzie knew it for the demon it was, for the fury it wreaked and for the death it would bring.

~*~

Lizzie found Deon, the only heroin dealer that side of Overtown, on a stoop playing cards with three black guys. She climbed the old white and slack-looking porch and stood quietly at Deon's side, waiting for acknowledgment.

"I need a little H on credit," she said.

Though she had some money, it was hardly enough to cover what she already owed him, what she needed, and what she was required to pay Snow.

Deon frowned at his hand. "Pay me for the last dope I gave you."

A few of the card players snickered. Lizzie recognized the one with dreadlocks as an old friend of her brother's.

"I'll get it. Money's tight."

"Money's always tight for a crackhead," Deon said.

More laughter.

Lizzie whimpered. She'd tried to cut back, wanted to cut back. But her quiet yearning had become a yawning hunger, and now, fingernails dug into palms in an effort to keep from picking at her flesh. Nervousness swallowed her. She had to have something. God. Please. Help.

"I'll do anything," Lizzie said.

Deon looked up, bored.

"Snow's inside," he said.

Fear sliced her, and Lizzie rushed from the porch, heels fumbling on stairs so that she pitched, facedown, to packed dirt. Howls of laughter taunted her, even as she scrambled up and into the night, never daring to look back with the fear of Snow on her heels.

She tried to get back to work, but by two A.M. Lizzie ached.

One hundred twenty dollars in her pocket and not an ounce of heroin or gram of crack in sight. Her nose ran, and her stomach snarled, forcing her to double over in the fury of convulsions. She couldn't walk and would've crawled, had she thought that even possible. So, Lizzie balled up, fetal position in the same alley her johns tossed cum-filled condoms. She lay there, nose near a yellowed and cracked needle streaked in blood, and an old Coke can, hollowed out and burnt. Sweat and dirt streaked mud on a still swollen face as her heart pounded an uneven tune of pain and panic alike. Shadows passed her eyes briefly as the world dimmed and pitched. Lizzie's bowels gave way and finally, blackness overwhelmed her.

When Lizzie woke in the morning, it was with the shame of lying near enough to feel the spray of a wino's hot piss as he relieved himself near her face. It was promptly followed by the realization that she'd shit herself.

CHAPTER TWENTY-THREE

Deena eased her gloss black BMW into the parking space labeled "D. Tanaka" and frowned at the empty adjacent one belonging to Kenji. She exited the garage and rounded to the towering firm, briefcase in hand, mind already weighing and dismissing tasks. She juggled two projects at the moment, a new wing on the home of a Miami socialite and a bowling alley in a not-so-nice part of town. Both were in the tail-end phase requiring only the overseeing of construction and an occasional meeting with her engineer of preference on all projects, Greg Knight from Knight Engineering. A third potential project required her to submit a design proposal and interview with a panel of judges from the state. She expected a final decision in the days to come.

Deena trekked up to her office on the seventh floor, same as Kenji's. It took her eleven years to get there though on a shortened route that coworkers claimed had everything to do with her screwing the boss's son. There were others on that floor, prized architects who'd been in the field longer than Deena had been on the earth, and a few of them were still unpacking potted plants and portraits.

But Deena knew the score. Her father-in-law's dream was to leave his firm to a Tanaka. When she'd married into the family, she made that a possibility; and when Kenji declared architecture his major, the marquee outside practically changed itself.

But her transition to heir apparent hadn't been smooth. When Kenji first came to the firm three years ago, as an intern postgraduation, Deena's job description changed from architect to trainer, despite the accolades she'd managed to acquire. Quickly, her father-in-law made clear that he trusted the task of molding Kenji to Deena and would equate his failure to a failure on her part. She'd done everything from helping him study for the AREs to intervening on projects he'd designed. Kenji's first week past the test he got a major contract, a fast-food restaurant that dropped into his lap, no doubt with pressure from upstairs. He slapped it together in a fit, selecting materials ill-suited to the job, overlooking obvious design flaws, and claiming tickets to the Marlins in the World Series as the cause. Later, Deena would go from patching his design to scrapping it and starting from scratch. Had she left it as it stood, it would've collapsed in a year, maybe less.

He was disillusioned. As the son of the world's most famous architect, he'd seen his father build structures that were both romantic and grand. But he lacked the discipline to learn his craft, earn his name, or take his time. The surname Tanaka bought him projects he couldn't hope to compete for on his own—Deena knew that, as her marriage certificate had done more than even Skylife could manage. Suddenly, Tanaka meant nary a question about qualifications and only an eagerness to get started. One client of Deena's equated it to having Ralph Lauren suddenly agree to become her personal stylist.

Deena dropped her briefcase on her desk, powered on her PC, and went for a cup of coffee. When she returned she went through e-mails systematically, made notations where necessary, and stopped to read the congratulations cards on her desk from those welcoming her nephew to the family. She sent a few e-mails of thanks and settled in for a morning of grunt work. There were the new building codes passed by the county she needed to review, codes that she'd planned on reading at home before Tony's arrival. As it stood now, two children in the place of one made the house way too hectic for meaningful work.

Pausing every so often to sip coffee or take a note, Deena read over the regulations for exhaust ventilation. She was halfway through when her door cracked and someone stepped in.

"Morning, Kenji."

She didn't have to look up to know it was him. He was the only one that barged in.

"Hey. You got here early."

"Mhm."

Deena turned the page.

"How was Disney?"

"Disney was interesting." She looked up. "Have you finished the book I assigned you? *International Building Code?*"

Kenji shook his head. "Thumbed through it. But I've got plans to read it this weekend."

Deena stared at him. He was in black slacks and a baby blue button-up, a gift from her if she wasn't mistaken. His jet-black hair lay

105

stiffened with mousse, manipulated into something new and stylish. Fatigue shadowed his face.

"You got a haircut," she said.

He nodded. "Yeah, I did."

She turned back to her book. "You should've read the book already. I gave it to you before Tony showed up. There's no excuse."

"It's a dry read, Dee. I start and can't finish."

Deena set her book aside and studied him carefully. She remembered him as a boy, first growing stubble on his face. He'd blurt random facts about engineering or construction as readily as he did the nuances of a Marvel comic. What happened in between was a mystery. Again, it struck her that he looked tired.

"Ours is a slow climb, Kenji. You won't get there if you don't dig in and start grappling."

He ventured to her window. "Dad won a contest. I could win a contest."

Kenji pulled the blinds. Wood woven, sliding panel bamboo. Outside, a Carnival Cruise liner pulled into dock at nearby Port of Miami.

Deena swiveled in her seat.

"Your father put in a lot of work before he won that contest," she said. "And the last thing you designed wasn't even safe for habitation."

"Just needed a few tweaks," he said.

Deena's gaze narrowed. "We don't do 'tweaks,' Kenji. You do this job wrong and people die."

Kenji sighed. "I'll do better, Deena. I promise."

She turned back to her desk, suddenly all business. "Start with the book. Read it. Today."

He had no projects because she'd pulled his father aside and bitched after the last fiasco. He still received his base salary, heftier than most, but would get no more until Deena gave the green light.

"Fine," he said.

There was silence between them.

"Guess I better go now," he said.

Sadness ate at the traces of his smile. How had she missed it before?

Deena stood, architecture forgotten. "Kenji? You okay, sweetheart?"

But he shrank from her. "Sure. Of course. I've just—I need to go. Bye."

Kenji whipped out the door, leaving Deena to stare and wonder.

CHAPTER TWENTY-FOUR

The end.

Lizzie found it through the pain of humiliation, the humiliation of pain. She found it in withdrawal and self-loathing. It came to her not in the ferocity of violence or the peace of death, but as reconciliation, betwixt and between.

There could be no going forward, at least not on this path. Before her was death, an Anthony sort of death, perhaps even worse. And yet, turning back made less sense. There was no one back there for her, no mother and father waiting to embrace a prodigal daughter, no praying grandmother who'd always believed. So, Lizzie stood, between two places, both of which led to nowhere.

And yet, she couldn't stay. There could be no more crack or heroin or mouth-foaming pain, no more men atop her thrusting, thrusting. She had but her own mistakes, multiplied and emphasized, bleeding the agony of her own demise. She had nothing and was no one.

She could die.

The suggestion came to her, soft as a seduction, alluring in its promise of control of determination. Finally, she would be her own, make her own way. She could die by her own hands, without pain and in peace. No one would miss her. No one would care.

Kenji.

She hadn't forgotten him, even before her heart whispered his name, slicing deep and through her muck of misery.

Kenji.

Tears formed, confusion of another sort, interrupted only when her phone began to ring.

~*~

Kenji gripped the phone at his ear, internally cursing in an effort to bully himself into hanging up. He had no reason to call her this way, angry, demanding answers to questions he couldn't rightly ask.

The ringing stopped, replaced by sniffles on the other end.

"Lizzie?"

He heard the fear in his voice but could hardly check it. Instinctively, a fist balled at his side.

"Help me."

And he ripped at the sound of her voice, her misery laying claim to him as certainly as if it were his own.

Kenji swallowed.

"Do you want me to—" He shook his head. "Is this it, Lizzie? Finally?"

He could hear nothing but crying, tears that ate through him to something soft and pitiful.

"Yes," she said.

Yes.

CHAPTER TWENTY-FIVE

Kenji stood in the doorway of Lizzie's apartment, gaze trailing as she zipped left and right, fingers hurriedly snatching for nothings—panties here, a sock there, a water bottle from the kitchen—all with trembling hands.

"What are you doing?" Kenji demanded. He cast a look of blatant worry at the door.

Lizzie tripped over a spiked heel boot. Trash piled in quaint landfills—threatening to consume.

"I'm getting my stuff!"

"With Snow on his way?"

He was willing to stand there and be with her, to work on calming the thud in his heart, but he would not, he could not, put his life on the line for a sock with no apparent match.

"He's coming," Lizzie said. "She called him." And jutted a thumb at the angular white girl who'd been eyeing him sideways from the kitchen.

Kenji had never seen such a rag of a woman. Skin sallow and hanging, hair both puffed and stringy dirty brown, pockmarks rounded her eyes and mouth. Lizzie's roommate, Kit, stood straight up and down without a whisper of change from shoulder to thighs. The track marks on all four limbs told him of the common interest she and Lizzie shared.

"He doesn't love you, and he doesn't wanna marry you!" the girl shouted, interjecting herself into an argument that wasn't happening. "Go with this guy and you'll be back on the corner in a month as his bitch! That plus a bounty on your head from Snow! Use your fucking brain for once!"

Bounty?

"Lizzie, seriously. Let's go. Whatever it is you're looking for, I can buy it."

"It's a picture of Anthony!" she cried. "I can't leave my brother behind!"

And so they'd die for it, die for a picture Deena no doubt had dozens of.

Kenji cursed and fell to his knees, rummaging wildly in heaps of trash resting on the floor, desperate in his search for a glimpse of Anthony Hammond. Outside, a door slammed and his bladder burned. Every gangster movie and graphic novel he'd ever seen told him that he had but seconds to live. So he snatched Lizzie by the wrist and whipped out the door, leaving clothes and trash in the same pile, fleeing down three flights of stairs before flinging her into the Audi. When Kenji peeled off, it was without the courage to look back.

~*~

Lizzie careened for a look at the fast unraveling interstate behind her, hair whipping in the wind, relief and madness flooding her in equal measure. When she turned back to Kenji, it was with the realization that he was going far too fast, and far too fast north.

He lived in the other direction.

"Where are we going?" Lizzie demanded.

Briefly, Kat's wild admonishments came flooding back to her.

"Palm Springs. There's a detox center that's expecting you," he said, fists gripping the wheel.

He'd had a friend at the University of Miami with a coke problem. One call to him, then to the posh unit where he'd stayed, had all been enough, done as he drove to get Lizzie. The mere hint of pro bono work from the Tanaka firm had made a six-month wait list dissolve to nothing.

Kenji took in her sudden, frightened expression—more afraid than when Snow was on his way—and had a moment's hesitation.

"This is what you want, right?" He slowed. "Right?"

Lizzie lowered her head, brown waves fluttering south like a

111

river downstream.

What would it be like to run hands through hair like that? To feel it whisper across his flesh?

"It'll never work," she said softly. And for a moment he thought she'd read his mind. "It never does. I'm broken. Past treatment."

He looked away and found himself aching for her. Kenji blotted out sudden, unexpected tears with a blink of the eye.

"One month," he said firmly. "One month is what it should take. And when you get out, I'll be the one at the exit, car revved and impatient for you."

Lizzie's face crumpled indecisively, halfway between a smile and tears. He couldn't bear that, so he turned to the road, far beyond an innocent bystander in her sorrow. When had it happened? How had it happened? He just couldn't tell.

Kenji squinted at the road, demanding discipline in the place of emotion. But she hugged him, something half clinging and searing and pushing him where he ought not go. He wrapped an arm round her, wind whipping those wild chocolate locks with the top down on the Audi. Lizzie snuggled into him, and they drove the hour and a half to Palm Springs in silence.

CHAPTER TWENTY-SIX

Kenji stood at the window of his office. Up seven floors in a carving arc of view that swept the building on two sides, he looked down at the bay, stripped of its sailboats. Clouds of steel painted the sky, swelling and threatening, yet again.

The morning after Lizzie checked into the drug treatment facility in Palm Springs, it began to rain. There was but little of it at first, liquid sunshine for a dry and thirsty landscape. But the days passed, and as they did, quiet showers fluctuated in intensity, as if mimicking the ambivalent beat of his heart. As he stared out at dark and brewing waters of the bay, a torrent rained down from the sky in an instant, as impassioned and unrelenting as the emotions awakened within him.

Was this how it had been for his brother? Sensing the folly of his heart but unable to resist just the same? Knowing the path, its likelihood of success, yet seeing every alternative, every morsel of reasoning as impotent against the strength of his yearnings?

It didn't happen all at once, like a fairy tale, where one touch did him in. He could point to half-a-dozen nights and see that no one had any more sway than the other. Were he truthful, he'd admit that he'd been attracted to her in the first second of the first time they met and had been secretly pulling for her triumph ever since. But this was about more than cheerleading from the sidelines. He'd sunk seventeen thousand of his own money into her rehab treatment the first month, and now that they sought to extend her stay, he wrote a second check for more without hesitation. Yes, he was rich, and no, he wouldn't miss it. But it was too much to spend and still call himself an innocent bystander in the tale of Lizzie Hammond.

She called him every day. After the first two weeks moratorium on outside communication, she was allowed to make a single ten-minute phone call every day at 2 o'clock. He never missed one.

Try as he might, Kenji couldn't equate whatever this was to what had happened between his brother and sister-in-law. Their only concern had been the reaction others might have. Back then, a racist Hammond family couldn't reconcile with the idea of Deena loving an Asian guy. Likewise, their father, while he loved Deena for her potential in the field, wanted to preserve their name, their culture, their history, by wedding his sons to Japanese girls. That was the long and short of their dilemma. But this wasn't exactly an equivalent. Kenji had gone, not just for a girl with a bigoted family, but a girl just as likely to relapse, rob, and leave him on the side of the road, dead.

Kenji smiled. He remembered his days in high school, angry about the lack of excitement in the undulating line that was a rich kid's life. Despite living in one of the most dangerous cities in the country, he'd yet to so much as see a purse snatched by his eighteenth birthday. And while so many years later, he'd yet to witness as much, he figured escaping with a prostitute from a murderous pimp pretty much fed that need, anyway.

CHAPTER TWENTY-SEVEN

Never in Tony's life had he been kept to such a rigid schedule. Monday through Friday, he rose and had a heavy meal that appeared to be neither here nor there. Ham croquettes and grits alongside oversized sausages alongside fresh fruit alongside half-a-dozen other shit he could hardly be pressed to name. It was all prepared by an old Mexican who fussed at Deena when she took only coffee and toast, praised Tak for his heavy appetite, and pinched Tony's cheeks endlessly, promising *hacer que la grasa*, which, according to Tak, meant something about making Tony fat.

After breakfast, the old woman, who'd once been Tak's childhood maid, piled the children into a black sedan and shuttled them to school, where he was expected to keep up a steady stream of classes until afternoon. Every single day after school he had homework to get done, homework that got checked by Tak or Deena faithfully. Monday evenings meant family counseling, where they crowded into a white lady's office and told her what she wanted to hear. Tuesdays and Thursdays meant drum lessons from Tak. Wednesday he had free time for the pool or basketball court after he did his homework, which always took forever. During the week he was only allowed two hours in front of the tube a night—an obscene allowance he was certain constituted a violation of his basic civil liberties, though he had to admit the game room and pool with volcano slide made for a pretty all right substitute in any case.

Tony ventured down the hall of Edinburgh Academy, stretched a head above other sixth graders, Jordans big and slapping like clown feet on tile. Halfway between art and literature, he kept his gaze down, never veering left or right for a glimpse of the polished, glittering, and scrubbed clean kids all around.

A porky one with flaming red hair pulled up alongside him.

"Hammond, isn't it?"

Tony shot him a hateful look. Back at the group home, it would've been enough to run a kid off. But this one only frowned.

"You did say your father was in architecture, right?"

Had he?

"Yeah, sure," Tony said blandly.

The fat kid rushed to keep pace, shouldering a tall black kid whom he shouted an apology to, before turning back to Tony.

"So they brought him in for construction on the Exchange Towers?"

He couldn't have said that. He had no idea what the Exchange Towers were.

"What makes you think that?" Tony said.

"Well, you said that your father was handling the skyscrapers under construction downtown. Those are the Exchange Towers. Ergo, your father is working on the Exchange Towers."

Tony stopped. What the hell kind of kid said "ergo"?

His fat hand shot out. "I'm Brian Swallows," he said. "My grandmother's Jennifer Swallows. You might've heard of her."

Tony looked down at the hand. Eventually, the kid retracted it. He was dressed in the worst sort of way: navy blue sweater vest, short-sleeved banana button-up, white slacks. What was the point of being rich if you had to dress like that?

"We better get going," Brian said. "We'll be late for art."

Tony, who'd already turned to leave, shot him a look.

"You're in art, too?"

Brian nodded. "Grandmother thought it'd be good."

"Grandmother?" What a dick.

"The Exchange is a major project," Brian said. "Your family must be pretty excited. Was your father part of the design phase, as well?"

"Um, yeah. Sure."

"Is your father independent or partner in a firm?"

"Inde—firm," Tony said. A firm sounded far more anonymous.

"You're not sure?"

Tony rounded the corner. "I just told you, didn't I? What are you, a narc?"

Brian slowed. "A . . . narc?"

"Go away," Tony snapped and shoved open the door to art class.

He didn't know why he couldn't go to a regular kid's school. Why he couldn't sit in the back and sleep like he'd done in Bismarck, Lincoln, Louisville, and Tulsa. No. He had to go to a place where the dads golfed, the moms had plastic tits, and the kids summered in Versailles.

No amount of forced acclimation could make him part of their world. When Matthew Tolbert volunteered to introduce him around as the new kid, Tony told him he hadn't planned on staying. And when Brett Moore asked him over for video games on Sunday, Tony asked him if he didn't think black folks had video games of their own. When Frankie Spencer offered to help him with math after an embarrassing episode at the blackboard, Tony told him that he knew of a guy's asshole in need of more attention than him. Eventually, the buzzards slowed in their circling, and the students of Edinburgh Academy began to put distance between Tony and them. All except the fat kid, Brian, that is.

"We should hang out sometime," Brian said as he dropped into the seat next to where Tony always sat.

"No, we shouldn't," Tony said and slumped down in his seat.

The man with the Jew-fro walked in. He wanted them to pull out their journals for a writing exercise. Good. Brian wouldn't have occasion to talk.

"I'd like for each of you to reflect on your readings of *Tower in the City*. In particular, I'd like you to discuss the relationship between Efran, our protagonist, and the adults in his life. Relate them if you will to the adults in your life, or the experiences you've had with adults."

Tony stared at the Jew-fro. There was no way in hell he was

117

doing that assignment. As it was, he'd spent the first few weeks of school nodding off to Nazi death camps and murderous Germans. Twice, he dreamt the old man whose nuts he'd busted on I-75 had ordered his capture as head of the Gestapo. Each time, he woke drenched in sweat and trembling. If the Jew-fro thought that Tony would relate *Tower in the City* to his life any more than his dreams had done, then he'd be the second one to catch a pair of busted nuts.

All around Tony, students began to write. Heads bent, pencils working furiously. To his right, Brian Swallows sketched an outline. To his left, the dark girl with thick black hair, whom he'd noticed on the first day, flipped through the pages of her book with a frown. Tony wondered what she'd be writing.

"Mr. Hammond? Are you having trouble with the assignment?"

Tony looked up. "No, sir."

"Then you'll need to begin."

He picked up his pencil. And hesitated.

"Mr. Hammond?"

"What?" Tony barked.

The room gasped.

The lit teacher took a step back and looked from one student to the next. Each stared at him in unadulterated shock.

"You will address me as Mr. Applebaum."

Tony snorted. "Yeah. Sure. Okay." He would make a point of doing just the opposite.

Applebaum stood frozen, as if wavering in indecisiveness. "Get to work," he snapped.

Tony dropped his head and began to draw. A huge fist was what appeared on the page, a surprise even to him. Sketched in and scarred, Tony busied himself shadowing in the edges when Brian leaned over, wide-eyed.

"Tony, you'll upset Mr. Applebaum."

A jagged tattoo shaded the knuckles of his fist. Slowly, the word "thug" came into view.

"It isn't appropriate for you to sit there and draw," Brian continued. "If you're having trouble with the reading selection—"

"Do you ever shut the fuck up?" Tony demanded.

Brian gasped. Again Tony had the stares of the classroom.

"Why, you little piece of trash! I—"

Tony tossed his pencil and lunged, flipping his seat and hurling both fat Brian and himself into the wall.

He would kill him. He would maul him, make him deaf, dumb, blind, and leave him lying in a pool of his own blood. Fists to mouth like a jackhammer—fist to mouth like a jackhammer; "trash" was going to make trash taste trash. Misery had a sweetness all its own. It was a lesson he was willing to share with Brian.

Applebaum peeled Tony back by the waist, dragging, struggling, and finally heaving him out the front door. Once in the hall, Tony's lit teacher faced him, bloodied and disheveled, the horror on his face made clear. It was then that they understood each other, for it was then that Applebaum's face transformed from sympathy and indulgence to fear, comprehending that Tony was fury and terror, misery and menace, and a thing unlike which he'd ever known.

~*~

Tak stared at a white-faced easel and blinked as if expecting it to change by power of the mind. Only faintly amused, he flourished a charcoal pencil as if poised with the first of grand ideas . . . and then dropped it in disgust. Ten years ago, when he'd been young and sculpted like a Roman gladiator—okay, not quite but close enough—he'd had the heart of an impassioned poet to match. His painting of Deena, *Unfolded*, had netted his highest commission to date, a comfortable seven-digit figure. His second painting of her, titled *Demure*, was inspired by a glimpse of her just hours before their wedding. It hung in the Japanese American Museum of Art, ironically enough, alongside works from names he hadn't

119

thought himself worthy to be near. Since then, he'd produced other artwork that sold well by any standard, but greatness was the treasure that eluded him.

He had no shortage of culprits to blame. Life with a five-year-old meant that spontaneity was all but nonexistent. Add a jack-in-the-box surprise of an eleven-year-old from Bismarck and Tak had given up on the idea of whisking his wife off for romantic romps in the Caribbean, or to their bedroom, for that matter. Both had once served as inspiration for art.

But it was more than the presence of two children which ailed him. Once, Tak could put brush to canvas and find beauty, revelation, paradise, already thriving within him. Now, the emptiness of his art reflected the emptiness within.

What was happening?

Regret was too strong a word. He loved his wife, loved his family. But what had they taken; what had he given—freely given, in his role as husband and father? And whatever it was, would he ever be fully Tak without it?

He stared at the blank canvas in wonder.

But the answer never came.

~*~

Deena stared at the official Acceptance of Proposal notification from the State of Florida, resting in her inbox. She lifted it, certain of another step, another interview, another panel, between her and the project she'd sought. Her design for what she'd touted as the most forward-thinking, technologically advanced prison in the world had been accepted. Having proposed a role in the design and construction phases, Deena stood to earn a commission of thirty-six million for the firm.

She let the letter drift to the floor.

The door opened.

It was her father-in-law.

Deena looked up guiltily.

"You heard," she said.

Daichi Tanaka stood a full head above her, silken black hair now graying gracefully at the temples, face suddenly as hardened and intolerable as the day they'd met in a snow-covered parking lot at her alma mater MIT.

"I won't permit you. You knew I wouldn't permit you," he said.

Deena's gaze dropped to his hands, curiously clenched in a fist. He had a sheet of paper there, no doubt the duplicate notification letter, filed with him as head of the firm.

She scooped up her own copy and disappeared behind her desk.

"It's not a matter of receiving your permission, Daichi. I'm a partner now. I don't need it." Deena's gaze flitted away, bravery wavering in the face of a Goliath.

Daichi closed the door and took a step toward her, surprising her when his hostility melted to tenderness. "Deena, please. I'm hardly speaking to you as a CEO in a supervisory capacity. I come to you as a father. Can you not see how *unhealthy* this is? I mean, to actively play a part in the imprisonment of your mother—"

"I have no mother," Deena snapped.

Daichi froze. The two looked at each other, mentor to mentee, boss to employee, father to daughter-in-law, always midway through the graceful dance from one to the other. But somewhere along the way, the advice of a father became the ultimatum of a boss.

He smoothed out his paperwork carefully.

"I would not do this. Whatever the pay, you have neither the need for it, nor for what it inevitably will bring."

Deena's gaze narrowed. "With all due respect, you have no idea what I need."

Daichi stepped closer, eyes on her, a specimen that suddenly seemed both familiar and peculiar to him.

"My *musume,* I can't even begin—"

She shot him a pointed look at the Japanese word for "daughter" and once again, Daichi went still.

"Let's keep things professional, shall we?" Deena said coolly.

Daichi exhaled. "If you insist."

She dropped into her seat with the rare victory against Daichi Tanaka, gloating internally, storing it away.

"So, tell me," Deena said enthusiastically, "how was Phuket?"

She expected him to drop down in a chair, eager to share stories that passed only between them—woeful tales of unexpected erosion, ineffective sediment control, countless delays, and the follies of construction workers who proved more pain than pleasure to work with. But Daichi Tanaka simply stood, a hand on the back of the chair she expected him to occupy, evenness in his stare, ice in his eyes.

"My apologies, Mrs. Tanaka, but professionalism dictates that I not dally." He gave a curt nod. "Expect to hear more from me regarding our disagreement."

Daichi headed for the door.

"Conference meeting in an hour," he reminded her, as if she suddenly needed such reminders, and disappeared from sight.

CHAPTER TWENTY-EIGHT

Deena entered the conference room, a massive and windowless space with an elongated table for twenty-four at its center. Around it were black leather swivel chairs, each occupied by the senior-most members of the firm. There was no board of directors at the Tanaka firm, no board for one of the largest architectural firms in the world, because, despite its size, Daichi considered it a family company. Only a Tanaka would sit at the helm of the company, and when one was no longer available, its doors would close. Such was the belief of Daichi Tanaka.

Deena took a seat at the far end, on what would be Daichi's right side, where he preferred her. The seat to his left and across from her was empty. It was where Kenji sat, and it would remain glaringly empty until his arrival. Despite the earliness of the hour, all partners were present and only two seats sat vacant. However, Daichi stood over his, surveying his partners with an always critical eye.

"Deena, I've been meaning to tell you. Your work on Kansas City National Bank was stellar. Guaranteed to win an award, I think," Jennifer Swallows said carefully.

As with any words she spoke, Deena took them in, turning and inspecting for the true meaning beneath. Given that there were but two women in the highest ranks of a near-exclusively male firm, it would've been natural to assume that Jennifer, the older woman, and Deena, would've bonded instantly. But from the moment of Deena's hire, the senior architect made it clear that she was a threat. Instead of the support Deena anticipated receiving, Jennifer criticized her loudly and often on issues both great and small, making a point of masking advice with obvious challenges to her intelligence. When Daichi first sought to mold Deena and prop her up, Jennifer and her flunky, Walter Smith, gossiped religiously and worked covertly to undermine her efforts. Finally, when it became apparent that Deena had surpassed her both in reputation and prestige, Jennifer sought out a more demure, though no less hostile, stance, despite her increasingly advanced age.

Seventy.

It seemed to Deena that seventy brought a maturity with it that should've admonished against malicious gossip, distasteful jokes, relentless criticism, and pointless insults. But Mia had been two years old before even the jabs about the inherent benefits in screwing a Tanaka finally wore off. At the height of it all, an openly gay Walter Smith approached Deena at the annual winter cocktail party and inquired as to whether Daichi's younger son happened to be homosexual. When she indicated that he wasn't, Walter insisted that Deena hurry up and get married so that the men of the firm would have means to screw their way to the top of the Tanaka firm too. Though Deena hadn't shared their exchange with another, Walter had been fired by Monday morning just the same.

Already, her thoughts were with the prison designs upstairs and all she needed to do. With a sigh, Deena skimmed the meeting's itinerary in an effort to gauge the amount of time she'd be forced to sit and wallow. Attendance, a call to order—as if anyone dared be out of order with Daichi Tanaka present—and a CEO/Principal Architect report by Daichi. There would be no way of estimating how long such a report could take. Deena did know, however, that any report by Daichi would be weighted with numbers, figures, percentages, and performance measures not just of architects at their principal location, but at Rio, Tokyo, Mumbai, and more. Each time Deena considered the twenty-six locations with the Tanaka logo at its helm, she remembered the meeting so many years ago, when her inattentiveness had caused her to inadvertently make the case for laying off fifteen percent of the architects, engineers, planners, interior designers, graphic designers, and administrative staff throughout the world—a number that totaled nearly fourteen hundred people. Both the guilt and hate mail she subsequently received served as catalyst for many a sleepless night.

With Deena's marriage to Tak, Daichi awarded her partnership as a wedding gift of sorts. The gesture was unmistakably clear. Tanakas did not, as a rule, believe in divorce. And Deena's marriage to Tak was as much a merger of her interests to that of the Tanakas, in so far as his father was concerned. Her career goals became Daichi's and vice versa. As a Tanaka, he could only benefit from any strides she made in the field.

Both Deena's expanded role at the firm and her marriage were still new when the economy finally began to turn up from its drastic decline. When Daichi sought to expand into new territory, this time Shanghai, Deena insisted on coming along. Her father-in-law took it as a sign of unshakeable ambition. A blushing bride with her career still in sight? It seemed to make him love her all the more. And so it was that the newlywed couple packed, halted work on the construction of their new house, and moved to Shanghai for two months. Now, as Daichi stood before her, he undoubtedly toyed with the idea of expansion once more.

Kenji stormed in, whirlwind that he was, adjusting his tie with fumbling fingers. Deena rushed to meet him, thereby blocking the board's view of the Tanaka they swore would be the end of the firm.

"Where's your briefcase?" she demanded, adjusting his knot with practiced fingers. "How will you take notes? And did you remember the research you were supposed to do on aggressive minority recruitment?"

"No time."

There was nothing he could have been doing more important. Nothing.

"Kenji—"

"Deena, would you move so I can sit down? I mean, seriously. You—"

She had a thousand questions for him, each more exasperated than the last, but his cheeks were scorched, and his father was glaring, so she scrambled back to her seat. A last look at the poorly adjusted fabric about his neck reminded Deena that it had been she who'd tied his tie the night of his prom, for his high school graduation, and for graduation from college.

Daichi rounded the room to Deena, slammed a hand on the hardwood table hard enough to make Deena jump, and leaned in, expression severe.

"I would recommend that you take your own advice, Mrs. Tanaka, regarding professionalism, and curtail your behavior so that it complies with standard decorum in *my* conference room. Any further distractions from you or Mr. Tanaka will result in both of you receiving a standard reprimand under Article III, Section 2.15 of the Effective Code of Conduct Policy. Do I make myself clear?"

"Yes—yes, Daichi," Deena murmured.

She glanced at a wide-eyed Kenji, who looked from father to sister, as if waiting for further explanation.

Daichi stalked to the front of the room.

"What?" Kenji whispered.

Deena shot him an exasperated look.

"Article III, Section 2.15 of the Effective Code of Conduct Policy gives him the right to levy disciplinary actions at his discretion, up to and including suspension and a monetary fine," she hissed.

Deena righted herself immediately and set about ignoring him, her attention now on Daichi.

He was one of those people who commanded attention when he entered a room. Dignified, masterly, refined—Daichi Tanaka gave off an air of importance, probably from the day he was born. Salt-and-pepper hair, steel-brown eyes, and a stubbornly square chin were more than enough to intimidate. Couple that with power, extraordinary wealth, and unequaled prestige, and the outcome was a recipe for unbridled fear.

Today, Daichi wore a twenty-five hundred dollar Armani suit, tailor-made, smoke-gray. His briefcase, of the same gray, was a limited edition Prada, retail price close to five thousand. He retrieved the bag from a chair and tossed it on the table as though it cost nothing, before jamming two big hands in his pockets and turning away from a stark and attentive audience.

"An architect by the name of Jayashree Verma has approached me with the aim of firm expansion into Sydney, Australia. I would like to hear partner thoughts before making a decision."

He faced them and waited.

It was always that way with Daichi. Testing, ever testing. Giving them little information so that he could glean what they knew, what they didn't know, and why.

No one wanted to speak. Deena could see it in the way eyes studied the brown swirls on the table, life lines of a tree that once lived. When she glanced over at Kenji, his eyes were downcast, not on the table, but a spot just below it.

Kenji smiled down at his phone. His buddies Zach, Brian, and Cody were heckling him for being absent as of late. Text message after text message rained in on him, each listing the plethora of activities they'd undertaken without him—all of which, coincidentally enough, happened to be far more fun without him. Their assumption was that he'd been getting lucky more often than not, with the blonde accountant, Paige. He hadn't corrected them, not because he wanted them to think him a stud, but because she required little explanation and Lizzie, by contrast, too much.

Zach, former college teammate and self-proclaimed ladies' man, now sought to tell him about the opportunity of a lifetime of which he'd missed out. In it, he and Cody had been at their usual South Beach haunts when a potential one-night stand indicated a willingness to go home, not just with Zach, but Cody, too.

THAT COULD'VE BEEN YOU, Zach concluded in a text.

Kenji thumbed in a response.

APPRECIATE THE THOUGHT, BUT LIKE 2 LEAVE THE RANDOM SEX 2 U.

The answer came instantly.

34" 26" 36", Zach wrote.

Kenji tried not to smile.

To his right, a frumpy old lady who Deena couldn't stand, stumbled over words. "Of course, I'm familiar with Verma's work. He's a—"

"She," Deena snapped.

Kenji looked up.

"What?"

"Verma's a 'she,'" Deena corrected.

"Oh." The old lady shifted. "That detail escaped me."

"Fascinating," Kenji's dad said, in the unmistakable tone that meant he was honing in for the kill. "Considering that her early acclaim was mostly due to being such a young and successful woman in

127

patriarchal India."

Kenji grinned, barefaced, as he looked from father to that old menace. Maybe she'd finally get fired after all. Lord knows she's tortured Deena long enough.

"Son, glad to see I have your attention. Now do tell us your thoughts on expansion into Australia."

Heat rushed through Kenji. Inadvertently, he shot a look at Deena. She stared at her lap.

"Well, Dad . . ." He took the time to swallow, grasping for snippets of conversation. Nothing. "It all sounds okay. But you'd know best."

Kenji waited, eyes on his father, who never even blinked as he watched his son. Finally, Daichi nodded his approval.

"Off the cuff, I'd have to decline the venture," Jennifer Swallows cut in. "A twenty-six office firm is pretty substantial already, I'd say. And we want to guard against artificially inflating ourselves."

Lines now creased the otherwise sharp-featured face of Jennifer Swallows. She reminded Deena of a bird at times—not the beauty of a majestic eagle, swarming high above others, or the charm of a sweet blue jay. No, Jennifer Swallows reminded Deena of a starving elderly vulture through both deed and appearance.

Deena shot her an impatient look. "Your argument is the same each time we consider expansion. 'The firm is large enough already,' as if each new job created somehow lessens your bottom line."

"We expanded into Buenos Aires," Jennifer said. "At your insistence."

"And we stayed out of Singapore, at yours!"

Strom Wilson groaned. "Please, could we not rehash Singapore, Deena?"

Strom was the newest partner of the firm, in position for two years, at the firm for seventeen. Hair a stark white, face a constant frown, he made no qualms about his impatience with younger, less-experienced architects, Kenji included.

"Seven percent of the world's top architects graduate from the National University of Singapore," Deena said. "Other firms with a direct presence are capitalizing, not only on those numbers, but on the cultural viewpoint which shapes the architecture of—"

"Stay on topic, Mrs. Tanaka," Daichi said, but there was no mistaking the smile of appreciation. She knew it well.

"Fine," Deena said. "What are we considering here? Expansion into Sydney. It's a great idea if the bottom line can support it."

"What a surprise," Jennifer said. "But then again, maybe I'd be perpetually interested in expansion, too, if I sought to profit."

Daichi silenced her with a hand. But it was a fair point. Up until very recently, the Tanaka firm only offered non-equity partnership. In it, partners received a fixed salary plus their rate of commission; however, their fixed salary proved significantly higher than that of the other associates. With Deena's marriage to Tak, she became the first equity partner in the Tanaka firm, garnering a stake in its operations, profiting when the firm did, and earning on every project, regardless of whether she'd contributed or not. And while non-equity partners had only cursory voting rights, Deena could weigh in on any subject, though Daichi still wielded power of the veto. Deena had, in essence, become the second-most powerful individual among the firm's 9,000 employees. Kenji became the third.

Kenji dropped his phone on the floor.

"It stands to reason that we'd want a strong presence in Australia," Deena said loudly, horrified that Daichi might see his son palming the floor for his phone. "The Tanaka firm has a reputation of excellence," she continued. "We should seek to expand that as far and wide as possible."

"Yeah," Jennifer snapped. "Except when you branch out too thin we end up having to lay off a few thousand employees at your behest."

Deena stared at her. "If I didn't know any better, Ms. Swallows,

129

I'd think you were blaming me for the state of the economy, too."

Daichi grinned deliciously, a rare smile, restrictive but still reminiscent of Tak's. Deena couldn't help but smile in return.

"Daichi," she said softly, turning to face her father, "we can't ignore the reputation or the caliber of students that typically graduate from architectural colleges in Australia, particularly, the University of Auckland. Their faculty is among the best in the world. To remain competitive, we'll need to tap into that."

Daichi nodded in slow agreement.

"And there's something to be said for a diversity of experiences," Deena continued, audience disappearing to one as she warmed to the argument. "But I'm not telling you anything you don't already know. Diversity is at the helm of your belief system. The arguments you make as you go from lecture to lecture. What do they say? That we're to embrace, nurture, and reflect the prevailing norms, belief systems, and richness of diversity in varying societies. Therefore, it only stands to reason that we can benefit from adding high-quality Australian architects to an already diverse family."

"Yes, but—"

Daichi halted Jennifer with a hand.

"Agreed," he said. He turned to Jennifer.

"Ms. Swallows, do us the pleasure of researching the feasibility of expansion into Australia. I hope you were paying attention to the points Mrs. Tanaka illustrated. I'd like them highlighted in precise format. In addition, prepare a list of architectural firms with the largest presence in Australia, as well as their substantial in-state projects within the last ten years."

A cell phone rang. Deena flinched.

Daichi's gaze swept the group, scathing, searching, stalking. Deena shrank in her chair, thankful for the OCD tendency she had to check her cell three or four times before each meeting started. Partnership in no way meant immunity. In fact, two former partners, Sam Michaels and Donald Mason, had been forced out after complaints from Tak following a few incidents between them and Deena. Actually, Tak had told his father that he could either fire them or watch him kick their asses. They'd received notices the same day, and with only a cursory severance pay.

Daichi came to a standstill just before Deena. She looked around in confusion before realizing all eyes were now on a statuesque, horrified Jennifer Swallows.

"Answer," Daichi demanded. "Answer before the blatant way you insult my intelligence further rouses my temper."

Jennifer reached into a dumpy and oversized black purse, fishing around blindly. Several moments of shrill ringing lapsed before Daichi snatched the bag and dumped its contents on the table. Crumpled receipts, old napkins, lipstick, mascara, eyeliner, a plastic knife, mints from the Olive Garden, sunscreen, two jumbo-sized Snicker bars, a pair of car keys, sunglasses, and a tiny silver vibrator clattered to the table.

Deena gasped.

"Answer," Daichi repeated.

It was only with effort that Deena's huge eyes slid from the silver bullet to its owner.

Jennifer rose from the table, face a nightmarish red, only to have Daichi shake his head in forbidding fashion.

"You've interrupted our meeting. We will interrupt your conversation. Answer now."

Jennifer dropped into her seat.

"Hello?" she croaked.

Silence followed.

"No, I—"

She reached for her items and hurriedly began stuffing them into her purse.

131

"*Brian? My* Brian?" she was on her feet. "No! I'll be there immediately."

Jennifer hung up the phone.

"I have to go," she said. "I'm so sorry. My grandson—my grandson's been attacked. I have to get to Edinburgh Academy."

The phone in Deena's purse began to vibrate. She looked down and saw it was Edinburgh Academy.

"Daichi, I'm sorry." She was already pushing away from the table. "Edinburgh's calling me, too. I better take this."

Daichi tossed aside his pointer. He said nothing, but stepped closer, as if watching a fascinating scene unfold. Deena answered her phone.

It was the dean, insisting on a conference at once.

CHAPTER TWENTY-NINE

Deena stepped into the dean's office at Edinburgh Academy and froze at the sight of Jennifer Swallows. Next to her was a portly boy with an ice pack affixed to his face. And to Deena's left, Tak and a scowling, wild-haired Tony.

"Deena," Jennifer hissed, her gaze following her as she took a seat next to Tony. "Had I known the riffraff who attacked my baby was yours, I would've given you a ride."

Tony's hand clenched in a fist. Tak placed his own hand over it.

"Why would you call a child names?" Deena said. "Seventy years old and ill-bred as ever."

"Ill-bred!" Jennifer sputtered.

Deena turned on Tony. "What happened? Did he attack you?"

Any offspring of Jennifer Swallows was prone to do just about anything.

Tony turned from her, focus now on a white stretch of wall.

"You heard your aunt," Tak snapped. "Answer. Now."

Tony sighed. "Yeah, I hit him first," he said proudly. "And I'll do it again if he bugs me."

Deena stopped. "But he . . . harassed you?"

Tony shrugged roughly.

"I only tried to be his friend!" the fat child blubbered. "I tried to help him with his work!"

"Other students in the class tell me that Brian offered to assist with a writing assignment that Anthony appeared to be having difficulty with. In response, Mr. Hammond attacked him."

Deena turned an incredulous look on the dean. "Well, that can't be all to it," she said. "Tell him what else happened, Tony!"

"That's all. That's it," Tony said simply.

Deena and Tak exchanged a somber look.

"He shouldn't even be here," Jennifer Swallows blurted. "There's an admissions process. Edinburgh Academy is the most exclusive private school in the Southeast, and I know for a fact that he shouldn't have been here."

"His reputation is horrible!" the fat child conceded. "All over the school he's alienated other people! Frankie Spencer told me just the other day their family's considering a lawsuit for public slander after something *he* said."

"Frankie Spencer's a doughnut bruiser."

"Tony!" Deena shrieked. "My God!"

She looked from the dean to Jennifer, the latter of which smiled like she'd just been blessed with the sweetest, richest, most indulgent dessert.

"Keep it up," Tak warned. "Keep it right up, Tony Hammond."

Tony shot Tak a look of impatience but said nothing.

"I promise you, we don't encourage this kind of behavior," Deena said to the dean.

"Oh, you can hardly help it," Jennifer said with mock graciousness. "After all, the whole office knows how he just showed up on your doorstep. How he was homeless just months ago."

"Homeless?" Brian echoed.

"Somebody better shut her up," Tony warned.

"Here, I was thinking the same," Tak said with a look of caution trained on Jennifer.

"Subject to Edinburgh Academy protocol, Mr. Hammond will

134

be faced with one week's suspension for his actions," the dean said.

"A week!" Jennifer cried. "That's hardly enough! Look at my grandson. He's been beaten!"

"It's the extent of our capabilities," the dean replied.

"Bullshit! You can kick his ass out," Jennifer said.

"For a first offense?" the dean said.

"For a kid who just got here!"

Jennifer turned a scowl on Deena. "Influence, always influence. What tempting nugget did the Tanakas offer to get their riffraff into the most prestigious school south of the Mason Dixon line?"

"I don't know what you mean," Deena said evenly.

"Like hell you don't."

Jennifer leaped from her chair, snatched her wounded grandson by the collar, which caused him to groan, and ushered him toward the door. Deena caught a glimpse of the furious shiner just beneath his icepack. It would haunt him for days.

"You know, Mrs. Tanaka, maybe if you spent half as much time keeping this hooligan in check as you did feeding some thirst for riches the ghetto girl inside you desire—"

"What?" Deena cried, heated and overheated in an instant.

An arm shot out from Tak. He stood, putting a body between his wife and a woman nearly her grandmother's age.

The dean leaped from his chair. "Ms. Swallows, I hardly think—"

"The PTA will know that you're harboring a thug on campus," Jennifer said, cutting him off. "Don't be surprised if Pepperdine gets an influx of students in the coming weeks."

Jennifer slammed the door behind her, forcing it to bounce with

135

her fury.

Silence followed.

"Well," Deena said finally, "we should probably go."

"I'm afraid there's one more thing. Something I didn't want to mention in front of her."

The dean returned to his desk. He picked up a simple black notebook and opened it before handing it over to Deena. There was a fist inside.

"This is what he spends his time doing while others are working."

Seconds later, Tak, Deena, and Tony burst out of the office.

"Room for two weeks!" Tak shouted. "And not the room as you've got it now. I'm talking no TV, no video games, no computer, no breathing without my okay! You got that?"

Tak turned on him midhall, daring Tony to contradict.

Head lowered, hands in his pockets, he found sudden interest in his reflection on the floor.

"Yeah," Tony said.

"*Yes*," Tak snapped. "And you're not gonna just be lying around, either. You'll pick up on the chores. Mrs. Jimenez'll let you know what to do. You give her a hard time, and you'll see that two weeks lasts as long as I say they do. You got it?"

"Yes."

Tak stormed down the hall with Deena just behind him. She glanced back only once to shoot Tony a glare of warning.

CHAPTER THIRTY

Tony rode with Deena, at her insistence, back to the house. She'd handled things this way to give Tak time to cool off and Tony a moment to express himself.

"If he did something to you," Deena said quietly as she merged onto I-95, "something you didn't want to mention back there, it's okay. You can tell me now."

Tony said nothing.

"When you were back at the group home—"

"I'm not gonna talk about the group home," Tony snapped.

Deena lapsed into silence. And it was in silence that they drove home.

When she pulled into the driveway, it was next to Tak's convertible. Silently, Deena and Tony went into the house only to be greeted by the sight of Tak pacing.

"Go to your room," he snapped.

Tony slumped off.

"What now?" Tak demanded the moment he was out of earshot. "What now, Dee? And what the hell is happening?"

"It was a fight, Tak. There had to be some reason why."

"Before you came, the dean was telling me about all this—this *shit* he does. Always cursing! Never paying attention! And you heard what he said about the gay kid!" Tak shook his head. "He's threatened other kids before."

"I don't know what you want me to say."

Tak turned away from her, retracting a look of breathless rage.

"I don't know," he said. "I just—I don't know." He headed for the door.

"Where are you going?" Deena called.

The door slammed in response.

~*~

Two hours of driving in circles and thirteen floors of stairs later, Tak burst through the doors to the lobby of his father's office. The cool, clipped, and professional voice of an automated woman welcomed him in English, Spanish, and Japanese. He trekked across Spanish marble, tossed a wave first at his father's secretary Angela, and banged on a massive door of African mahogany.

"Takumi!"

Angela, ever anxious, rushed around to meet him.

"Your father's on a phone call from Madrid! I don't think he'll—
"

Tak barged in.

Daichi Tanaka held the phone to his ear.

"I need to talk to you," Tak blurted. "And I can't come back later."

Behind him stood Angela.

"I tried to tell him you were on a call—"

"It's all right," Daichi said and switched over to fluent Spanish. "*Lo siento. Estoy obligado a retomar esta conversación en otro momento.*" Daichi paused. "*Por supesto. Tenga un buen día.*"

When he hung up, his gaze traveled to Angela. She backed out of the room, and Tak lowered himself into a seat.

"Mia's all right?"

Tak nodded.

"Then this is about what happened at Edinburgh."

Tak massaged a brow. "I'm in over my head, Dad."

Daichi sat back.

"You react from your heart and do so without exception. In this case, you've taken a child you know nothing about without thought of the potential consequences."

Tak boiled. "What was I supposed to do, Dad, since you know everything? Trash him? Leave him to be raised by taxpayers?"

"Certainly not. But you were supposed to give adequate thought to the issues that might arise."

Tak sighed. "He's in counseling. We all are."

Daichi paused. "Then you're not here about him. You're here about you."

Silence passed between them.

"I'm confused. And angry. He does things that make no sense. Steals what he doesn't need to. Lies about what doesn't matter. It goes on and on. Little things. Like whether he ate the last of the strawberries. I would shake him if I thought it would rattle some sense into him!"

Daichi scratched his head. "I'm afraid I don't have anything of value to offer in the way of psychological assessments for troubled children, and you don't need me to tell you I've been an inconsistent father."

"Get to it, Dad."

"Well, even parents without troubled children go through these emotions—confusion, uncertainty, anger, doubt. We wonder whether the job we've done is adequate, and we long for moments back so that we might correct perceived mistakes. These feelings are magnified when juxtaposed against stress of any sort. Your stress, of course, being the newness of your role as father to a troubled son."

139

Tak sat back with a snort at his father's choice of words. "Father to a son?" he echoed.

"You don't think of yourself as his father?" Daichi said, surprised.

Tak looked up, thoughts interrupted.

"Oh, it's not that," he said. "I just think it's painfully ironic that I'm raising the son of the man who tried to kill me."

His father smirked.

"You know, as far back as Hammurabi, a woman's chastity was deemed to be a tribute *to* and a thing of value *for* her family. Perhaps Deena's brother anticipated your desire to, uh, take that."

Tak grinned.

"Think of Anthony Hammond as the man who brought you to the woman you love. Or rather, forced you to look at her via gunpoint."

The two laughed. Life had a way of being funny, even when it shouldn't have been.

"You have regrets?" Daichi finally asked.

It was the question Tak had been too fearful to pose himself. "I don't want regrets." It was the best he could do.

Daichi nodded.

"Well, he's your son now. For better or worse. And as I've found, we often must get through the worst with our sons to enjoy the best."

Tak shot him a rueful smile, paused, and then headed for the door. On his mind were thoughts of the strained father-son journey they'd shared, culminating, of course, in the accident that nearly took his life.

"There's something else," Daichi said. "Ordinarily, I would never do this, but . . ."

140

Tak waited, a hand on the doorknob.

"It's about Deena. You should know about the project she's on."

CHAPTER THIRTY-ONE

When Tak returned home, night engulfed the city. Were he pressed, he could hardly account for his whereabouts after leaving his father's office. There'd been some driving, much of it circular, but there'd been long patches of nothingness, too. Parked on an endless stretch of sand far from his house, he'd looked out at the waters and asked, "What now?"

He was a husband, father, son. Each came with a shitload of expectations. But suddenly, he could only think of his wife.

Tak found Deena poolside and soaking in the Jacuzzi behind their house. Head resting against the ledge, two-tone toffee curls spilled and hung damp from the steaming water. She lifted a sleepy gaze at the sight of him.

Tak peeled off his shoes and stuck feet in the water. Khaki shorts soaking from the damp edge on which he sat. Content with watching his feet submerge, he toyed with just how he should begin.

"I talked to Dad today," he said finally. "He told me about the prison project."

Deena lowered her gaze. With it came a silence so long that Tak gave up on earning a response.

"Do you realize," she said softly, "that I'm a thousand times more likely to murder you because my mother murdered my father?"

Well, he wasn't expecting that.

"Mariticide," she said softly.

Tak sighed.

"You're not going to kill me, Dee."

She looked up at him. "Your father sent you to talk to me. To talk sense into me."

"Well, yeah. He's worried about you. I am, too."

She stood up, water rushing in currents from her body.

"For twenty-five years I've been on my own, since my mother decided I had no need for parents. I put myself through school, got a job at the best damned architectural firm in the world, and oversaw a multimillion-dollar project by my twenty-fifth birthday. I think it's safe to say I don't need you or your father wringing hands over me."

"And that means what? That I forgo my right to worry about my wife? Or him his daughter?"

She looked away. But Tak studied her, studied her till fury melted to uncertain sigh.

"Come here, Dee." He held out a hand.

"No," she sulked. "I don't want to."

He pulled her to him anyway, suppressing a smile. How long he held her, he couldn't say.

"It's no good, baby," Tak told her and planted a kiss on her forehead. "Any project that has you caging up your own mother is no good. You've got to leave it alone. Okay?"

She never did respond.

CHAPTER THIRTY-TWO

Just as the rain stopped, Kenji came to a realization. He'd lost his mind.

Yearning to have a girl like Lizzie Hammond was like hoping to grasp grains of sand even while watching them slip from his fingers. And while he could fall to his knees and thrash wildly for more sand, inevitably, it too would fall away like the last.

He would leave her alone. As much for her good as his. They could be friends; hell, they were already family. But they could never be more, no matter how many times he thought of those sweet, gold-flecked eyes widening in astonishment at the slightest things, or her little chin, set stubborn in everlasting defiance.

With each day her treatment stretched on he found that his patience unevenly stretched with it. Common sense told him that a decade of physical and mental abuse didn't unravel with a pill and dose of impatience from him. Skepticism told him that his yearning to hear her voice or see her smile was a testament to his physical attraction and nothing more. But that argument only lasted until 2 P.M. each day, when she made her daily phone call, causing him to inadvertently smile without a hope of doing otherwise.

In the months they were apart, Lizzie had become an unmistakable part of Kenji's life. Seven days a week they talked. About small things at first—the niece they shared, the weather, how much they both anticipated their talks. She rarely went out, and so, he'd taken to explaining each day in stark clarity—the bleeding red of sunsets, the molten silver of a storm, bold and ever intensifying. They talked of her treatment and her troubles. Cravings made her fear that she could get no better, no matter how much he encouraged. Kenji learned the name of her therapist—Dave, who was himself a recovering alcoholic. It was with Dave that she talked about her addiction, prostitution, her family, and Snow.

"Sometimes I think that none of this matters," she admitted to Kenji. "That the moment I'm out, Snow will kill me anyway."

He promised her that they'd conquer that problem together. Still, he stood ever amazed by the little chivalrous knight inside, eager to emerge for Lizzie Hammond and Lizzie Hammond alone.

They never talked about what they were or weren't, and for that, Kenji was grateful. There were too many truths in that conversation—about what he wanted, what he anticipated, and what he could fairly expect from Lizzie at this juncture.

CHAPTER THIRTY-THREE

Deena frowned at the results of the soils samples she'd sent for analysis, taken from one of three future sites for the new women's prison. The first reported flaky particles, the second excessive moisture: leaving only the third as a true option for construction. She tossed aside the stacks of paper with a snort. When she looked up, Tak looked down at her.

"Working still?" he said and pushed her feet off the coffee table. "Been waiting for you in bed."

Deena stacked the papers and filed them neatly in her briefcase, facedown so that the bold type stating "Project 9 Women's Correctional Facility," would be conveniently out of view.

"Okay. I just had some things I needed to get out of the way."

Tak dropped down next to her so that the couch jerked with his weight. When he picked up a document labeled "Financial Analysis" next to a box of pizza and a bit of leftover change, she snatched it away, out of fear that he'd read the prison reference underneath.

"Well, you just answered my question," he said dryly.

Deena shoved it too in her briefcase. "Stay out of my work, Tak. It's really none of your business."

"It is when it affects our home life."

She turned on him. "And who says it does? Your father? The all-knowing Daichi Tanaka?"

Tak raised a brow. "You're the one who acts like he's omniscient, not me."

"Just mind your damned business," she warned.

Haphazardly, Deena stuffed financial reports, legal reports, building ordinances and designs into a Louis Vuitton briefcase she'd purchased years ago. Though her hands trembled and her temperature rose as if her very body threatened to overheat, Tak sat next to her, a foot propped on his knee, arm draped behind the back of the couch, watching her as if she were only minutely interesting.

"You've been dreaming about her again," he said quietly. An observation. An accusation.

As a little girl, she used to relive the same moments in her dreams: strange men, her mother's screams, Deena running, running, running. And then the bang.

There was always the bang.

"I have not," Deena snapped, voice betraying with the slightest of a tremble.

Tak picked at a piece of lint on his jeans. "All right then," he said, "tell me what else is happening at work."

She hesitated. "Your father is thinking of expanding into Sydney."

"And you?"

"I think it's great."

Tak sighed. "Of course you do."

Suddenly, he was on his feet. Deena looked up at him in wonder.

"What does that mean?"

She stood, never at ease with a man towering over her.

"It means Shanghai, Copenhagen, Houston, and now this."

"Now what?" Deena demanded in exasperation, though she suspected she knew.

"You'll want in. Ground floor. Site development. New hires. All of it."

He searched her face. "Yeah," Tak said, "just like I figured."

But Deena shook her head. "And what's wrong with that? What's wrong with ambition?"

"Ambition?" he cried. "Is that what has you seeking new and better ways to punish your mother? Out to show you're even more of a heartless hard ass than the original Tanaka?"

Deena rolled her eyes. "Listen, Tak. Don't make this about whatever happened between you and your dad, okay?"

Disbelief etched his face. "You have got to be kidding me." He stared at her but a moment before stalking off in a huff. Halfway gone, he turned back.

"You know, your family could use some of that passion and perseverance that you've got on short order for work. Maybe even a little of that devotion. As it stands, I haven't quite figured out how to be both mother and father, much as Tony and Mia would appreciate it. The excuses you give for them? The total absence of discipline, no matter what it is they do? Yeah. Turns out it doesn't help much."

Deena gasped. She lacked passion, perseverance, and devotion when it came to him and their children? After all they'd endured to be together? After all this time, he still needed her to prove something to him?

She had only two words for that.

"Fuck you."

Tak threw up his hands in surrender, turned, and stormed off. When Deena headed for the bedroom, it was just in time for him to brush past her, favorite pillow and blanket in hand. Seconds later, he slammed the door to a guest room behind him.

~*~

Darkness.

Darkness and the wail of a baby: as sharp and piteous as that of any wounded creature. Deena couldn't find the baby, and blackness engulfed her, consuming with eerie totality. It was more than a light extinguished, more than the mere absence of it. This dark meant emptiness. Emptiness, isolation—except there was the child that

148

sobbed. Where was she? How was she? And why wouldn't she stop crying?

Panic seized Deena, thrashing her heart and forcing tears to her cheeks. The baby. She was expected to get the baby. Mommy said to hurry.

"Dee! Dee, wake up."

Deena's eyes flew open to face Tak staring down at her.

"Are you okay?" he whispered.

She sat up.

"The baby," she said. "There was a baby—"

He shook his head.

"Was a dream. You're awake now."

He brushed dampness from her face.

Deena snatched free, her wound renewed with the memory of his earlier words.

"I know, I'm awake now," she snapped, embarrassment fueling her anger.

Tak stared at her, disbelief plain. "All right then," he said. "Guess I'll head back to the guest room."

He stared at her and she stared back.

"Night," Tak said and slammed the door behind him.

~*~

Deena rose in the morning and dressed to a silent home. Having woken late, she missed the morning rush where Mrs. Jimenez hurried food down the children's throats before ushering them out the door.

Going in late would mean another late evening, later than usual this time. She needed to notify the state that they needed a new round of possible sites for the prison less she be forced to go with the only one even remotely acceptable. There was also the need to visit a construction site in Hialeah, where a miniature plaza was being built in accordance with her specifications. There was the expansion report from Jennifer Swallows—hopefully Daichi would want to move on her results quickly. Deena knew that she did.

Dressed in a featherweight wool suit from the Armani collection, she ventured to the living room for the purse and change she'd left near a half-eaten pizza the night before. Mrs. Jimenez had removed the box, as expected, but moved the money and purse, it seemed, too. When asked about it, she directed Deena to the master bedroom for the handbag but warned that she'd seen no money on the coffee table.

It was an oddity. Not only was their no cash in the living room, but there was none in her purse either. She hadn't the time for a bank run. Food sources at construction sites were notoriously fickle—chances were there'd be little more than a poorly cleaned truck serving lukewarm sandwiches and taking cash only.

Deena ventured to the study, where she found Tak facing a blank canvas.

"Did you take my money from the coffee table?"

He sat on an oak stool with his back to her.

"Nope."

"And from my purse? Did you take—"

"If you lost your money, Deena, there's some in the top drawer of my dresser."

She pursed her lips in irritation and stomped off for the room again. Once there, she threw open the drawer in question, sifting past stack after stack of neatly folded Calvin Klein boxers, and coming away with nothing. She returned to the study yet again.

"There isn't anything in the top drawer! And I had money last night—"

"If it isn't there, then you've already spent it. Now excuse me, but I'm trying to work, hard as you may find that to believe."

With a humph of disbelief, Deena stomped from the room a second time, rocking the door on its hinges when she slammed it. It flew open again, quick, surprising her.

"If you can find time in your oh-so-important day, you'll want to be here for the meeting with Tony's social worker!" Tak shouted after her. "It's only required to adopt your nephew!"

Before she could retort, he shut the door in her face.

CHAPTER THRITY-FOUR

Thursday afternoon, Tony sat on the edge of his bed, eyeing the lines of his Jordans. Sleek, alternating red and white, a tiny airborne legend plastered to the back side. He didn't know much about the man behind the shoe—had only once seen a YouTube compilation of some sublime but grainy dunking, but still, he must've been phenomenal. Leslie from the group home had once told him that Jordan had screwed up and played baseball for a little while, messing up what probably would've been his best years. But Tony never did hold much stock in what Leslie McConnell said, not so long as she swore her real name to be Luisa Fettuccine of the infamous Fettuccine crime family in New York. Being in a group home was part and parcel of the FBI relocation program, if you let her tell it.

Tony looked down at his Jordans once again. They and his thoughts were the only entertainment he had. Tak had insisted he needed to be alone with his thoughts before ripping out everything Microsoft and Sony ever made from his bedroom. Tony, having counted himself at least mildly lucky, waited until his departure to pull out the new T-Mobile Sonic with long-range wi-fi capabilities from his pocket, only to have Tak return with a hand outstretched expectantly. So much for the fighter pilot game he'd just downloaded. He wondered if he'd ever see it again.

How much longer did he have at the Tanaka house? It was hard to say at that point. Tak and Deena were fighting, probably because of him, especially because of him. After all, that was the way it worked. Tony looked down at his socks bulging with the money he'd collected so far— two hundred forty-seven dollars to date. How rich did you have to be to not notice two hundred forty-seven dollars missing from your house? Tony smoothed out the bulge carefully. He wore socks with money in them at all times, in the event he had but a moment to leave. It was his greatest idea yet, because when the social worker came and took you away, there was never any time for suitcases and good-byes. Tony touched the emblem of his Jordans. If he was wearing them when she came, then he would leave in them. For that reason, he made sure he wore them as much as possible each day. And since he hadn't reconciled himself to the notion of leaving, he assumed it would be with the aid of a social worker when he finally made his departure.

Tak and Deena didn't allow him to leave the bedroom much, on account of his punishment, which he supposed he could understand. Earlier, while going to the bathroom, he'd heard Tak on his cell with what he guessed was the social worker, confirming the time of her visit. They exchanged pleasantries, and somewhere in between, Tony heard the word "concerns." He knew what that meant. He knew it well.

Tony smiled. He would miss the meals the Tanakas gave him; they always came with aggressive Spanish lessons. Mrs. Jimenez brought weighted plates three times a day on weekends, and he ate them at a desk with nothing but books on it for entertainment. Yesterday morning, seven A.M., she burst in with a few shouts of *levantarse* and a huge wad of eggs, tortillas, and spiced chili, all stacked. Right beside it had been a sliced avocado, refried beans doused in yellow cheese and salsa, alongside a huge cup of orange juice. She returned forty-five minutes later with a look of disgust and a few barks of *más, más*. When he shook his head that he couldn't do more, Jimenez sucked her teeth and snatched the plate away as if appalled at having been charged with feeding such a wuss.

No matter, because she'd returned less than three hours later with a braised chicken overdosed on steroids and a few meager vegetables on the side. Back when Tony had first come to the Tanakas', he would swallow whatever Deena or Jimenez put him in front of him. But Jimenez went too far. She brought breakfast, lunch, dinner, and snacks, as if fattening him for a date with Charlie the Cannibal. He would miss Jimenez when the hunger came back.

Tony jumped at the sound of a door slamming. He didn't dare go out. Easygoing as he looked, Tak had gone over tougher than anticipated, never letting up on the solitary confinement. On the first day he tested him. Tak went out and came back to find Tony on the living-room couch, feet up and watching *The Simpsons*. Without a word, Tak plucked him up and carried him under his arm back into the bedroom. Tony kicked and punched, but it was against the strength of a guy with his own personal gym and the muscles to prove it.

He dumped Tony in the bed like a boy, told him to holler if had to pee, and locked the door behind him. Tony had screamed in rage at being treated like a toddler, but it did no good. And when Tak stuck his head in, asking politely if Tony needed the bathroom or food, he'd heaped a slur of curse words on him to provoke him. Far from the beating he expected, Tak only looked at him as if mildly disappointed.

"Hmm. Let's add a week to your punishment," Tak said cheerfully, "till we figure how to clean your mouth."

When he closed the door it was on a second helping of curses.

Deena was home early. Tony could hear her heels on the wood floor in the hall. She had a quick step, as if always needing to be somewhere other than where she was. Louder, louder. And then it stopped. There was a tap at his door.

"Tony? The social worker's here."

Tony took in the first room he'd ever had to himself. He could've easily brought two friends and played a half court pickup game. As it were, he didn't have any and didn't need them, with the motion sensor console game that let him leap around the room with a thousand simulated ones. It would've been nice to take the console with him wherever he went next. But with the money in his socks, the Jordans on his feet, and Deena waiting in the hall, Tony said good-bye to the room.

He would always remember being a Tanaka.

Deena led Tony to the dining-room table, where they joined Tak, Mia, and a middle-aged black woman. Mrs. Jimenez excused herself to put on coffee as they took their seats.

They exchanged pleasantries before quickly switching over to business.

"You should have a number of documents for me. We discussed them in court."

Jesus, Deena's thoughts circled around to a memory of court. There'd been a mention of something not long after the hearing, a follow-up phone call by Allison—but somehow it had escaped her.

Deftly, Tak produced a stack of papers from underneath the table.

"It's all there," he said. "Marriage certificate. Birth certificates, copies of driver's licenses, verification of employment and financial statements from the bank. Three character reference letters, proof of insurance, and a background check for me."

He looked at Deena. She colored.

"Mrs. Tanaka?" the social worker said, shuffling through papers. "You don't have a background check for me?"

She didn't, of course. Thankfulness segued to annoyance as she silently cursed Tak for leading her to this moment without reminding her. He'd wanted to humiliate her, to show that it was him and not her who'd forged ahead in this matter. Well, now, he'd made his point.

"No, I actually . . ." Deena faltered. "I'll have it for you soon. There—there was a delay."

The social worker's head lifted swiftly. It was the wrong thing to say.

"You know what?" Tak said. "I *do* have her background check. Our attorney got it for us, thank goodness." He shot her a superior look. "Here you go."

He handed over a paper from under the table. Clearly, it had been resting in his lap with all the others.

"Very good," the social worker said and scanned the contents of the report before shoving it in the stack.

They turned to talk about their experiences in the home. Despite their insistence that life with Tony and the Tanakas bordered on euphoric, the reports from Edinburgh Academy told a different story—one that included disruptive behavior in class, bullying, and assault. The social worker now wanted to hear how the Tanakas doled out discipline.

Deena expected Tak to parse his words, as she'd found his quarantining a little harsh. However, he detailed Tony's days, spent without fail in his room as punishment for the latest fiasco, and explained that while Deena had grown up with corporal punishment being the norm and him without it, he wasn't beyond a firm hand if he thought it necessary.

"But you haven't used one yet?" she said.

"Don't say 'yet,'" Tak replied with his trademark smooth smile. "It implies you think they'll be a need for it."

She smiled with her eyes and mouth. He was charming her as he charmed all women.

"Let me show you around," Tak suggested.

155

And so it was that Tak stood and the social worker followed, with Tony, Mia, and a thoroughly useless Deena bringing up the rear. He swept her through the house, showing her not only the master bedroom and the two for the children, but the guest rooms, three restrooms, game room, theatre, office, kitchen, and spacious backyard. He pointed out little things, like the child-safe lock on the medicine cabinets, the strategically placed fire extinguishers, the fireplace screens, the coverings for the Jacuzzi and pool, the smoke and carbon monoxide detectors, and first aid kits, not only in the bathrooms, but out back in the cabinet of a locked bar. Deena frowned at the last, not having recalled putting it there.

As they walked, the social worker inquired as to how they handled stress, both individually and collectively. She was curious about which relationships they considered most important and past experiences of loss. Tak rambled on as if chatting with a good friend, pointing out his paintings and instruments as the ultimate in stress relief and carelessly mentioning that Tony had taken up guitar and now showed promise. Finally, when he talked of relationships he held dear, he glanced at his wife with a subdued smile and admitted that even after all these years it was her he couldn't do without.

Tak told her of an awesome extended family, including a cousin and best friend who lived next door, a father with the world's best advice, and a little brother he could still count on for a good race around the block. And when it seemed that she would turn the question on Deena, he added that it seemed she held his family even closer than he did, and would routinely call on his aunts for advice.

By the time they walked Miss Kingston to the door, she had both an offer of staying for an after-hours drink and a standing invitation to go out on the bay with them one Saturday. On her departure, she threatened to take them up on the latter before promising to return for a second visit soon.

The moment the door slammed, the smile slid from Tak's face.

"Go back to your room," he barked at Tony.

The child opened his mouth to protest, thought better of it, and disappeared down the hall.

"Daddy—"

"You go to your room, too. Miss Parker tells me you had a tantrum today during math."

"But it wasn't my fault!" Mia cried. "Toby Martin—"

"Room," Tak said, and Mia stomped off, Mary Janes abusing the hardwood.

"Tak—"

He brushed past Deena before she could say more and veered for the west wing, leaving her standing in the living room, unmistakably alone.

CHAPTER THIRTY-FIVE

The center released Lizzie at twelve noon that Friday. In a slight variation on his promise, Kenji met her in the lobby, instead of the revved car in the parking lot. He stood there looking tall and awkward and unsure until she emerged from the main hall with a smile.

He hadn't expected her to look like that. Hair damp and heavy on her shoulders, plumper in the cheeks, thighs, and middle, she wore a simple white sundress, pure against butterscotch skin. She bit her lip at the sight of him, shylike, and something in him awakened.

Down boy. Down.

"I just—I have to sign out," she explained after their weird, greeting-less greeting.

He wanted to say something. About how beautiful she was or how healthy she looked, but his tongue simply lay there, useless. So, he led her to the car, opened her door, and climbed in, wishing courage would find him some way. Without a word, he started off.

He imagined that it would be like it was when he'd dropped her off, but it dawned on Kenji that such a thing was impossible. The woman he'd fallen for had been high and abused, while the one next to him might be little more than a conglomeration of medications. In other words . . . a stranger.

"Where are you taking me?" Lizzie asked.

He glanced at her.

Why had he left this conversation for so long, the one where they determined what was best for her? They'd made no arrangements, and now they coasted . . . on a ride to nowhere.

"My apartment, everything I owned, was all from Snow. I gave up everything when I left him. I don't have anywhere to go. Or even any clothes to wear."

She looked down desperately at herself. "Even this stupid dress is from the center."

Shewanda Pugh

"You can stay with me," he said quietly. "No strings attached," he added, when she gave him a distrustful glance. "I have a spare bedroom that never gets a guest. And as for clothes, I can just buy you more."

"No."

Kenji glanced at her.

"This is the way it starts with men. You need something. They get it for you. Now you owe them. I don't—I don't want to owe anyone else."

Had he asked for anything? When he'd spent twenty-five grand on her drug rehab, did he ask her for an IOU?

Her comment was like a dash of acid. Still, he figured she must've had a lot of self-healing to do. Better to let her reach her own conclusions about him than to force-feed her any of his own.

"All right," Kenji said. "Wear the same dress every day. See if I care." He did, of course.

A flicker of skepticism wrinkled her nose. But, like that, it smoothed again. "Good," she said evenly.

Kenji glanced at her again. Before inviting an ex-drug addict and prostitute to live with him just a moment ago, the most spontaneous thing he'd ever done was to call Aimee Winchester in the tenth grade so that he could ask her to the Spring Fling. He hung up, of course, at the sound of her voice and with the realization that through twelve years of school they'd spoken only twice, the last time when she'd bested him in the sixth-grade spelling bee. In the end, he'd skipped the dance altogether, but got to hear from his buddies later about how she'd arrived on the arm of Marty Sams, starting fullback for the Miami Beach Hi-Tiders.

"I've been doing some reading," Kenji said. "On your situation."

She gave him a look.

"Your recovery," he tried again.

No better.

159

"I, uh, know it's going to be difficult," he said. "But I want you to take it easy. Concentrate on taking care of yourself and staying healthy."

"What are you, a doctor?" Lizzie smiled.

Kenji couldn't help but return the favor. "Yeah. I'm a doctor. Dr. Tanaka. And here's my prescription. There's a stretch of beach behind my condo. You can only access it from the building. Or rather, our building. I want you out there every day that there's sunshine."

Lizzie blinked.

"What do you mean you can only access it from the building?"

"It's private."

Lizzie sat back in her seat, face thoughtful with some private revelation. "And what would be the point of going to the beach every day?"

He wasn't sure, exactly. But he knew that in the days after Anthony had been killed, in the days when Deena battled grief, old hurts, and resistance to courage, the beach was where his brother brought her, day after day, it seemed. Their father had always said that the beach was where *chi* met *sui,* or rather, earth met water. As two of the five elements in Japanese philosophy, *chi,* or earth, represented the solid, hard, and unchangeable, whereas *sui,* or water, was fluid, forming, and formless. It was where resistance to change met change itself.

"You'd be surprised," Kenji said quietly, "of what a little beach could do."

Lizzie had a nightmare her first night at Kenji's house. Her screams made him leap from bed and skid down the hall, thumping his toe on the door jamb like an asshole. What started as a serious bid to rescue ended with him limping in and sitting humbly and painfully on the edge of her bed.

She'd been about to shoot up. It was the best kind, high-quality, none of that black tar shit that Snow sells. There'd been a long moment of hesitation before starting—and after—goodness could she feel the high, like a jolt of intensity jump-starting her nervous system. But just as that magnificent sort of happiness found her, skeletal hands did the same, out from under the bed, groping and disappearing. When she went to look, the floor fell out beneath her. Lizzie tumbled in darkness, screaming in a descent that should've ended in death, only to land intact alongside her dead brother. Anthony sat up and called her a fool.

Kenji expected her to cry, but a few sullen blinks were enough to chase the tears away. Still, he hugged her, stayed with her, and fell asleep sitting up in her bed after she climbed back in and turned out the lights. When he woke, he was underneath the bedspread too.

CHAPTER THIRTY-SIX

Deena spent the morning in her office devouring the Sydney report from Jennifer Swallows. Already, a handful of the world's most prominent firms were in Sydney or Melbourne gobbling up work in greed. Government projects, corporations, art galleries, shopping malls—the list of missed opportunities read like a horror story for the wallet. Deena flipped to the stats on recent graduates from two Australian institutions—they had the distinction of being among the top in the architectural world. It was no surprise that most remained home in Australia, some at less-than-prestigious firms. She imagined the Tanakas could steal them without much effort. There were a few she had her eye on in particular, young upstarts who'd earned recognition through local write-ups. In a margin, she jotted down the few who came to mind. Afterward, she read through the summary of economic conditions in Australia while subconsciously counting the days till her arrival.

When hunger finally overcame Deena, she ordered Thai for delivery. On arrival, she took her Hot & Sour soup, Pad Thai, and report and ventured down to the break room. Unlike her early days at the firm, she had no trouble finding lunch mates now. Firmly wedged between a second-year intern from Bangkok and a veteran five years her senior, Deena confirmed the rumors of possible expansion into Sydney and swore them to secrecy. When she left, it was with the knowledge that half the Miami office would be privy to the news by quit time.

Back in her office, she skimmed through a copy of *Skyscrape*, the leading periodical on tall and supertall construction. In it, an article about the skyscraper boom in India caught her eye. She read through all nine pages without hesitation, noting points of contention in the margins. Quickly, she typed up a formal response and e-mailed it to the editor, knowing that the Tanaka letterhead guaranteed its publication.

It was now time for her masterpiece.

Modeled after the infamous supermax federal prisons, the women's correctional facility Deena designed to replace the crumbling one which housed her mother would be buried entirely underground, with each inmate in a cell unto themselves. Perforated steel doors would open and close on the command of another, and everything—bed, stool, desk, and toilet—would be formed of concrete.

Gloria Hammond would want death over her daughter's prison.

Deprived of the most basic human interactions, even her food would come and go without need of human intervention. Mandated exercise would demean her further. Deena's mother would circle a concrete concave, a hollowed out pool dug on the orders of her own daughter, made to flex useless legs in a useless life that should've ended twenty-five long years ago.

Deena folded her designs and stuck them in a drawer, locking it in for safekeeping. Secretly, she had always known she'd win the contract. Both Deena and the state were in a dangerous game with the same aim: maximum punishment for minimum dollar. An architect could only understand one of those goals; someone affected by murder the other.

It just so happened that Deena Tanaka was both.

CHAPTER THIRTY-SEVEN

Right from the beginning, Lizzie sought to earn her keep, cleaning with enough bleach to flare the nostrils and burning dinner every night. Miss Alvarez, the widowed Cuban woman who usually cleaned and cooked for Kenji, cursed in Spanglish and muttered about wasted food and cleaning products. In fact, most everything about Lizzie irritated her, right down to the way she incessantly washed and wore the few clothes she'd permitted Kenji to buy. More often than not, Miss Alvarez complained of Kenji placing too much stock in appearance, instead of searching for a girl who better met his needs. Clearly, she wasn't as enamored with Lizzie as he.

Though the two of them didn't talk about it, Kenji knew Lizzie spent her days walking the beach, judging by the amount of sand he crunched underfoot each evening after work. Even on the days when sand proved absent from his foyer, the complaints of Miss Alvarez, incoherent to Lizzie, told Kenji that she'd been to the beach nonetheless. They spent the evenings watching cheesy anime, which she studied and asked too many confused and only slightly exasperating questions about.

There were also the action films, which she argued were appallingly unrealistic. That lack of realism, however, did little to curtail her obvious interest. When they weren't on movies, they were into old board games like Clue, Monopoly, and Life. On evenings and weekends, the sun would disappear from the sky and reappear again, casting rays of light on a bleary eyed pair, neither willing to declare loss, bankruptcy, or hopelessness. When their games did end, either by Lizzie flipping the board in a poorly orchestrated accident or Kenji inquiring of her fatigue so many times that she quit in irritation, the two of them would retire to their own beds, sleep in late, get up, and do it all over again.

Those were the better evenings. Other nights, she proved restless, listless, cranky, piteous, or just plain annoyed. Knowing her mood shifts to be part of the healing process, he ignored them when possible and crossed swords when temperament got the best of him. But it seemed that when he'd been taken to his very worst, when he muttered and slammed doors and told her to piss off, Kenji would close himself in the room, fume, and then open it to find her waiting on the other end. "Kenji?" she'd say, the pain in her voice unmistakable. And he, feeling like three parts ass, would give a deep sigh and bury an apology somewhere in the midst of a hug.

Though he was quick to rise with Lizzie, he was quicker to mellow out, so easy was it for him to go soft over her. So pathetic was Kenji, in fact, that he rarely needed an apology for her less-than-ideal behavior. For him, it was enough that she fed him a heartrending look, complete with the softest, most doelike brown eyes possible.

Paige stopped by unexpectedly one night. On opening the door, Kenji's first reaction had been to shut it on her nose. But immediately, she began talking.

She stood before him with her sweeping, swooshing curls pinned up to emphasize a pale and slender neck. Dark makeup rendered oversized eyes dramatic, peach lips looked unexpectedly lush. A cream tank fell just short of her jeans, revealing floor-flat abs in peek-a-boo fashion.

"Kenji!" Paige said a hand on the door frame. "I've been thinking about you so much."

A hand on the doorknob, he peeked out of the corner of his eye for so much as the shadow of Lizzie.

"I swear, after what happened between us, I felt so bad!" Paige gushed. "Almost immediately I wanted to come see you—"

Go away.

"I wanted to make things right—"

Go away.

"But I didn't know how you'd take it!"

Goawaygoawaygoawaygoaway.

"Given everything that's happened and is happening between us, I thought it best that—"

"Kenji?"

And . . . shit.

He turned ever so slightly, absurdly really, at the sound of

165

Lizzie's voice. Eyes widened in agony, she looked at him, only him, demanding, without speaking. Like an ass, he looked away. Slender golden feet pounded in their retreat.

"Kenji?"

Unlike Lizzie, Paige's inquiry only forged emotion, mocked affection, pretended hurt. He harbored no delusions that he was just as robustly attractive to her without the benefit of a multimillion-dollar trust fund or the eventual inheritance of the architectural equivalent of Coca-Cola. So he raised his gaze in annoyance.

"What?" Kenji snapped.

"Who is that?" Paige cried.

"My sister-in-law!"

"And what? She's *living* here? Right under my nose?"

Kenji snatched Paige's hand from the doorway, whirled her around, and on her gasp of perplexity, slammed the door on her backside.

"Lizzie!"

Kenji tore through the house to her room, shoved the door open, and froze at the sight of her dormant on the bed.

Funny, he thought, how a woman pulled the collar of her dress way down and her hem way up in the hopes of achieving something sexy. He'd seen Lizzie in the short, ripped, barely there, and graphic. But for Kenji, nothing topped Lizzie Hammond in things that belonged to him, that still managed somehow to smell faintly of him. That day, the handful of items she now owned were in the wash, leaving her to wear his fitted tee and boxers.

"Lizzie—" he started again, only to have her turn completely away from him, head on a pillow.

"She's my coworker—"

"And I'm your *sister-in-law!*"

166

Kenji flinched. It was true and not true. She'd made a point, and yet in doing so, had missed the obvious altogether. Paige *was* his coworker, and Lizzie his sister-in-law, and yes, he'd taken the easy way by describing them with the truth's bare minimum. But he hadn't taken the easy way with Lizzie, not literally. Not once.

"Jesus, Lizzie! You know that I never get it right! That I always say and do the wrong thing! But can't you see how I look at you? Can't you figure how I feel about you by now?" He stared at her, at her back, waiting, hoping she understood.

Nothing.

With a snort of frustration, Kenji burst from the room, down the hall, and into the kitchen. There he paced, paced, and paced some more. And finally, he turned.

"Lizzie."

"Kenji." Her voice trembled with emotion.

He took a step at the sound of his name, spoken with something so potent he didn't dare name it but checked himself almost immediately.

"I feel like . . . like I'm bursting a thousand times over," she whispered. "Is this—the way it works?"

"Yeah," he breathed, and closed his eyes against the tremble within him.

She took his hand, hers small and slender next to his, fingers lacing. She leaned up and into him until their lips met deliciously.

Something unleashed.

He submerged with her, lips meeting, conquering, desperate in an instant. With a hand in her hair and the other firmly locked in hers, he swept her round till her back faced the counter. She met his eagerness and swallowed it, hand in his hair, pressing, a mountain of desire, hunger overwhelming. It was as if another second disconnected from him was a second she couldn't bear. And there he was thinking the same thing.

He pulled away.

167

"Lizzie—"

She moved in again. To stop her from kissing him, he took both her wrists in his. "We should get some sleep, Liz. We'll talk later."

He fled from her before she could convince him to stay. Lord knows another word from her would've done so.

Kenji lay awake for far too long before falling into a deep and uneven sleep. When he woke, it was to Lizzie, tucking in next to him. No doubt she'd had another bad dream. So he made room, muttering something sleepy and incoherent, before returning to abstract shapes and a hopefulness he couldn't quite understand.

When morning came, Kenji woke to find that he and Lizzie fit together easy as lovers. Her snoring and partway on her stomach, legs spread; him behind her and to the side, a leg draped lazily but parting her thighs. His hand cupped one rounded breast through fabric of his orange UM shirt. It rode high enough to expose the swell of her ass, clad in simple white panties. Kenji swallowed at the sight of all that flesh. Cursing himself for waking from a sleep so sweet, he pulled away in regret.

"Don't," Lizzie said. "Not yet at least."

She rolled onto her back and sat up, moving in so close that their noses nearly touched.

"No?" he said, gaze locked on her mouth.

She licked her lips.

"Kiss me."

He did as he was told.

Mouth claiming hers in slow and thoughtful fashion, he took his time with her, moving in when her chin tilted upward and climbing atop when she leaned back. Light and teasing painfully, he reeled from the taste of her. She was unbelievably soft beneath him, and he stirred, nibbling at her lips, relishing deliciousness.

How bad had he wanted her? Fear had kept him from knowing. But he knew now. Hunger escalating to madness, Kenji's open mouth

168

feasted on Lizzie's, lapping, longing, pressing for more than even this. She swallowed his kisses as if desperate for them, tugging on his shirt till he tore it off, pulling off hers and returning again.

She wrapped arms around him and drew him in quick, as if even his brief parting was too much. Her kisses were slow and drugging, urging him as she parted legs for him, encouraging with a hand in his hair as she leaned back.

He could kiss her forever that way; easy, indulgent, savoring the velvet of her mouth, or hard and hungry, grinding and surging fire through to their very cores. It was almost as if she'd never been touched, never teased, as every whisper of flesh against flesh brought a never-ending surge, an ambush of emotion. Lizzie had no answer for how a whore could quiver from the caress of a man, or find tears at words that were sweet. After all, hadn't she been told she was beautiful before? Perfect? Worthy of worship?

She hadn't.

Lizzie thought she might drown with him, drown from him, so submerged she was in his scent, taste, and hardness against her body. Every inch of him was masculine, every morsel man, from the bristle of his face to the ripple of his chest. She had been with others, so many others, but never had she felt all woman and helpless altogether, overwhelmed and emboldened, in one.

Lizzie reached for him, and he pushed her aside. When she reached a second time, he drew her fingers to his lips and kissed. Fingertips, first; then palm, wrist, and upward: even there where heroin had scarred. He shushed the beginnings of her protest and silenced her to whimpers when his lips trailed from arm to nipple, flicking with a tongue. Lizzie stiffened in an instant, head back, jolted and breathless. Kenji returned, teasing her with his tongue, flicking, hardening, sucking two tender peaks. He massaged her, caressed her, and ran lips across her body, before returning to her mouth once again. The warmth of her mouth and its willingness made him stir, hard between damp, sweat-laden legs.

Lizzie curled at his touch and moaned with his kisses, driving him to agony in his desire. He ran a hand down her side to sopping white panties, removed them, and followed with his boxers. For all the sex she'd had, all the moments, never had one hinted at this—the silent promise of Kenji's mouth, the constant shocks of pleasure. Heat rose in Lizzie in new

169

and foreign fashion, stockpiling and threatening a magnificent release. She crushed underneath him, thrusting to meet his slightest motion.

Dangerously they moved, one against another, bodies one in heat and desperation. She arched for him, torturing by begging with her body. He met soft wet flesh between her thighs with the brush of a finger and a ragged moan escaped her. Kenji stroked, gently, just there, and bit a lip at the whimper of his name.

He dug a condom out of the top drawer and slipped it on, fingers trembling. Hardened beyond reason, stirring in anticipation, he climbed atop her and pressed his hungry lips to hers tenderly.

He pushed and pulsating softness enveloped him.

Goodness.

Eyes shut, he was inundated by the feel of her. Soft. Quivering. Damp. Even on entry, she lifted for him, begging him deeper with that, the first thrust. He held her, and she clung and instantly, he needed all of her. Kenji pushed back a feeling of greed with weak resolve and moved against her slow, stoking moans with each deepening stroke. Breathless and haggard, he ran a hand through her hair, fingers tangling and loving it. Hands on her ass, filled and overflowing—he loved that too—and knew he could have it no other way. He wanted no other girl.

It wasn't her fault.

She had thought that he would be like the others; that he would take only his fill. She had wanted it, if for no other reason but to have his nearness. But she hadn't anticipated the inevitable. Scorching and bursting, she could withhold nothing from him, not even her trembling, as she rushed to peak frantically. She had come to him the fool, thinking herself the experienced one. After all, she had nothing to give that another hadn't had, nothing so far as she knew. But he'd taken what hadn't been there; what was his; what was promised.

CHAPTER THIRTY-EIGHT

Kenji sat on the edge of his bed, head lowered, bile and regret coalescing in furious fashion.

How had he let passion consume him so completely? Let it evict rationale, sanity, and the need for peace of mind? What Lizzie needed was a friend, a confidant, a guy who could see her instead of her body, who could find worth without lust. He'd thought himself that man. But his cock had shown him different.

"Kenji?" Lizzie said.

It wasn't that he didn't care. Damn, it was just the opposite. But by acting on it, by acting on his emotions, he'd mangled what he wanted with what it was Lizzie needed.

Then there was Tak and Deena.

What would they make of it? What would happen when they found out? Would it happen as it did with Tak and Deena, when his father stumbled in, hurt, outraged, furious?

No.

Because he would tell Tak now.

Kenji leaped to his feet, shrugging Lizzie's touch from his shoulder. He snatched his cell from the nightstand and burst from the room. Once in the hall, he hit two on the speed dial and waited.

"Bad time, Kenj," was Tak's greeting.

"What's happened?"

Never in his life had Tak been too busy to listen to him. Neither spoke for a moment.

"Nothing," Tak said with false brightness. "Nothing that can't wait. So, what's up?"

Kenji inhaled and knew that his big brother wouldn't have

missed even that. After all, this was a guy who'd been his mother and father, when Mom doused herself in alcohol and Dad chased glory further and further from home. Here was his only brother, who'd managed to be both parent and friend. Never had Tak hurt him. Yet he suspected that was about to change.

"Okay," Kenji said. "You're definitely gonna lose it when I tell you this, but I need to do it anyway. Even if this goes somewhere or nowhere, it's important to me that I don't do it behind your back."

"Talk, Kenj."

The breath Kenji took was mile-deep, and with it, he snatched all the nerve he could muster.

"I slept with Lizzie."

Tak chuckled. "What?"

Kenji cringed. Would he really have to say it again?

He would.

"I slept with Lizzie," he said quietly.

"Lizzie who?"

"Lizzie Hammond."

Silence.

The pregnant kind, heavy with unspoken words.

"Kenji."

"I know, Tak, I know."

"No, you don't know! Not if you thought that shit was a good idea!"

Kenji leaned against the door, chest clenched with the worst of internal conflict. "Tak, I'm crazy about her. I—"

"What are you talking about? Are you insane? The girl's on drugs! She's a prostitute! How could possibly be crazy about—"

"Don't," Kenji said, and his voice trembled with the warning. "Just—don't say it."

Tak froze. And though they weren't speaking, Kenji knew that he'd picked up every ounce of emotion in his voice.

Tak sighed. "What are you doing?" he demanded tiredly.

Back against his front door, Kenji drew a foot to it and lowered his head. There was no way with Tak, save the honest one.

"I don't know. We've been spending so much time together."

"What? Why?" Tak snorted in exasperation. "You know what, Kenj? Don't tell me. I'm terrified of the answer."

But he would tell him anyway.

"She came to the firm looking for Deena." He dropped his leg and took up a pace in the hall. "I took her out to dinner and a movie. Afterward, we kept seeing each other. We both wanted to see each other."

"And how much did that run you an hour?"

Kenji stopped. "Come on. Cut me a little."

Tak exhaled. In his mind's eye, Kenji could see him roping in the temper, soothing it for the sake of a little brother. But a misplaced word from Kenji right then would earn him a string of never-ending curse words. Tak had their father's temper, minus the eloquence.

"She wanted out," Kenji explained. "Out of the drugs, the prostitution. I sent her to rehab for a long while, and we talked every day. When she got out there was nowhere to go. So she came home with me."

"Came home with you," Tak echoed dryly.

The wryness sliced him.

"Yeah," Kenji snapped. "She's living with me."

173

Tak snorted.

"Lizzie Hammond doesn't live with anyone. She visits for a while, steals your shit, and sells it for crack. Then dumb-asses like me or you go driving up and down the streets looking for her, putting our lives at risk so we can get cussed out when we find her."

"Tak, come on. Listen—"

"No, *you* listen. Yeah, she's cute. Beautiful, just like her sister. But I know you, Kenj. You don't go further than that. And this is no game, you hear? This is my wife's sister. You can't just dip your toe in the water and then decide you don't wanna get wet!"

"I don't wanna dip my toe in anything!"

"Yeah, pardon the censorship," Tak sneered. "But you're kind of missing the point. Even if you are serious—which would be the first time in your life—she isn't. I've been dealing in Lizzie's shit for a long time. She doesn't fall in love—she falls in opportunity. Lizzie takes what she needs and says fuck whoever comes up short. Are you listening to me?"

"Yeah, I'm listening," Kenji snapped.

"Good! Because I don't know if she's told you, but she's been in rehab before! I've personally driven her to Key West, Orlando, Tampa, and Naples. I've taken her to the airport for a five-star rehab in California that I paid for. Do you know what she did?"

"What?" Kenji said tiredly.

"She got clean. She always gets clean! For a week, a month; it makes no difference. Then she's always back, worse than ever."

This was the part he couldn't understand. Could Tak give up on him, too? Turn his back the moment Kenji failed to live up to some standard?

"You guys just gave up on her. The only family she's ever had and you abandoned her."

He never thought that silence could sound like murder. But it

174

did.

"I'm gonna stop you there, Kenj, because I'm not actually trying to hurt you. It's just that you're young and don't know what it is to put someone else before yourself. You don't know what it is to have the joy of a baby on the way on one hand and a pregnant wife so grief stricken that she won't eat on the other. You don't know the hard choices of life, because you've never had to make any. And you damned sure don't know what it is to be motherless and fatherless and parent all at the same time, when you should only have to be a kid yourself. So, I'll forgive your stupidity just the once and call it luck, or good fortune, or whatever—you can pick. But what I won't do is sit here and give you a pass on judging me or Deena."

Kenji swallowed. He hadn't meant it that way. Hadn't meant to imply blame or worse, that either Tak or Deena somehow owed their siblings more than they'd already given. And now he'd exasperated things by siding with Lizzie on something that ran a lot deeper than he'd ever fathomed.

"I know you mean well," Tak said, "but you've got to understand. You don't save someone who wants to drown. You drown with them."

Drown. Was that what they'd do together?

"Not this time," Kenji said softly, his voice absent of conviction. "Not this time."

"Yeah. Okay," Tak said. "I'll leave you to your movie life in a second. But let me give you some parting advice. When she steals your shit, when she goes missing, don't wake me up to find her. And I swear to God, if you call my wife and upset her after we've managed to move on from Lizzie, then I promise you, I will pencil you in for one hell-of-an-ass whooping. Do I make myself clear?"

Kenji sighed. "There's one other thing."

"What?" Tak shouted.

"She needs clothes. She doesn't really want me to buy any. I thought, maybe, that if Deena had anything—"

Tak hung up the phone.

Kenji's older brother came over that evening with a sack of clothes, some still bearing tags, and a scowl on his face. After only a cursory hello to Lizzie, Tak pulled his kid brother aside and lectured him on the necessity of safe sex and the importance of STD testing. Only once Kenji had managed a shade just slight of magenta did he stop. It was then that Tak offered a muttered apology for his harsh line over the phone, regretting any implication that Kenji had ever been a burden to him, and admitting that things were a little out of sync at home. Though he was curious, Kenji couldn't bring himself to ask, so used was he to being the kid next to the decidedly adult big brother. They never talked about the things that shadowed Tak's eyes or made his smile come a little slower on occasion. Kenji figured it was Tak's constant need to protect him that served as the reason, and now he liked to think the same. Sometimes though, a contrary voice told him Tak said nothing because his brother thought him a child, or worse, an imbecile in need of protection. Strangely enough, that guy sounded a whole lot like the one who pointed to the extra stretch of gums evident with Kenji's every smile.

On his way out, Tak told him to call if he needed anything.

Chapter Thirty-Nine

Backpacks weighted with work, students of grossly varying heights roamed thick in the corridors of Edinburgh Academy, talk of television, vacations, and gossip mounting like a swarm of bees in a hive. The halls bustled like a Times Square subway station on New Year's Eve.

Times Square subway station. That beauty belonged to Tak. More and more, Tony found that it was he that he quoted.

The bushy brown-haired girl from class fell in step alongside him. Funny, he thought, that he should call her bushy-haired, when his own tresses were only tamed by Deena's sizzling hot comb and a series of braids done as he squirmed. The last one to braid his hair had been Ms. Reynolds, his foster mom.

"You're back," she announced brightly. With massive ponytails on either side of a large head, wrangled in with a mess of baby blue ribbons, the girl walked alongside Tony, shifting to avoid older kids as they passed. In contrast, Tony shouldered those who didn't get the hell out of his way.

"They're saying you were homeless before you came here," she bubbled. "Is it true?"

Tony shot her a look as they rounded the corner. "Yeah."

Her eyes widened. "That must've been so cool."

Tony stopped. With kids rushing past on either side, conscious of the final seconds before bell, it was like standing neck-deep in fast-running waters.

"I was hungry," he said simply. "Hungry, cold, dirty, and desperate. All the fucking time."

He took off.

By the time she caught up to him, her face had colored fiercely. "I'm sorry," she gushed. "I'm not usually that stupid."

"Yeah. Okay," Tony snapped.

They rounded another corner and stopped at the entrance to science.

"I'm glad you hit Brian," she said before the closed door. "He's pretty obnoxious."

Tony smirked and shoved open the door to the classroom. The fat kid in front jumped at his arrival.

"We'll be starting our group projects on the solar system today," the bushy-haired girl explained. "I'll have to be your partner since no one else will want to."

Tony veered to a desk far opposite of the one she grabbed and sat. As the kids filed in, they took seats up front and to the right, fanning away from him purposefully. Briefly, Tony entertained the thought of pretending to lunge at a nearby student, if only to see half a dozen of them fall out of their chairs. The thought made him grin . . . before the memory of Tak's punishment set his face to a scowl.

Mr. Keplar was a deathly thin and pale man with eyes as blue and round as a lagoon. He wore his fine, coffee-colored hair combed straight back, revealing a compromised hairline in the form of a severe widow's peak.

"Today's the big day!" Keplar clapped with his entrance to the room, step-stuttering only briefly at the sight of Tony.

No doubt the careful gaze that followed counted the number of children within striking distance and verified the evacuation plan crafted in Tony's absence. When Keplar's blue eyes met Tony's brown ones, he blushed with the embarrassment of a man whose mind had been read.

"Glad to have you back," Keplar said shrilly.

Tony snorted.   "Like a pack of warts," he guessed.

Keplar eyed him a moment longer before turning back to the class.

"Today we'll go over chapter six in your textbooks, and then pair off in twos. Each group will then be responsible for a report on the solar system and a scale model re-creation, as per the instructions on your syllabus. I'll be up here if you have any questions."

Immediately, each person flipped the texts, already on their desks, open to chapter six. Tony slung his backpack onto his desk and rummaged blindly, even as Keplar began to lecture.

"The solar system, boys and girls, consists of a beautiful yet fiery sun and the astronomical objects gravitationally bound to orbit. Our readings today will shed light on this fascinating subject."

Keplar ceased his frantic introductory notes on the dry erase board and whirled to face them.

"Mr. Hammond, begin reading chapter six, please."

Tony looked around. To his left and right were students who waited, books open, hands folded in some cases, poised and ready for the passage. Tony, however, had just found the right book. It sat unopened on his desk.

"I haven't found the page yet," he answered lamely.

"Oh! Well, we'll wait."

Again, Tony looked around, this time scowling. With a heavy sigh, he cracked *General Science: Everything You'd Want to Know about the World (Almost!) With Practical Application.*

He flipped to the table of contents, and then to chapter six. The first paragraph stopped him. There were more ten-letter words in it than a stack of foreign passports. There was no way in hell he was reading that.

"The page is missing," Tony said, aware that he'd been given cellophane-wrapped books in every class.

"What?"

Keplar took a tentative step forward. "That doesn't seem possible. Perhaps a manufacturing error—"

He was halfway down the aisle when Tony tore the page from his book. Keplar froze as page 127 floated to the floor.

"Oh, wow. Looks like you better pick someone else," Tony said calmly.

Keplar swallowed, Adam's apple bobbing. Eventually, his gaze shifted right, to a wide-mouthed white girl with slanted blue eyes.

"Ginerva. Please."

Her voice came in crisp, confident. "Our solar system is comprised of the sun, eight planets, and a multitude of celestial bodies formed from the collapse of a giant molecular cloud 4.6 billion years ago. The astronomical objects gravitationally bound to orbit the sun . . ."

Tony's mind drifted. Leaning back in his seat, he closed his eyes, the bush of his hair made like a pillow for his neck. Behind his eyelids, Tony stood at the helm of Tak's ship, sailing the *Darling* like a rogue pirate. He had a crew of twelve—no girls—and a map that would lead him to treasure in the South Pacific. Though he didn't know where in the hell the South Pacific might be, he figured south and toward the Pacific were as good a direction as any to start. Tak's wuss of a red sail had been taken down and replaced with the Jolly Roger. A bout of cannons lined the sides in the event he met enemies. He would've liked to have met enemies.

Tony opened his eyes at the sound of desks scraping the floor. He hadn't heard the announcement, but apparently it was time for them to break into pairs. Friends found friends; neighbors scooted over, until only he and the weird, bush-haired girl remained. She grabbed her backpack and found the back of the room.

"Told you," she said and dropped into a vacant seat.

Before, Tony had looked at her as a mere matter of annoyance, but now, she was a curiosity. Where was her fear? Her loathing for him? And why was it that during the pairings, that she too wound up alone?

"Why are they avoiding you?" he asked.

She shrugged good-naturedly. "They say I talk too much."

"I can see that," Tony said.

"They say worse things about you."

180

"I can see that, too."

Smiling, she pulled out a psychedelic notebook of red, white, and blue. Across the front, "Science" had been stenciled in, in large black letters.

"It's very important that I do well in science," she said matter-of-factly. "I'll need it to be a doctor like my mom and dad. Oh! Before I forget, they both have erratic hours, so we'll be working at your house. I think you'll agree that your house would be best."

Tony blinked.

"Work? At my house?"

"Yes, on the model. We have to complete it. Anyway, I was thinking I could just ride home with you some evenings, and my mom could pick me up when she finishes her shift."

Words fired from her lips like bullets. Had she always talked so fast?

"Ride home with me?" Tony echoed.

"Yeah. In the black car you go in. I assume that's your nanny or maid. It must be pretty odd having a nanny after you've been homeless. Daddy says that homelessness is a very serious problem that pervades the nation."

"Okay," Tony said.

"You must be very rich. Richer even than Brian Swallows, though he likes to act the part. He likes to act like he has a lot of money, but in my experience, the people who act as if they have the most money are the ones who hardly have any at all. Also, Brian says that your foster mom is a Tanaka. Now is she your foster mom or your real mom, because she looks an awful lot like you, and you have a real particular look, you know? I like it though. It's very handsome."

Tony blinked. And suddenly she had a cell phone in hand.

"She's my aunt," he mumbled. "How do you know her?"

"Oh, I saw her when you were in trouble." She punched buttons with a thumb. "How's Mondays, Wednesdays, and Thursdays for you?"

"Huh?" Tony said. Talking to her made him feel as if he'd been thrown in a wash cycle—on spin.

"The project, Tony. Please, concentrate. Daddy says that I can be exasperating, but you don't appear exasperated. In any case, it's important just the same that you try to focus so that we can make plans to complete the project."

Indeed, the conversation was getting away from him. He thought quickly. Monday nights they had family counseling. Tuesdays and Thursdays were drum lessons. Wednesday was his free evening, and she sure as hell couldn't have that. She couldn't have his weekends either.

"I keep a busy schedule," Tony said. "It's hard to say."

"Oh. Do you take lessons?"

He shifted, suddenly uncomfortable. What did she care what he did with his time? Hadn't he said he was busy?

"Drum lessons, yeah."

"I could watch. I could ride with you to your lessons and watch. Then afterward, we could work and have dinner and watch TV or whatever. It's lonely at my house, anyway. That would be so cool. What do you watch? I like M*A*S*H."

Tony shook off her suggestion and looked up to find Keplar moving up and down the aisles. When he approached them, caution etched his face.

"And how are you two making a go of it, Wendy?"

Wendy. Briefly, he thought of his Bismarck textbook tattooed with "Wendy takes it up the ass." For some reason, it now made him blush. Tony lowered his gaze.

"Oh, hi, Mr. Keplar. Here's what we have so far. We'll be at Tony's house every Tuesday and Thursday night. I'll watch him practice drums, first. Then we'll work, have dinner, and watch M*A*S*H together."

Tony sank in his chair amongst snickers.

Good Lord, he thought. Pretty as she was, he would keep from watching M*A*S*H if he could.

~*~

When three o'clock arrived, the sleek black Lincoln that usually retrieved Tony and Mia was replaced by a pearl Benz. Tony sighed. So, he hadn't got away with tearing up the science book after all.

"Daddy!" Mia squealed.

Tony snatched her when she attempted to pitch into traffic. He'd heard enough times that Mia was his responsibility to know that he'd get much more than a smack in the head should he stand around and watch her run into the street.

"Hey, baby," Tak said and knelt down on ripped jeans to squeeze his daughter.

When he stood again, his eyes were on Tony. It was the eleven-year-old who looked away first.

"So, how was science today?" Tak said evenly.

Tony studied the blades of grass. They were a deep, forest green, wide and evenly cut, with just a twinge of dampness.

"Science was okay. We talked about planets and stuff. And there's a project I have to do. I got paired with this weird girl. Oh and—"

"I'm tired, Tony. So, get to the part where you mutilate your books and check out for forty minutes."

"Forty minutes! It was more like—"

Tak whacked him in the back of the head, palm open. It was becoming his signature move, painfully reminiscent of his mother.

"Get in the car!"

183

Tony skulked to the front seat, climbed in, and waited for Mia to buckle herself into the booster under Tak's supervision. Tak then climbed behind the wheel, started the car, backed out, and whipped into traffic.

"Tomorrow, Keplar'll give you a photocopy of the page you tore out," Tak announced. "In exchange, you're going to give him a handwritten apology. Then you're going to copy—by hand—every word, diagram, and picture on the front and back of the page you decided was worthless. You'll have plenty of time, what with your phone and video games missing."

"What! But I just got the new *Eternal: Art of War* and—"

"Yeah. Thanks, by the way. Your aunt gave me hell for letting you get something with a mature rating. And you repay me by lining the floors with your schoolwork."

Tony dropped his gaze. He'd screwed up again, of course. It wasn't that he'd wanted to, it was just—he didn't want to be laughed at. Already, they knew he'd been homeless and that he didn't have parents. He wouldn't entertain them further by bumbling stupidly through passages on the solar system.

Tak held out an expectant hand. "Phone."

Tony sighed dejectedly, dug out his cell, and surrendered it.

"You now have tutoring Saturday mornings, too," he said. "Until you feel more secure about your reading."

Tony shot him a surprised look, but lowered it when Tak half-smiled at him.

Chapter Forty

Monday nights meant counseling. But for the rest of the week, Deena arrived early and worked well into the night. She called impromptu meetings with in-house engineers, designers and electricians, consultants who verified that her prison was functional if nothing else. When the hour grew late, Deena ventured upstairs to her father-in-law, the only other individual sure to be working. They discussed her letter to *Skyscrape*, Sydney, and even Jennifer Swallows's subsequent threat to sue for battery.

"She'll do nothing," Daichi assured her. "Ms. Swallows is far too ambitious for something so alienating. Trust me, she's as astute as she is old."

Deena snickered.

"She also realizes that I could drop dead from overwork, leaving you at the helm of the firm. After all, no one expects me to actually leave Kenji in charge."

He went back to shuffling papers.

And there it was. The confirmation she knew would come, yet she still found almost impossible to believe. One day, the largest, most prestigious architectural firm in the world would be hers. She thought back to the day she met Daichi for the first time, ambushing him in a snow-covered parking lot at MIT. Back then, she hadn't thought herself worthy to ask for an internship. Now, she would one day inherit the place.

Daichi shot his daughter-in-law a look of unadulterated impatience. "Please," he said. "Try not to look so thrilled by the idea of my death."

Deena giggled and clamped a hand over her mouth in shame. Soon, Daichi was laughing, too.

"You probably take this news to mean that you'll get the nod on Sydney should we expand," Daichi said.

Well, she had anticipated that he would want to move on expansion into Sydney and would possibly even reconsider Singapore, too. Over the years, Deena had contributed so much to the expansion process that she expected to work on opening markets in both cities.

Looked forward to it, in fact.

"You mention it, frequently. Sydney and Singapore. I'll have you know that I aim to take your advice. We'll expand into both territories within a year."

Deena grinned. "That leads me to my next point," she said.

"You'll not be part of either," Daichi said.

Deena froze.

"What do you mean?"

"I mean that I plan on leaving you behind when I go to both places. You won't be playing a role with either."

"But I want to."

"I'm aware of that."

Tak.

"You've been talking to your son. He told you not to let me. He told you it's been causing problems."

"All I know I've learned by watching you. For two weeks you've come early and worked late, even when the reason for doing so wasn't readily apparent."

Deena opened her mouth to protest; however, her father-in-law held up a hand. "Long ago, I had a conversation with a young and ambitious woman who believed she could balance the roles of wife, mother, and architect. At the time, I was naïve enough to think it impossible. But she showed me otherwise.

"Go home," he said. "And face whatever demons you hide from."

Deena rose, her stare never wavering from Daichi. She turned and strode for the door.

"There's one more thing," he said quietly. "A reminder, I

186

suppose. 'Vengeance is mine, thus saith the Lord.'"

Deena turned in confusion. "What?"

"The passage. It's from your religion, is it not?" Daichi rose and rounded his massive desk before leaning against it, studying her.

"I know what's happening," Daichi said. "Your hatred is malignant, eating away at you as a cancer, at what is both good and bad, leaving nothing but the vengeance it nurtures. You will not poison your soul with the help of my name, nor will you use my firm to exact a retribution certain to consume both donor and beneficiary alike."

Deena's gaze narrowed. "I'm a Tanaka," she said. "And I can work on any project I choose."

Daichi smiled. "Of course you can. But as I'm sure you're aware, policy dictates that you disclose any conflict of interest the moment it's apparent. Since you indicated none on your initial filing of intention with the firm, you're now required to notify senior management the moment your conflict became apparent."

He continued to smile, even as Deena's lips parted in horror.

A full meeting, where she would be required to disclose her conflict of interest—her mother—confined in the prison she wished to design. She would need their approval before work could begin. She would need the approval of Daichi, of Jennifer Swallows.

"In the morning, you'll contract another firm to complete the project. Then you'll go on vacation. A week. No, two. And when you return, it'll be with a renewed vigor for your first love—organic architecture."

"You're suspending me?" Deena cried. "For what?"

Daichi shrugged. "Technically, others may call it a breach of policy for failure to disclose. However, I prefer to call it saving my family. Go home, Deena. And come back in two weeks."

CHAPTER FORTY-ONE

Punishment for Tony lasted four days, with time off for good behavior. After he'd sulked the first night, he got a second book from Keplar at a cost of seventy-five dollars according to Tak, and spent two days copying the tight script of the two columns that comprised the front and back of the wayward page. There was also a picture with the sun and its planets, which Tak made him draw. When his punishment was over, he got back the much-missed video games and the phone. It was only then that Tony realized how quickly he'd grown accustomed to a better life. At the group home, there'd been no cell with downloadable games and an app to order pizza when Mrs. Jimenez cooked tripe or some other weird shit. And there'd definitely been no *Eternal: Art of War*, *NASCAR Legend*, or a host of basketball, football, and baseball games to tide him over. There'd been other kids, and that was about it. And of the dozen or so he'd come to know over the years, Tony missed not a one. Not a single goddamned one.

No sooner than did Tony peel the wrap off *Eternal: Art of War*, than did Tak tap on the door. He said he was just checking on him, but he'd checked on him in the same way when Tony got *NASCAR Legend*, *Medieval Summons*, *Agent Operative*, and the NBA half-court game with motion sensor detection.

Tak dug the second controller out of a drawer and took a seat next to Tony.

"It says that we'll be in the same 'legion.' I don't know what that is," Tony said.

"It's a military squad," Tak said, adjusting the battery pack onto his handheld device. "I'll be commander," he added.

"No way! I'm commander."

"Then I'm going rogue," Tak said. "See you on the battlefield."

Tony grinned. "Rogue? Well, bring it, *otosan*."

It came out of its own accord. Tony blushed. How could he have been so stupid as to call his uncle his father? Sure, Tak spent loads of time with him, but he had no dad. The world knew that.

Tak's mouth curled into a small, heartened smile.

"You're gonna die on this battlefield, Tony Hammond. Repeatedly. So don't try and sweeten me with your talk of *'otosan.'* It's too late to make me commander."

Tak powered on the console. "And anyway, 'dad' works just fine."

~*~

For Tony, there was no shaking Wendy. She rode home with him on the days promised and watched him play drums and thumb around on Tak's guitar before plopping down at his desk and reading aloud her findings on the solar system. She would print out double copies of everything, giving him more work than even the crap he had before.

And the questions she asked. Caesar Augustus fucked that! Always in your brain, kicking around and being weird. *Tony, where's your mom?*

Dead.

Well, where's your dad?

Dead.

Where's your grandma?

Prison.

Where's your grandfather?

Dead.

That's terrible, Tony. No wonder you exhibit all the classic signs of abandonment. You've never had more than a shell of a family.

What kinda kid talked like that?

Tak thought her cute and every so often nudged Tony toward her for the sole purpose of unnerving him. And it worked.

On the day that Wendy read aloud their typed report, and Tony stood by her side, lamely holding a stationary model of the solar system, Tak expressed disappointment at her absence that evening. While Tony was relieved that her constant chatter, which he likened to a boat's propeller—quick, slashing, and always going in circles—had ceased, he would admit only on threat of irreparable physical distress that he missed her a little, too.

~*~

Home. Shower. Bed. Gaze upward at the ceiling, Deena thanked money and good fortune for the maid in her employ. They allowed her to slink in, in a funk of self-loathing, tuck the kids into bed, and return to her pity in peace.

Suspension. And she could do nothing. Even then, Deena bit her lip on outrage, tears stinging her eyes. How dare he interfere in her marriage, in her home life, in any of it—father-in-law or not!

Hadn't she shown that she could balance work and home? Hadn't she proven indispensable to both?

But even as she thought, a memory tugged at her pride. It was of Tak at the table, clearly abreast of the adoption proceedings, making her out to be the fool. She'd been angry at him, was still angry at him, for propping himself up by standing on her. True, she hadn't remembered the documents they'd needed, but it was hardly an indication of neglect on her part. It was easy for Tak. He was home, could work at his leisure, or not work, she supposed. Either way, he knew the wealth would keep coming. But for her, being wife and architect, mother and corporate executive hardly came with built-in vacation time. It was only natural for Tak to pick up her slack.

Deena slipped into uneasy sleep with these thoughts on her mind, fists clenched at her side.

~*~

Darkness.

Darkness again.

Deena's heart pounded in fright from the unnatural stillness. Nothing before her, nothing behind: just a void where things should've been. Even the baby had stopped crying. She could hear her heart beat, pounding in her ears. Her mother's face slipped out from blackness.

"Run!"

Deena woke with a start.

The next night she dreamed of men—five of them, at the door for her father. No more, no less, just . . . men.

And yet she woke with a scream.

Three nights in a week Deena woke, sweat drenching her in a bath of fear. Twice Tak came to her side, and twice she pushed him away. On the third, however, he refused to move.

"What is this, Deena? What's happening?" he demanded.

"I don't know!" she shrieked. "I don't know what's happening!"

She grabbed fistfuls of her own wild hair and let out a traitorous sob, unable to mask the torment of frayed nerves and little sleep. Tak pulled her hands from her head.

"Dammit, Dee, talk to me. What's happening when you sleep?"

She shook her head, overwhelmed in her search for the words. "Nightmares. Memories. I can't even tell."

He stared at her. "Would it help if you talked to someone? Someone who could give you something to sleep? Be a listening ear?"

But a doctor wasn't the answer, so she shook her head before he could finish.

"I need answers, Tak. Answers a shrink doesn't have."

He stared at her. He knew. Already, he knew. "I'll go with you," he said.

She looked away. "I need to go alone."

Tak opened his mouth, but shut it automatically. "If you need me," he started again. "Scrap that, if you *want* me, I'm there for you. No matter what."

Deena knelt before him and took his hands in hers. "I love you for that," she said. "But I need to visit my mother alone."

CHAPTER FORTY-TWO

Quite a few years ago, Lizzie walked out of school for the last time. Poised to become a ninth grader for yet another go-around, she found a world of quick highs and fast cash more compelling than stumbling through Shakespeare and squinting at the kind of math that called for letters and numbers. She never thought of dropping out as quitting, but rather, getting on with the business of her life. Early on, her clientele consisted of boys with a crumpled fist of cash, willing to blow a week's allowance on a quick rub off from her. Later, when the right people understood that she was, in fact, a whore, her customers expanded to include a portly gym teacher, an old janitor with piecemeal teeth, and a guidance counselor who'd initially approached her with a then-sincere wish to help her sort out her life. That conversation ended with Lizzie on her knees and an out-to-lunch sign on his door. A few weeks later, with a little encouragement from Snow, Lizzie realized the money she could make by forgoing her façade of an education and devoting herself to whoring twenty-four seven.

Lizzie squinted at the series of thick blue books lining the shelves of the bookstore. There was no deciphering one from the other. *GED Prep in 30 Days, Ace the GED, A Complete GED Study Guide.* She looked to Kenji for help.

He shrugged. "Get whichever. I don't care."

Lizzie turned back to the books, her gaze settling on *GED Prep in 30 Days.* It would be great to have her high school equivalency that fast. But how smart did she already have to be for that? She remembered a statewide assessment they had to take in the ninth grade. Results indicated that she read on a fourth-grade level. The shame of the moment colored her cheeks, still. Even after all he knew about her, Lizzie couldn't bear Kenji finding out that she sounded out words and counted on her fingers.

"Never mind," Lizzie said. "I don't need anything."

The smile slid from Kenji's face. "What do you mean, 'never mind'? It's a high school diploma. You kinda need one."

Lizzie had a memory. Some poem, some stupid, stupid poem about a raven—and her standing—standing and sounding out aloud.

Whore. Stupid whore. Sounding out like a dummy.

She's a retard! You let a retard suck your dick! Hope you don't catch it!

She's best at sucking dick, Teach. Just leave her to her talents!

Lizzie choked on the memory.

"Liz?" Kenji said uncertainly.

He reached for her, but she couldn't bear for him to touch her—not with those voices wreaking havoc in her head. Lizzie recoiled, choking on the memories, and took off. She blasted through an old man on her way out of Barnes & Noble. Her lungs burst with the fill of outside air.

It appeared she would have time to calm herself. With a hand on the brick face of the bookstore, Lizzie scowled at the glass doors she'd nearly shattered. Where in the hell was Kenji? Why didn't he come after her?

When Kenji pushed open the doors, he held a straining plastic bag in one hand as an old man sparked off wildly, arm flailing behind him. A squint revealed that he was the man Lizzie had shoved.

Kenji appeared at her side.

"I, uh, bought a couple of selections. And I apologized to your friend." He shot a careful look back. "But I think we'd better go."

He placed a hand at the small of her back and led her to the Audi. Lizzie glanced behind her, just once, and in time for the old man to flip her the middle finger.

~*~

Kenji didn't know a thing about tutoring. As it turned out, exceptional grades were but one more Asian stereotype he didn't adhere to. In high school, he was far more likely to be at baseball practice or Heroes & Villains, his favorite comic book store, than cracking the books on any day. And then there was always TV to consider. At any given time there were at least half a dozen new shows worthy of at least cursory attention. Cancellations, schedule shuffling, and firings meant constant changes in the prime time lineup, which he prided himself on keeping abreast of. It would've been nice to say that even after all that, school came next. But there were the latest hip-hop releases and friends to hang

194

out with. Only once he'd exhausted all that did he turn to books.

In high school, Kenji had been a solid B student. To him, his grades proved not that he was some budding genius, but that school was some bullshit operation that most could eek by on with at least consistently minimal effort.

Which led him to Lizzie.

She'd asked him where to start. So, Kenji thumbed through the book atop a stack, *Ace the GED,* and suggested she begin with a few of the assessments. He plopped an alarm clock on the table to time her and left to put on a pot of coffee. Grinds in the filter, water in the machine, Kenji leaned against a solid granite counter and watched her watch the clock. She looked at it. And looked at it. And looked at it. Finally, Kenji marched around the counter and snatched the clock from sight.

"No clock," he said. "Just . . . take your time, okay?"

Lizzie turned back to the book. Eyes wide, she inhaled so deeply her chest bloomed in response. How long she held it, he did not know.

"Breathe, Lizzie."

Him, book, him, book, her gaze flitted back and forth. Finally, *finally*, she settled on the book.

"O-P-E-C, or the or—or—"

"It's O PEC. The letter 'o' and then 'pec' altogether. Like a bird pecks."

She looked up at him.

"It's an abbreviation. See? O-P-E-C."

She held up the book at him. Kenji took a seat. "Just trust me, okay? It's O, and then PEC."

Lizzie turned back to the book with a scowl. "OPEC," she shot him a look. "OPEC, or the or—or—"

He leaned over. "Organization."

195

"Right. Organization of puh—puh—pet—"

"Petroleum," Kenji said.

Lizzie looked at him.

"They make gas from it."

Lizzie leaned forward, faced pinched as if constipated. "OPEC or the or—organization of petroleum eh—ex—ex—puh—por—ting cuh—countries is a per—per—"

Lizzie sighed hopelessly.

"Hey, listen," Kenji said, "it's okay. How about this? I'll write down every word we have trouble with. Then we'll work on them one by one."

It's what I should've been doing, instead of fucking her. Helping the girl figure out how to read, how to be self-sufficient without selling her body. Not getting your fill.

Color drained from his cheeks.

"Maybe you and me can just hang out," Lizzie said with a weak smile.

She placed a hand on his thigh and squeezed. It felt obscene. After all, somewhere in her passion for him had to be realities of which neither could avoid. She had to realize that it was he who fed, clothed, and provided a roof over her head. She had to realize that it was he that protected her from what she perceived as her only other option: Snow. And she had to be grateful for the stupid rescue mentality he'd taken on, whereby he whisked her from poverty and into rehab, and even now, taught her to read and write. How, then, was it that he could treat this as love, when a romance comprised free will and a willingness on both ends? He'd all but bribed her into loving him, it seemed.

"Liz, let's focus on the schoolwork, okay?" He removed her hand from his lap.

CHAPTER FORTY-THREE

The drive to Broward Corrections took forty-five minutes in relatively minor Saturday-morning traffic. Deena drove with the windows down and the wind in her hair, keenly in tune with the tremble of her hands. Nearly two-and-a-half decades stood between Deena and her mother, two-and-a-half decades between that moment and the one when she murdered her father.

Who knew that anxiety could seize her like this—stiffening her spine, dotting her forehead in sweat, parching her throat in pain? The sun was especially brilliant this morning, emblazoned against a lackluster sky, blinding and heightening her unease. But where fear and anticipation mingled for a powerful potion, determination propelled her forward. Years of unanswered questions, of a life damned at the hands of one woman. Her brother, her sister, her own pain, even—she blamed her mother for it all. She had a right to know why it'd happened.

Deena exited the interstate and veered left onto Sheridan. What she expected, she couldn't be sure. But the sheer normalcy of the short trek that lay before her was perhaps the most obscene thing of all. Clusters of single-story, pastel suburban homes on the right and left, a McDonald's here, a library there, unnerving in its ordinariness. And at the end of it all, at the end of her yellow brick road, stood a concrete complex of captivity, unassuming in the morning sun. It lied to Deena as it stood there, belying a sense of safety, hiding the horror of society's truths.

Deena pulled into the parking lot, eyes focused on the fortress before her. For more than twenty years her mother remained there, caged in confinement with killers.

Good.

Deena abandoned her purse to the trunk of her car and headed for the looming guards at the prison entrance. Already a small line had begun to form, toddlers and children a part of the queue. She frowned distastefully. Never would she bring Mia to such squalor. And what would be the purpose anyway? To remind her of the poor choices others made? Of society's wrath for those who rightly deserve it? She could turn on the TV for that.

A tall and broad-shouldered man with a star tattooed on the backside of his skull cut off Deena in line. She opened her mouth to protest and shut it, deciding she'd prefer any spot out of his view anyway.

Despite the usurper's height and girth, Deena could make out the line's destination: a narrowed entryway bathed in light. She looked from it to the guards just before. Vaguely disturbed by the restrictive nature of the hall, the men with guns at the entrance, and the curt, skeptical nature by which they raked gazes over each member of the line, Deena experienced an unfounded feeling of terror.

Claustrophobia.

But was it possible? She'd never had it before. However, now that she inched forward, toward that compressed, threadlike hall, she felt something like panic titillating her senses.

It was what they wanted, she realized; it was purposeful. After all, hadn't she designed a prison in which every wall, ceiling, and floor was created to incite this overwhelmingly oppressive feel?

A guard gestured to her with massive hands, demanded her name, and nodded for her to step forward. Immediately, she was stopped by a second guard near a table, unseen from her place outside. He too demanded her name and checked it against a short list.

"Gloria Hammond?"

Deena gave a curt nod and looked away. Her mother's name still held power it turned out, even after all those years. She supposed, in some way, that the truth of what she was doing had not occurred to her until those words had been uttered. Before then, she thought herself in a fairy tale of nightmarish proportions.

"ID," the guard barked as if she'd been stupid in not producing it thus far.

Deena slipped her driver's license from the pocket of her slacks. He scrutinized it, turned it over, and handed it back.

"Go," he blurted, impatient that she had not instantaneously moved on to the next step.

Deena walked alone, down a hall that stretched on, walls grungy white and narrow enough that her fingertips would sweep both sides should she extend her arms. At the end waited a metal detector and two more guards. When she slowed, one waved her forward impatiently.

A pat down. Fingers in her pockets, under her armpits, sweeping her breasts. Two men who could've been thumbing a grapefruit for all of the attention they paid to curves they so generously touched. The lack of acknowledgment, the gruff handling, was but one more indication of humanity's absence.

"Go," one said and nodded at the metal detector.

She stepped through.

Silence.

Deena pushed through a set of double doors. And into sunlight.

She blinked in surprise.

For all their touching and searching and double checking, they'd led her to believe she'd be admitted into the very depths of confinement, and certainly not this bastion of open-aired freedom. But then, commonsense set in and Deena's gaze flitted upward, till she caught a glimpse of a guard tower shaded in the trees.

"Take a seat at a bench and wait."

Another voice: a surprise waiting to the right of the door.

Deena dully registered a woman that could've been a man, or vice versa, and headed for the picnic tables. She took a seat at what she hoped was an indiscriminate location in the middle, folded her hands in her lap, and waited.

Underneath her, smooth metal stretched out both left and right, bolted to a concrete slab poured into grass. One table away, a toddler burst free of his mother and laughed as the distance grew between her and him. She retrieved him from under a tree just next to the canteen. Were it not for the guard in foliage and the now plainly visible electronic fence that threatened them, she would've thought herself in a park or playground.

"Deena?"

She snapped to attention. A voice—lost to memory, lost to nightmares, now addressed her in daylight.

The woman before Deena was a cruel caricature of her mother. Once tall and graceful with milk ivory skin, high-perched breasts, and the slimmest of hips, this woman had sallow, pitted features, brassy limp locks, and slack, wrinkled skin. Brilliant, Carolina blue eyes were now flat and lusterless, as if belonging to the dead. The fiery orange jumpsuit draped over her hollow frame and patted-cake breasts were scandalous to a girl who'd first learned of designer fashions by watching this woman dress in the morning. Words escaped Deena.

"You're beautiful," Gloria Hammond whispered.

She reached out a hand, trembling, as if she might dare to touch her daughter, after all this time. Deena stared at those outstretched fingers, revulsion curling her stomach.

"Don't," she managed. "I . . . can't stand for you to touch me."

Gloria's hand snatched back, eyes pooling for a fast-flooding stream.

How dare she! Instinctively, fists balled in Deena's lap.

A guard to the right of Gloria Hammond placed a hand on her shoulder. "Come on now. Take a seat," he warned.

Everything they said sounded like a warning.

Deena's mother sat automatically, and the guard left. Suddenly, they were very much alone.

"I can't believe how beautiful you are," Gloria Hammond said again. Her voice was like a flutter of dried leaves, dead, a simpering sigh devoid of life.

"I look like you," Deena snapped.

It was obviously not a choice.

Gloria placed a hand on the table. Fingers curled and uncurled, as if massaging the metal tabletop. It was with horror that Deena realized it was her left hand. The wedding ring was gone.

"I—"

Gloria's hand went still. She looked up, saw Deena's face, followed her daughter's stare to her hand, and snatched it from the table.

In the distance, a child laughed.

"I never thought I'd see you again," her mother began. "I never thought I'd see your face. And Anthony's . . ."

Gloria broke off and put a hand to her mouth. The right hand. No doubt the one that killed Deena's father.

"I didn't come here to reminisce," Deena said. "Or to embrace you like some brokenhearted daughter desperate to have a mother. I only want to know why you're a murderer; I only want answers."

For a long time, Gloria didn't speak. The toddler who cavorted to and fro giving his mother hell was now cradled serenely in the arms of an inmate, as angelic as a sweet-cheeked cherub. The inmate smiled, murmured something that had to be love, and stroked the child's hair tenderly. Deena looked up from the pair with tear-filled eyes. They were mirrored in her mother's own, glistening gaze.

"Don't you dare cry," Deena spat. "You have no right. You murdered a man who meant everything to me. Do you know what's happened because of that? Did you ever bother to find out?"

Deena rose only just slightly, before a look of sit-your-ass-down from the guard calmed her.

"Anthony sold drugs," she hissed. "Trying to provide a life for the family you abandoned. He was only a boy! A child trying to do a parent's job. He died like a dog because of it."

Gloria looked away, tears spilling freely over now-hollowed cheeks.

"You look at me," Deena demanded. "It's the least you can do after what's happened to us."

201

Again, her mother faced her. She was used to taking orders.

"Lizzie's a whore," Deena continued. "A ten-dollar whore that stands on the corner and takes less if it's all she can get. She needs it for the high, you know. Crack. Cocaine. Heroin. She does it all. You wouldn't believe what she's done for a high."

Gloria wept pitifully, face buried in her hands, audible sobs so violent that visitors from other tables kept casting curious looks. Deena only vaguely acknowledged them.

"Stop putting on a show. You must've known that Anthony was dead. Only Lizzie would've been a surprise." Deena's lip curled in disgust. "You always did have a flare for the dramatic."

Gloria wiped her face with the back of her hand. "I cry easy," she said. "Same as you."

Deena didn't care. The verbal lacerations felt gruesomely rewarding, like slashing at a victim and dancing in the wounds.

"I'm not like you. I abhor you."

Gloria laughed.

"So, what now? You think you're like your father?" She shook her head. "You always were in love with him."

Deena glared. "What the hell's that supposed to mean?"

Her mother leaned back, the tears on her face now dry. The smile on her lips smug. "It's not your father that you're like, Deena. It's me. Anthony was like his father."

"What?"

Her mother sighed. "Come on. Have you never wondered how Anthony, as just a boy, was able to rise so quickly in the RIP gang? Or why grown men coalesced behind a child, almost overnight?"

Deena withdrew. "No."

Gloria eyed her. "Yes, you did," she said quietly. "Your father was one of them."

"He was not!" Deena cried.

Gloria stared. "Of course he was. Think. Remember. You already know."

"He worked for the city," Deena said frantically. "He did maintenance . . . for the city."

"And yet you lived in a beautiful white house, four bedrooms and a spacious yard, all in Coral Gables. How do expect we paid for that, Deena? I didn't work. And you're old enough to know the salary of a . . ." she paused as if to recall. "Maintenance worker."

Deena sat back. "You're lying."

"He went away sometimes. Do you remember?" Gloria said. "A maintenance man away on business?"

Deena suddenly had an image, her father, smile bright and hopeful as he hugged his sugar bear and promised to see her soon. Away on business, he'd said.

Tears filled her eyes.

"You didn't have to kill him."

But Gloria met her gaze. "You have no idea what I've had to do." Gloria folded her hands on the table and cleared her throat.

"Five men came to the house that night. You answered the door and came for me, just as you'd been taught to do. The moment I saw them, I told you to take Anthony and Lizzie and run. You already knew where to go; you'd practiced before. Our visitors marched me to the bedroom where Dean lay and pulled out guns. I was given two choices. Shoot my husband or else. 'Or else' meant that a sixth man, now watching my ten-year-old struggle down a back alley with my toddler and baby, would off the little ones and sell you to a man named Mondo who specialized in pimping children. Ten thousand was what he could get for a girl as pretty as you.

"There were supposed to be round-the-clock guards. Three guys

203

in the gang, lower ranking, who would keep watch since Dean had earned a bounty on his head. But they disappeared, still, to this day. Most folks figure they were killed, though bodies were never found." Gloria paused.

"In the end, it was Dean who told me to do it. 'Just do it,' he said and nodded toward the gun. He couldn't bear the idea of someone hurting his children. Even for a minute." Tears welled in her eyes.

"I love Dean. Still," Gloria said fiercely. "*Still.* And we made the *right* choice."

Thick and humid air enveloped Deena, suffocating her in sadness. She rose, stumbled, flailing as if trapped. Desperate to get away. Images of the moment she returned to her parents' home, the gun, the blood, her mother shrieking, melded like a syndication on madness. She could take no more. But then her mother said it, and even that was too much, too.

"I love you, Deena," Gloria said.

Deena fled. From the table and between a bookend pair of guards who snatched her back and patted her down properly. The moment they released her, Deena broke for the hall, rushing, ever rushing, to make it to sunlight. She stumbled into the parking lot, blinded, fleeing for her car, until an emphatic thud and slice of pain made her howl and fall back.

Tak emerged from the passenger side of the car she'd run into.

"Hey, whoa, slow down, honey bun."

He scooped her with firm hands, and she submerged in his embrace shamelessly, sobbing, nauseated by a sudden upturning of life.

Long moments passed, moments where he soaked up her tears and held her in silence.

"What are you doing here?" she managed into his chest.

Tak tilted her chin so that she faced him. His smile was unmistakable. "Hey, you said I couldn't come with you. Not that I couldn't come after."

She smiled faintly.

"That's better. So much better," he said, nodding in approval.

It was then that Deena noticed John Tanaka behind the wheel of Tak's BMW, drumming out the beat to some muted and awful-sounding metal song.

"He'll drive my car," Tak said. "I'll take yours. Let's go."

It was as if he'd known what she'd discover that day, as if he knew how uprooted she'd be. But even she hadn't known.

But on the car ride, she made sure to tell him.

Deena stared at the ceiling of a bedroom whose price tag comfortably sat in the six-figure range. Next to her lay a husband who tossed frequently and woke every hour or so to see if he could help in some way. In his willingness was but one more reminder of the sweepingly dismissive attitude she'd taken with everything and everyone.

Never had she thought to ask the "why" of her father's murder, or to fathom that he might've somehow played a role in his own demise. For her, it was enough to dismiss a once-loved mother as evil and move on to the next concern. If she were honest, she knew that to be the mantra of her life: Lizzie was determined to be a prostitute and drug user, decisions her sister made willingly long ago; Tak was a once celebrated artist whose glory had waned; certainly he had time to pick up the slack at home. Hadn't those been her beliefs? How faithless had she been to the truths of her heart, to the truths that lay bare before her, in thinking that way?

Lizzie's decisions were a predictable by-product of neglect and abuse. In fact, it amazed Deena that a young girl which the law deemed a victim unable to give sexual consent on the one hand, could suddenly become a willing participant worthy of prosecution with the acceptance of a few dollars. But Deena was as guilty as society for such obscenely flawed thoughts. After all, hadn't she believed Lizzie disgusting, or at the very least, wholly culpable, for what was happening to and with her? But what had she, her own sister, done to protect her? Never had she sought to eradicate the source of Lizzie's ails; Deena had only sought to bandage them with rehab and shouting. Some part of her feared she knew little of her sister's real life; rumors and innuendos pointed to a relationship with

Snow that shouldn't have been. When he became her pimp, Deena berated herself for not doing more to intervene. Eventually, though, she sank back into her cocoon of dismissiveness, insistent on a sister who lived in accordance with what made her happy, thereby freeing herself of any real assessment of reality.

It was the same way with Tak. When his art began to wane, Deena thought him not working hard enough, losing interest, or both. After all, he'd never had her fire, her desperate ambition. Food and shelter had always been predictable mainstays for the son of Daichi Tanaka. And so, in her easy way, she'd dismissed even her own husband's woes, though she could never bear for him to do the same. Never had she questioned where his creativity had gone and why or whether there was anything she could do to change that.

She could go on, of course. Her dismissals of Tony acting out; her insistence that something or someone else had to be at fault. Never had she been one to wrangle with an issue that couldn't be fixed in a single setting. Hadn't that been what her long drawn out affair with Tak was all about? She hated the difficult—no, scratch that—*loathed* the difficult, drawn out impositions of life, especially those that called on something other than keen intellect to solve them.

Which brought her back to her parents. Lying awake, Deena pieced together the cheerful puzzle of her childhood and found that the missing portions were absent of her own accord. However, now that she'd seen her mother's face, they came back willingly, accusingly; calling her out for her faithlessness to the mother she once loved. How had she let others determine her mother's worth? How had she let others write the story of their existence, when all along, her memories insisted on another version?

Overprotective, doting, affectionate, slow to rise in anger. She had so many recollections—of smearing on her mother's Chanel lipstick 'til she resembled a drunken clown, of weighing her neck, arms, and fingers in precious pearls and gemstones before stumbling about the house, of pressing her face to her mother's in a mirror, in the hopes of noting even the faintest resemblance. She'd always adored her, until she'd been given reason to do otherwise.

Deena's gripe with herself had nothing to do with being angry about her father's death—she certainly thought that still within her rights. No, her gripe had everything to do with her reluctance, all those long years, to find out the truth. Didn't she owe it to someone she once professed to love, to at the very least know their motivations? Even then, the moment that propelled her forward and into Broward Corrections had been fueled by her own nightmares, instead of any sense of loyalty to her mother.

She thought she'd known her father well. Certainly, Deena knew things about him—like the zealous sweet tooth he harbored or the way he was prone to sleep in, but the more she looked back, the more she found jagged pieces unable to fit itself into the proper puzzle. For example, her father never missed a spelling bee, Young Architects Competition, or parent-teacher conference, no matter whether day or night. How could blue-collar work be so flexible?

She'd gone to the City of Miami's website after that visit, and perused all jobs under the title "maintenance." Half came back as positions for engineers and technicians, the sort that required a college degree. The other, as menial labor. Even a supervisory position, listed as senior maintenance, paid no more than what a department store clerk would get. Still, memories of a postcard-perfect home pervaded her. Mother didn't work, and father, according to her research, should've been on public assistance. Even for a fool it became plain that something was amiss.

"Dee? You all right?"

There he was again, sweet as ever, giving her even then what she didn't deserve. After all, hadn't she made a mockery of his art, implying that creativity was simply an act of volition? Or worse, that it made no difference at all whether he created or not? As an artist herself, she knew better than such crass thinking and had resorted to it only because he had stopped producing. But by looking only at the bottom dollar, she'd implied that his work had no intrinsic value, other than that which could directly benefit her.

She couldn't remember when her hunger for security had become a thirst for riches.

"I owe you an apology," Deena said. But even in the dark, her next words wouldn't come.

Had Tak been faced with the choice her father had to make, he never would've given her a choice either. In true life as in conjecture,

207

Tak's unequivocal priority would always be their children, their lives together, and their love. Those things had always come first for him even when career blinded her.

Dean Hammond had asked to die. In that unceremonious way that had always been his, he told his wife to "just do it," as if already impatient with her hesitation. In the complicit moment when both mother and father sacrificed life willingly for Deena, Anthony, and Lizzie, Dean Hammond died—and not one, but two parents became willing martyrs for their unsuspecting children.

Deena remembered little of what followed her father's death. There was her mother's arrest, almost immediately. An admittance of guilt. The foster home. But why? Certainly, police would've searched for suspects, found some corroboration for her story. Deena couldn't even recall being questioned about the men at their door.

Unless her mother's silence had been part of the agreement.

"Dee?"

Deena thought she might drown; drown in the pity of regret, of a want to forget a hatred so intense that it seized her like violent bits of nausea.

Her father's murder had been born of love, it turned out.

Love and hard choices.

But a life led wrong had led to those choices.

"Dee, baby, please. Get some sleep," Tak said, and took her into his arms.

She was crying in her sleep. It was something he hadn't seen in years, and it confused him, waking him out of a baffled stupor and causing him to grope stupidly. But when he realized where he was and what was happening, he reached for her automatically—as natural a thing as breathing.

She stirred in his arms, struggling, then stilling, body recognizing him without waking. He couldn't help the smallest smile of satisfaction, prompted when she snuggled in without so much as opening her eyes.

"You comfortable yet?" Tak asked her teasingly.

"Almost," Deena murmured and made a show of fluffing his shirt and adjusting him.

"You were crying," he said.

She went still.

"I know."

Hurt twisted his heart.

"You keep shutting me out," he said. "Let me help you make it better, Dee. Tell me what I can do."

She opened her eyes, and he could see little more in the dark.

"Love me," she whispered. "Despite all the mistakes I've made."

Tak smiled. "Gladly," he whispered and brought lips to the beat of his heart: Deena Tanaka.

Morning came and Tak parted his wife's thighs for the third time since her nightmare. She giggled, but it was cut off by a kiss on the swell of her lip.

Eyelids heavy, she looked up at him in smoldering expectation, open to him and vulnerable in a way that was only his.

Tak ran a hand across the silken swell of her breasts and teased a single chocolate nipple to hardness. He ran lower, hand over the curve of her abdomen, a reminder of his seed, accepted, loved, and nurtured. He found her core and grinned when she purred in response. Though he'd planned on teasing, tasting, and tracing the length of her body all morning, apparently Deena thought differently. She pulled him to her with urgency despite the long night, back arching to hasten his entry.

Seared on entry, Tak slumped forward, hair sweeping into his eyes. Pumping, gliding, throbbing, he found an easy, familiar rhythm, as heady as their first time, as agonizing as any.

She cried out in delight. He threw a hand over her mouth,

certain the kids might hear. But instead of stifling her cries, it emboldened her all the more, muffled moans fuel for the blasts from his hardness. Deena stiffened with her orgasm, her never-ending moans of fulfillment electrifying Tak and heaving him over the edge. When he did roll away from her, reluctantly, it was with an exhale of utter exhaustion.

CHAPTER FORTY-FOUR

Getting Deena's kitchen back from Mrs. Jimenez was no easy task. The woman was enamored with the duties of caring for "her Tak," a task of which she constantly reminded them, had been entrusted to her since he was all but twelve. To say that she took pride in her work was to misunderstand Mrs. Jimenez together. The Tanaka family was no more her "work" than they were Deena's work. As far as Mrs. Jimenez was concerned, the Tanakas were her own. Should anyone ever believe this misguided thinking, Tak had long since settled the issue of mutual amicability. Two years ago when their maid's husband fell sick, Tak paid for his bypass surgery. When the Jimenez's eldest daughter, Adriana, began her studies at the local community college, Tak paid for two semesters after their savings dried up. And when Mr. Jimenez had a second heart attack and passed away, it was Tak who'd paid for his funeral. After his death, he offered Mrs. Jimenez a room in the house where she was welcome to live should she need to or visit should she ever feel lonely. Their maid had cried herself to embarrassment at the gesture, causing Deena to follow suit, so moved was she by the magnitude of her husband's heart.

But Mrs. Jimenez's insistence that she'd all but birthed Tak made for a very steep climb between her and Deena. After the wedding, she decided to come and work for him and let his father look for a new maid. With her, she brought a whole set of hard and fast rules about what Tak would eat and how things should be cleaned. Each time Deena fought with Mrs. Jimenez, she couldn't shake the feeling that she was arguing with a mother-in-law instead of the person whose checks she signed. Finally, it was Tak who intervened, gently so, by setting out a clear series of compulsory practices that made Deena the unequivocal woman of the house. Only then did Mrs. Jimenez succumb to a life of employment under Deena.

With two weeks home, Deena decided that she would prepare dinner for the family each night. Mrs. Jimenez sulked, but busied herself scrubbing walls and fussing whenever the children sped by. Twice Deena noticed Tony chasing Mia and her laughing, slowed in her effort to escape him.

"There should be another visit from the social worker soon," Tak said. "I've been thinking of asking how we could speed things up. Can't really see any reason why it would be helpful to take forever."

Deena looked up from the hall the children scampered through. She had no idea how long Tak had been there.

"Speed things up?"

"The adoption," he said and headed for the fridge. "I think if we hurry up and get it over with, it'll go a long way toward making Tony feel like he belongs here."

Deena lowered her gaze. "You don't think he already feels like he belongs?"

Tak took a carton of juice from the fridge, lifted it partway to his mouth, stole a quick glance at Deena, and went in search of a glass.

"I'll bet he's been in lots of houses, Deena. And I'll bet lots of people have told him that they'll adopt him. What makes us any different?"

Juice-filled glass in hand, he leaned against the counter.

Deena frowned. "Well, we're his family. He must know—"

"How do you know there wasn't 'family' before? Or someone who told him to think of them as family?"

Deena lowered her gaze.

He chugged down his juice in three greedy gulps.

"Nothing we say will matter anyway. For somebody who's been disappointed, or lied to, or whatever, the only thing we can do is prove it to him. Maybe then he'll slow down with the acting out."

Deena bit her lip. "And you think hurrying through the adoption will help things?" In her mind, nothing but time could bridge a lapse of trust.

"It's the best I've got. And in the meantime, we take *Heavyweight Knockouts* away. We don't want him getting any better with the right hook."

Deena shot him a look. She hadn't approved that game.

212

Tak blushed with his blunder. "Don't worry," he said quickly. "In a few short years, we'll be arguing over whether he's going to UCLA or MIT."

He looked up and locked eyes with a frozen, gold-flecked pair in the hall.

Tony.

He scurried away.

Tony turned a corner and collided with Mia, or Baby Mia, as he liked to call her, since she had the temperament of a newborn.

"I still have it, Tony! And there's only one way to get it!"

A high-pitched giggle wafted down the hall, distant from the enormity of the house. Tony scowled. He was tired of playing with her.

"I'm not kidding anymore, Baby Mia! Give it back before I get mad!"

She disappeared into a room. Her head popped out. "No!" she squeaked and disappeared again.

Tony started down the hall, refusing to run after her again. Refusing to play her childish game.

"Give it back, Mia! *Now!*"

"No!"

Head popping out of another room, down the hall and opposite the other. They were in a fun house, minus the mirrors, it seemed. He would've broken any mirrors at that point, anyway.

"Mia!"

"*No!*"

She dipped into another room. He broke into a run.

213

She had his money. All three hundred sixty-two dollars of it. Stolen from the bathroom counter while he showered. She was always entering without knocking. How many times had he yelled at her about it? He should've known better.

Mia screamed at the sight of him barreling toward her and took off, sliding stupidly on hardwood in her Mary Janes. Thick hair bouncing, head whipping in horrified anticipation, she cut right, the frills of her lilac dress last to escape. Mia slammed the door shut, only to have Tony burst through it.

"Give it to me!" he roared on entry.

They were on the far side of the west wing in a room he'd never been in. Burgundy and gold swirls on the floor. Intermittent light and dark gold striped the walls glittering on its rise to the vaulted ceiling. Dangling chandeliers of a million crystal pieces hung like icicles waiting to pierce prey. Tony turned on Mia. A ballroom. In the house.

"Give me that goddamned money," he hissed.

He would return it if she gave it back to him now. Scatter it around the house so that the maid found and returned it—anything to deflect blame from him. He couldn't fuck up now, now that he was so close to adoption.

Mia blew a raspberry and bolted.

Tony sprang in fury, blurring across the ballroom and tackling the five-year-old to the floor. She hit it facefirst with a thud, him atop her.

For a moment he thought he'd got away with it. Or killed her. Silence stretched on.

And then she wailed.

A wail as loud and piteous as a grieving mother pierced the air. She was like a siren, never breaking, endless in her howl of sorrow.

Beneath Tony was Mia and sprayed out before them like a drug bust gone bad was an assortment of twenties, tens, fives, and ones, some splattered with blood. Tony stood, trembling as bad as the day police came home in the place of his mother.

He looked up. Both Tak and Deena were in the doorway.

It would end like this. With him having broken Mia's arm or some other terrible thing, with Deena wanting back every hug she'd ever given, and with Tak looking down at him in disgust.

They would make him leave. And he wouldn't take a dime with him.

Deena rushed to Mia, who bled from the mouth onto the lace bib of her gown. But Tak's eyes were on him. Hard, scowling, harsh. Still, he said nothing.

It would be Deena who spoke first.

"Baby, what happened? How did you get like this?"

Feverishly, she prodded and inspected Mia's mouth, before exhaling in relief. "It's just a busted lip," she murmured thickly.

Mrs. Jimenez appeared at the door, hissed something in horrified Spanish, and scurried off again.

"What happened?" Tak demanded. Still, his gaze was on Tony.

"We were—playing," Mia managed through shuddering sobs. "Running through the house—"

"How many times have I told you about that?" Tak snapped.

Tony glanced at him in surprise. Was he really concerned about that with the evidence of robbery right before him? Robbery and assault and God only knew what else. He didn't know how it all worked.

And then it occurred to him. This *was* robbery. Robbery, assault, abuse of a minor. And those were only the charges he could think of. They wouldn't be sending him to a group home. They'd put him in prison.

"Well," Tak said dryly, gaze even with Tony's, "if nothing else, we've found the missing money."

Deena looked up in surprise, and instinctively, Tony took a step back and made a survey of the exits. There was the one that Tak blocked and another, eons away. He could make for it, but would have to slip past Deena. He wondered if he could slow down enough to snatch a little money from the floor on the flee.

Jimenez returned with the first aid kit. Deena took it, leaving the old lady to scowl. She was good at it, anyway.

"Why don't you go with Mrs. Jimenez, Mia? We need to talk to Tony," Tak said.

"He didn't mean to hurt my lip!" Mia burst. "We were only playing!"

Tony's heart twisted in response. *She* was only playing. He had been figuring ways to murder her and dispose of the body.

"It's okay, baby," Deena said, eyes on her child.

Now she was standing, too. Both she and Tak faced him. They moved in closer.

Mia followed Mrs. Jimenez out. Once at the door, she turned back once more. "I shouldn't have played with his money. I should've stopped like he said."

"Agreed," Deena said. "We'll discuss it more in the hall."

Mia looked up fearfully. Deena nodded toward the door, and both mother and daughter exited from sight.

He was alone with Tak.

"Pick your money up, Tony."

He didn't dare move. "What?" he said weakly.

"Your money. I said, 'pick it up.'"

Tony blushed. "It's—it's not mine. It's yours. I took it."

"You mean stole it."

216

The boy turned a rich shade of ruby. "Yeah," he mumbled.

"What?" Tak took a step closer.

Tony couldn't get back fast enough.

"Yes, I stole it," he whispered, heart jackhammering.

Tak shrugged. "Go ahead and pick it up. It's yours now."

Terror stiffened Tony. Nobody let you rob them and get away with it. But when the punch line didn't come, Tony bent to get the money, an eye on Tak and an expectation of a blow to the back of the head.

"Count it," Tak ordered once Tony collected the bloodstained bills. "Out loud."

Tony could think of nothing scarier than the calmness with which Tak ordered him. Quickly, he did as he was told.

"Three hundred and sixty-two dollars."

Tak let out a low whistle. "Lotta money for an eleven-year-old."

Tony lowered his gaze.

"But I'm gonna let you keep it," Tak said. "Minimum wage is about seven bucks or so. How many hours you think it'll take you to earn that much?"

Tony's eyes rolled upward with the math. "About fifty hours," he said. He'd always been good with the thing he never had enough of: money. "Maybe fifty-two."

Tak shrugged. "Sounds about right. Now, Mrs. Jimenez is your boss. You'll cut grass, pull weeds, scrub windows, and polish silver till you've earned every bit of your three hundred sixty-two dollars."

Tak snatched it from Tony's hands. "*Then* you can keep it."

Just outside the door, he heard Deena fussing at Mia about not purposely annoying people.

217

"All right," Tony said softly.

Tak jammed the money in his front pocket. But when Tony headed for the door, he put a hand up to stop him.

"Help me understand you, Tony. Three hundred and sixty-two dollars. What could it possibly be for? What haven't we given you already?"

Tony sighed. There was no point in lying. No point in manipulating. Neither had helped him so far.

"If I had to leave, if you wanted me gone, I'd have something. Something to eat, maybe something to wear. I don't know. Just in case you got tired of me."

He looked up to see not just Tak but Deena in the doorway.

Tony's vision blurred. To his horror, hot, humiliating tears threatened, then spilled over onto reddened cheeks. He swiped them before attempting to shove his way through Tak and Deena and onward to his room. But he couldn't get through. Struggle as he might, he simply couldn't. It had to be Tak restraining him with muscles only a private gym could make. He fought and thought to scream, so enraged was he at the notion of being held hostage.

"Tony! Tony!" Deena cried.

He opened his eyes.

He'd mistaken his uncle for his aunt and a hug for imprisonment.

CHAPTER FORTY-FIVE

Kenji got a dozen children's books from his big brother, accompanied by the usual warning that he was in over his head with Lizzie.

They started with *Vandy Gets a Lion,* the story of a girl who is convinced to babysit a newborn lion for only an hour; however, an hour turns to days, and days, weeks, as the mysterious man who's given her the cub fails to return. Vandy raises the lion in secret in the confines of her bedroom, smuggling food, grooming him, and attempting to mask his roar.

Lizzie fussed when Kenji explained that they would read the same book every day until she did so flawlessly and could demonstrate comprehension. Their first time around, he counted four words that gave her serious issue.

Kenji continued to spend his days crammed in the office, thumbing through the International Building Code Deena had assigned him. He also took a stab from time to time on the minority recruitment report he'd been given long ago, though at the last meeting, his father had suggested that one of the other suits assist. That meant that at the next meeting, a typed twenty-page report, complete with PowerPoint presentation, would miraculously appear with Kenji's name on it, right above the poor sucker who'd actually done the work. Eventually, Kenji figured, all good deeds would be rewarded.

While at work, Kenji's mind usually drifted to some Lizzie-like thing. The burned dinners she insisted on making, the cute smirk of accomplishment when she read through *Vandy Gets a Lion* without stumbling, and that wild bray of a laugh she'd give each night they watched *South Park, The Simpsons,* or *Family Guy,* her new favorite shows.

Sometimes, at night, when the hour got late and his eyelids drooped, Lizzie would scoot over and caress his thigh, or worse, reach right into his shorts. Always, he would push her away. And always, the hurt would be plain.

CHAPTER FORTY-SIX

Among the duties of children with aging parents is accompanying them to doctors' visits. In the Hammond family, it was a task left to Aunt Rhonda, dumped on her under the guise of being the only one with "medical expertise." Now, driving from one of the many visits Deena's eighty-four-year-old grandmother was subjected to, Rhonda turned to a topic Deena had intentionally avoided: the idea that her grandmother could no longer live on her own. She had just been diagnosed with Alzheimer's.

To her credit, Deena's aunt Caroline had been the first to note that something was amiss, pointing to Grandma Emma's tendency to confuse and forget her grandchildren and great-grandchildren. Deena went on the defensive, shouting at her family that if they hadn't sought to replicate the twelve tribes of Israel, then maybe she could be expected to remember. But only a few days later, her grandmother had failed to recognize her and asked if her dead son Dean would be home for dinner. A tearful Deena could no longer deny she needed help.

Rhonda decided to call a meeting of Hammonds to discuss what was best for Grandma Emma. Bouts of insomnia, depression, inconsistent difficulty with everyday tasks, and failure to remember old friends, children, and even her husband, once, when shown a picture, had given the doctors cause for serious concern. So, Deena's family decided to gather, to discuss the future of her father's mother.

Despite an ever-swelling family, Aunt Caroline, Aunt Rhonda, Deena, Tak, Aunt Caroline's daughter, Keisha, her son Tariq, and his on-again off-again girlfriend, Pauline, were the only ones to show up. Deena quickly thought it best, however, when they began to argue at once.

"Well, she can't live by herself," Rhonda said. "Already, she's in the moderate phase of the disease, demonstrating persistent memory loss, bouts of confusion, and a whole list of other symptoms that I've already told you about."

She looked pointedly at her older sister, Caroline, who looked away.

There was a time, of course, when Grandma Emma didn't live by herself. Shortly after Lizzie moved out for the last time, other Hammonds came and went, taking children, sometimes leaving them. But eventually the Public Housing Authority decided that only Emma Hammond was officially on the lease, and they moved her over to a one bedroom no larger than a matchbox.

"Maybe the medication will help," Deena said, not exactly thrilled by the idea of having to house her overbearing grandmother. "Maybe then she won't have to move."

Vaguely, she registered Tak's hand under the table and on her knee. He gave her a squeeze.

Rhonda, a maternity nurse at Jackson Hospital, nodded. "It should. But how much we won't know yet. I think it's best if we play it conservative and put her somewhere where we know she'll be safe."

"She'll need a nurse and round-the-clock," Caroline said and dug a Newport from a tiny, patent leather cherry purse.

Rhonda glanced at her.

"And you a nurse," Caroline pointed out, lighting up her cigarette. "You could do the job."

"I don't think that's warranted this early," Aunt Rhonda snapped.

Caroline jabbed the cigarette between two meaty, painted lips, and smirked. "What's a matter, little sister? Afraid you gonna have to put your girlfriend out?"

Keisha hooted.

"Caroline, I don't think—"

"*Aunt* Caroline," she spat at Deena and fed her a long look. "I'm still your daddy's older sister, you know, no matter how much money you and Pork Fried Rice got."

Deena's mouth flew open, curses perched on the edge of her lips, but in a single motion, Tak snapped it shut again with a tap under her chin.

Across the table, Tariq stretched out long legs and sighed, head falling back with the weight of exasperation at the Hammond family.

"*Aunt* Caroline. *Aunt* Rhonda," Tak said with a smile that betrayed his odd sense of humor, "let's stay on topic just this once, shall we?"

Aunt Caroline shot him a look. "All right then, nephew," she said unconvincingly.

Deena glanced first at Aunt Caroline, fat and shiny, simpering; Newport jutting from thick red lips, to Aunt Rhonda, who still looked as if someone had just thrown open the door on her mid-shit.

"Can't we just go ahead and get this out in the open?" Caroline said loudly. "We all know you gay. Momma, me, Deena. Even Daddy knew, back when he was alive. Been knowing since they sent you home from summer camp on account of you fiddling around with some girl." She made a crude gesture with her fingers, and Rhonda colored fiercely. Caroline sat back, satisfied.

"They didn't have money to send nobody but you to camp, and *you* get kicked out 'cause you can't keep your fingers outta pussy."

Deena sank in embarrassment, both for herself and Tak, who, she wagered, would never grow used to the raw vulgarity of her family.

Rhonda burst from the table, and Deena shot after her, leaving Caroline to sit, smirk smug and self-satisfied to the tune of Keisha's, Tariq's, and Pauline's wild laughter. Only Tak sat motionless, color drained from his face.

"She's horrible, I know," Deena said, when she finally caught her aunt outside. "But we've known it for years."

Tears swarmed Rhonda's oversized eyes; she dashed them away blindly. "I don't have to tolerate her," Rhonda said. "Not anymore. I put up with her when we were kids. Hitting, cursing, humiliating me. I won't stand for it one more minute."

"So, don't," Deena said. "Don't put up with her. But don't run away either."

Deena shot a rueful glance back at her grandmother's building.

222

"We need you. And you know what else?"

"What?" Rhonda said harshly.

"You know she's not right. You know she's not all there is. Me and Tak and Mia, we love you regardless."

Rhonda's gaze shifted to the front door skeptically.

"Try again?" Deena said hopefully.

Rhonda heaved a deep sigh, and then nodded. "Try again," she breathed, and followed Deena inside.

"So, I been thinking," Caroline said, the moment they reentered, "Momma needs a nurse. Rhonda's a nurse."

"She wouldn't live with me and Mary Ann," Rhonda said.

Caroline smirked. "Is that right, now?"

"Haven't you had enough fun, yet?" Deena flared. "I, for one, don't have all day to watch your show unfold. So let's discuss Grandma, only Grandma, and get back to our mutually preferable and separated lives!"

"Here, here," Tariq muttered.

Deena blinked at the unexpected support.

"All right, then," Caroline said. "What about your house then? You could throw her in one of them back rooms. You got so many."

In her last visit alone, Emma Hammond had wondered aloud what Tak and Deena were trying to prove with such a spacious place. She also criticized the landscaper for a flower that had tilted over, asked Mrs. Jimenez if she could even cook black people's food, informed Tak and Deena they spoiled Mia and would suffer the consequences, and suggested, for the umpteenth time, that Deena's pants suits were of the devil. On her return from the restroom, she announced that Mrs. Jimenez had missed a spot when cleaning the bathroom.

Tak and Deena exchanged a muted, horrified look at the thought

223

of Deena's grandmother becoming a permanent resident.

Deena sputtered. "We—"

"—are hardly ever home," Tak blurted.

"And I wouldn't want her there—" Deena said.

"—alone!" Tak supplied and shot a look of veiled amusement her way. "We wouldn't want her there alone."

"You kidding? Man, I remember when we brought the kids over for Mia's birthday party," Tariq said. "You had that maid, the dude that cuts the grass, and some Russian nanny. That's three people right there."

"Only Mrs. Jimenez lives there," Deena mumbled.

"And they don't exactly get along," Tak offered.

Tariq shrugged. "Well, nothing's perfect. But she'd have her own room, nice house, everything. Shit, that's good living. *I* want that."

Indeed, he did. Caroline's oldest son, born when his mother was 16, had his first child at the age of 17 and followed with 6 more. Tariq's eldest son, following in the example of his father and grandmother, had his first child at 19; a responsible age according to the Hammonds. Tariq Jr. now had two children, as did five of his siblings, leaving Caroline's oldest son in the possession of 11 grandchildren. And he was only 48.

Deena sat up straighter. As it was, a house on a bay with serious distance from the Hammonds meant she could control her contact with them and thus her sanity. Moving her grandmother in would change all that.

"All right," she said. "So, Grandma Emma moves in with me. Who pays her bills? Me?"

A survey of averted gazes and shrugs confirmed as much. Only Rhonda looked directly at her, as if trying to ascertain if she'd gone loopy enough to consider the offer.

"So, I get dumped with the *whole* thing?" Deena said. "No friggin' way."

Tariq shifted uncomfortably. "I mean, not the whole thing. I got this security job I'm supposed to be coming into—"

"How you gon' work security when you got a record?" Keisha demanded.

Tariq blushed. "I mean, I know the dude. He's supposed to be hooking me up."

"What happened to that job at the dry cleaners you were supposed to get?" Caroline asked.

"And that stocking job at Target?" Keisha spat. "'Cause I'm tired of your baby momma calling me with the bullshit."

That was the other thing. Though Tariq's children were generally all in their twenties, his youngest child was a five-year-old named Peach. The drama that Peach's mother, Vera, stirred, however, was the stuff of legends. Among her greatest moments were supermarket fistfights with perceived rivals, threats of suicide, vacillations concerning whether the child was his or not, and declarations of marriage to an otherwise baffled Tariq. This was in addition to accusations of forgotten birthdays, and, of course, the absence of child support. Deena didn't think she had the patience to discuss Vera, especially when Pauline, her biggest rival, sat just across from her, raring for a fight just as certainly as if she were in the supermarket.

Rhonda cleared her throat. "Why don't you take her in, Caroline?" she asked. "You're always going on about Momma this and Momma that, and we can't even count how many times you and your kids have had to stay with her. Why don't *you* make some space?"

Caroline stared. "Much as I wish I were in a position like you two, where I could just take Momma in," she looked from Rhonda to Deena, "and much as Momma knows I would never put a man in front of her like you're doing with this Mary Jane—"

"Mary Ann."

"Mary *Ann*," Caroline snapped, "I don't have the space. Shakeith just moved back in with his daughters Sara and Window, and both their mommas."

As was always the case, Tak glanced at Deena to confirm that Window was a person's name. It was.

"You have four bedrooms," Rhonda reminded her.

"Yeah," Caroline said, "since we counting what *I* got," she shot an accusing look at Deena, "I'm in one. Keisha's stuff's in another. Curtis Jr. in the third cause ain't no way he living with his daddy, Snow, 'cause he say he can't stand 'em. And neither can Tayshon Jr., who'll be in the fourth room."

"Curtis Jr. ain't say that," Keisha hissed. "You always keeping up some kinda mess."

"I ain't keeping up nothing," Caroline retorted and tapped ashes on her father's prized table. "But Curtis don't like him, and Tayshon say you stupid for marrying him."

"You always running your goddamned mouth, but who gon' marry you? Seven years Andre Petit been staying at your house—"

"Don't worry 'bout how many years my man been there!"

"Well, don't you worry about how the fuck my man been getting on with his son!"

Tariq snorted. "Just don't come home with no diseases," he muttered, "'cause everybody know how Snow is."

Keisha whirled on her brother. "I *know* you ain't talking! Them six kids ain't but the ones you claiming! And anyway, Deidra Dee down at Winn Dixie told me you got three kids wit' her sister, and the youngest ain't but a year old!"

Pauline jumped up. "She a motherfuckin' lie! Tariq ain't been wit' nobody but me!"

"Jump up stupid, you wanna," Caroline said.

Pauline turned on her. "Momma Caroline, Deidra Dee don't know nothing. What, was she in the bed with 'em? Stood watching to make sure Tariq bust a nut? And she one to talk! She don't even know who her baby daddy is! Been so many niggas running up in there, can't nobody get 'em straight!"

Caroline and Keisha exchanged a look of scandalized delight and burst into laughter.

"Okay," Tariq said. "Back to Grandma," and cast a cautious glance at his trembling girlfriend as she lowered herself into her seat.

It occurred to Deena then that the Hammond family was a wash, a waste, an unequivocal parasite on society. Jobs were a novelty, education an oddity, welfare an entitlement for them. Killing Caroline Hammond by her fifteenth birthday would've saved the U.S. government money spent on a lifetime of welfare for what had to be upwards of forty recipients by now, including children, grandchildren, and great-grandchildren. Deena thought that she could kill them now and save society at least some money. Or, she could kill her aunt and cousin and make an example out of them. Deena massaged her temples tiredly. Anytime she had thoughts of mass familicide simply meant it was time to go.

"If someone in the family can make room for Grandma Emma," Tak said, glancing at her with a knowing expression, "then Deena and I can make sure we cover her expenses and compensate for the person's trouble."

They leaped at once, Caroline surmising that Shakeith, who was still to move in, could crowd into one room with baby mommas and babies alike; Keisha, that she and Snow could have her three daughters in a single room, and Tariq wondering aloud if maybe his oldest son, Donte, was ready to move in with his baby's mother as he'd been planning.

After lots of shouting and a little rearranging, Caroline's place was agreed on, with the caveat that Keisha's children would move faster than originally planned, and that Keisha's house would be open to Shakeith's ex-girlfriend and her daughter Sara, should the two-baby-mamas-in-one-house thing not work out. In exchange, twenty-five hundred would be given to Caroline a month, in addition to the burden of expenses Tak and Deena would shoulder. At the agreement's end, Deena left her family with a deep sense of fatigue and overwhelming relief.

227

CHAPTER FORTY-SEVEN

Keisha blew into her apartment and came to a full halt at the sight of her man. It was rare for him to seek her out in the evening.

"You coming from seeing your family?" he asked, and took a drag on a blunt so weighted that it swelled at its center. He sat at a small round table made for four, the home of countless plots and plans.

"Yeah," Keisha said and dropped her purse on the couch.

"See Lizzie there?"

Keisha sighed and headed for the kitchen. "I told you I wouldn't."

"And I told you money is short without her!" He stubbed out his blunt and rose to full height. "You my girl; you're supposed to help me when I need you."

Keisha threw open a stained freezer door and scowled at the contents. Feeling his gaze, she finally turned to face him. "Find another hoe, Snow. Can't be that hard."

He closed the space between them, quick, and slammed the freezer door shut in her face. "All right," he said. "But maybe I won't go far to find her."

Keisha met his gaze head-on.

"What the fuck's that supposed to mean?"

Snow held eye contact a fraction of a second longer, and then dropped it. He dissolved into a smile. "Nothing. I've got some new girls, some young girls, so that's good. Niggas always like doing crazy type shit to 'em. They like all that tightness and crying."

Keisha forced an image of Lizzie underneath her fiancé squirming and crying out of her head and turned back to the freezer. She decided on some ground beef and set it on defrost in the microwave.

"Help me find her, Keish. It's the only way we to pay for this big-ass wedding you want."

Keisha smirked. What seemed an eternity ago, she'd sat in on a shoreside ceremony, where the smiling bride's wild and curling hair fluttered in the wind. Afterward, they'd sailed aboard a yacht, drinking their fill of champagne and eating shrimp cocktail, steamed lobster, and oysters Rockefeller while a seven-piece band played the hits. Once again, she'd wanted the thing that had been promised Deena. Once again, Keisha would settle for second best.

She would take her wedding the best way she could get it.

~*~

Tony pursued Tak and Deena the moment they entered the front door. In the months he'd been with them, he sprouted a full inch—hair, limbs, and feet alike, shoulders broadening to accommodate an ever-changing boyish build. Deena had taken to braiding his hair, fat cornrows from hairline to shoulders, walnut with the occasional streak of rust. She was now a pro, having dropped tears in his scalp on only the first two occasions. Every day, he looked more like her brother, she kept saying.

"Tak, I cut some of the grass," Tony declared at the door stoop. "But I couldn't finish. It was too much."

Indeed, dirt striped his face, while a single winter leaf rested in his hair.

"Good thing about grass," Tak said, "is it'll be there later."

He shouldered past Tony for the kitchen, ignoring both the look of scorn on his wife's face and the disbelief on Tony's. He'd give him another day of torment, allowing him to think that he'd be expected to cut two acres of grass alone. Anyway, Deena would've killed him if he got anywhere near the botanical gardens.

Tony looked from Tak to Deena, the latter of which set about making coffee. She had a special airtight canister that she used, and when it emptied, Mrs. Jimenez ground coffee beans from a vacuum-sealed bag that smelled intoxicating. As he stood, peering over her shoulder, she'd told him in Spanglish that they were the rarest beans in the world, imported from Indonesia, but only after a four-legged civet ate the coffee beans and shit them out later.

229

Tony hadn't believed her, of course, so he Googled as much with his cell. Sure enough, he found a four-legged mammal, like a long and disturbing raccoon, and a description of the digestion process—a necessary first step in processing the four hundred-dollar coffee. It was with horror that Tony recalled sipping Deena's coffee behind her back when she'd told him he was too young to have his own. And it was with horror that he realized what it now meant. He'd drunk shit and liked it.

Deena made two cups of coffee, set one before Tak, and sat down across from him at the table. Tony pulled out a chair for himself. Without asking, he spooned two large heaps of cream into Deena's cup, and then three into Tak's. He followed it with sugar.

"Why couldn't I come with you guys?" he asked. "They're my family too, aren't they?" Tony looked from Tak to Deena.

The two exchanged a look of constipation.

"Yeah but . . ."

Deena shook her head. There was no way to tell a kid the family he'd just found was hardly worth his trouble. That they were worse than the worst caricature of black people. Crass and ignorant, boorish, without hope or ambition, they were content with gaining sustenance on the milk of society's crudeness. Poor didn't equal ignorance, but a thirst for nothing did. The Hammonds weren't the norm, not even by impoverished community standards. They were only the loudest and most visible, a sideshow from life's true experience.

She couldn't protect Tony from Caroline's crude assessments, Keisha's foul and indiscriminate mouth, or the three dozen children that rotated them in a gravitationally compelled orbit. She could only prolong it. But holidays would come. Weddings would come. Funerals would come. And the Hammonds would come out.

"They're basically assholes," Tak said.

"Tak!" Deena cried.

Tak sat up straighter, as if warming to the conversation. "You go over there and it's like sinking in a sea of assholes."

Tony grinned deliciously, as if thrilled by Tak's use of profanity.

230

"Is it really?"

"Absolutely. There's Dee, and then there's Rhonda and Grandma Emma. I think there's a cousin—Crystal?"

Deena nodded, tight-lipped.

"And she keeps away. Lives in Daytona Beach or something. You'll notice that any Hammond with a shred of self-dignity puts some distance between them and the brood."

"Tak!"

He was teasing . . . but serious, and while he hadn't said a word untrue, she'd thought they'd break it to Tony a little gentler.

"Back to the distance. For Crystal, it's a few hundred miles, so she's safely away. For Rhonda, it's working 80 hour weeks so she can always look busy. And for Deena, well, Deena built a moat around the house. Dragon should be here shortly."

Tony giggled. He had a broad smile, reminiscent of his father's goofy grin. When his smile faded, his eyes were on Deena.

"I must look an awful lot like my dad," he said.

Whatever whispers of a smile Deena's face harbored soon melted. "Why . . . why do you say that?" she said.

Tony shrugged, gaze averted. "It's like you think I'm haunting the house, the way you look at me sometimes. At first, I thought the worried looks were 'cause I was always screwing up. But I can see by your face it's 'cause I look like him. 'Cause you think I am him. Sometimes you make me feel like Pinocchio trying to convince Geppetto he's a real boy."

Shame lowered Deena's gaze and kept her from seeing him even then. How much of her bliss at Tony's arrival had been because she felt she'd been given a second chance? Hadn't her first thought at seeing him been that Anthony had come back to her? She'd seen Tony and not seen him, seen through him to a father now dead. How different had that been from the Hammonds, looking at Deena and seeing her mother for all those long years? Just because hate marred their version and love buoyed hers didn't mean he'd been any less invisible to her. Still, she couldn't look

231

at him.

Her first thought had been to get up, to separate herself from them. She could hardly think of a destination, yet knew her next moments had to be away from that table and away from him. The foul mouth, fighting, and stealing had all been Anthony Hammond's early mantra. From there it was the drugs, girls, and guns. Three paths: all rushing him to the same destination. It was there that he lay.

But Deena stopped at the door. She was doing it again: behaving like a Hammond. Sins of the father, or in her case, the mother, burden of the child to bear. Anthony Hammond was dead, and the dead ought to be left dead when there was so much life to live. Deena turned to face her nephew.

"Would you like to see the deadliest animal on the planet?"

Tony raised a brow.

"What do mean?"

Deena and Tak exchanged a whiff of a smile.

"I mean an animal so ferocious he's responsible for hundreds of human deaths a year in America alone."

Tony blinked. "It's not like, a dog or something, is it?"

Deena grinned. He was a sharp one. "No. They keep him caged. We have to see him at the zoo."

This perked him.

"All right," he said. "Just let me grab my jacket."

It was November now, closing in on his birthday, and a Miami breeze occasionally necessitated a windbreaker.

Once Tony was out of sight, Tak rose to clear the coffee cups from the table. "Taking him to see a few deer, huh?" he said.

Deena grinned. There were still a few months left on her annual passes to the zoo. "Yeah and maybe ice cream afterward."

232

"Make sure to promise him that you'll capture a monster responsible for murdering millions each year."

He'd terrified his daughter with just such a declaration not long ago, before returning to her bedroom with a common mosquito.

When Tony reemerged, his long face set solemn, as if preparing for battle with the wild.

"Hundreds of deaths a year, huh?" he said as they headed for the door.

"Absolutely." Deena grinned. "Maybe more."

Chapter Forty-Eight

Deena woke with the feeling that she'd overslept, temporarily forgetting she had no job to go to. She sat up with a start before Tak's hand shot out to slow her.

"Whoa," he said and pulled her back to the bed.

Deena fought back the momentary panic at the sight of an insistent sun just outside her window, and only sat back against a towering walnut headboard when Tak applied pressure to her shoulder.

"Hungry?" he said.

Still in his variation of pajamas, a ribbed tee and gym shorts, Tak nodded toward the nightstand. Only then did Deena notice the breakfast waiting for her. Belgian waffles, whip cream, heavy on the strawberries.

"Cliché, I know. But the six-piece Mexican Mariachi band couldn't make it on such short notice."

Deena blushed.

"I don't deserve this," she said, even as she reached for the food. "Breakfast in bed after the way I carried on?"

Tak shrugged.

"Then I should probably get rid of the car," he said.

"You bought a car?" Deena blurted.

"No," Tak said. "Were you expecting one?"

She hurled a pillow at him. He caught it and set it aside.

"You're never serious," Deena complained, cutting into the buttery soft waffle with the silverware once resting on her nightstand. "It's what drives your father crazy."

Tak snorted. "Leave my father out of this," he said and plucked the fork from her hand. "He's the last thing on my mind."

He guided the waffle into her waiting mouth. When whip cream dripped onto her lip, Deena paused with a memory of more than a decade ago—him, her, Atlanta, and loving him always, it seemed.

"You were sloppy then, too," Tak whispered and kissed her.

The food could wait.

Deena's Belgian waffles were cold by the time she returned to them. But when Tak rose as if to get her more, she pulled him back to bed.

Tak, without the energy to resist her pull, had collapsed next to her in bed. Now, Deena nibbled his neck.

"Man down, Dee, man down."

She shot him an unimpressed look. "You'll be up again. You always are."

Deena nipped at his earlobe, sucked it, and trailed a tongue down the length of his throat. Tak smiled sleepily.

"You're frisky," he said.

She climbed atop him. Already, they were naked.

At night, when they were together, fear of being overheard restrained her. But now, there was nothing. With the children at school, it was just Tak and Deena, as it had been so many years before.

"I want you again," Deena said and brought her mouth down on his.

Lips, tongue, taste, they wouldn't need more than this. With a moan of longing, she guided him in.

~*~

Only three times in her life had Deena had such lazy days. The first was on a cross-country road trip she'd taken with Tak—begun as friends but ended as lovers. The second was a week in Mexico they spent mostly making love a few years later. The third was their honeymoon in the South Pacific. Here was the fourth.

A suspension from work for Deena had meant a suspension for Tak. He'd taken to bringing her breakfast each morning and pounding her after, as if one required the other. Sometimes, the pounding came first, but either way, it sat on one end of breakfast like the most erotic of bookends. He'd pinch her ass while she packed lunch for the kids, whisper about inserting himself in any number of places, and once, even swept her onto the counter for a quickie the moment Tony and Mia were off to bed. Deena suspected that the mere mention of receiving a few dozen desperately hurried pumps had been enough to rush her halfway to orgasm. But his breath in her ear, hands on her body, and her very own voice, bold and divorced from her usual subdued self, hurled her to abandon. Fuck her, harder, faster, begging, needing. She was wildly his in a way she never had been before. And it thrilled them both.

In the evenings, Deena spent time with the kids, sitting in on Tony's drum lessons, the new guitar lessons he'd volunteered for, or, doing things on a whim— miniature golf, Dave & Busters, boogie boarding. And while Deena did see all the ways Tony was like her brother, she saw the divergence as well—direct, where his father was rude; aggressive, where his father was reckless; headstrong, instead of abusive.

"Funny sometimes," Tony once told her, "how the simple stuff really isn't and what's complicated really is simple."

"Take that building, for instance," he said and pointed to a gleaming skyscraper in the distance. "To most people, that's real complicated. Takes a lot. But if you think about it, it's really not."

"Tony, I don't think you understand—"

"Now take the stuff everyone's supposed to get, because everyone's experienced it. Everyone's seen something beautiful, loved a parent or friend, whatever."

"Okay," Deena said.

"Now there's a formula for that," he said, jutting a thumb back at the skyscraper. "You can go to school, sit down, pay attention, learn about the beams needed to support the weight, how to make it stay straight up and down, 'cause it must be easy to tilt since it's really just a tube. But where do you go to learn what's beautiful? Who loves you? Who you are? There's no school for that. So is it always an experiment? Never knowing, just guessing?"

She'd been struck by several things at once. One, that he'd been incredibly astute in his assessment of the skyscraper—referring to beams and weight support and even going so far as to call it a tube. Phenomenal, considering this particular skyscraper did have a tube frame.

Then, there was the other thing, far more impressive than his spatial aptitude. His assessment of the intangibles of life: beauty, love, uncertainty. Children tended to be blank slates, canvases filled with what adults chose to illustrate. She had known him to be smart, but never had she guessed at this astuteness, this propensity for reflection.

And reflection, more than anything, separated him from his father.

CHAPTER FORTY-NINE

Tak lifted his gaze from the Arts Section of *The Herald* and followed her with his eyes. If there'd been a moment where she'd stopped talking about Tony, it had been too small for him to notice.

"Sounds like he's gonna be a philosopher," Tak said, jumping in the brief gap of chatter about Tony's keen insights. He then returned to his newspaper. "We'd better get his trust fund together. He'll need it."

Deena turned on him, a banana sundress in her hands. She'd been going to and fro between it and a flirty white one for sailing the next day.

"Get John's friend to do it," Deena said. "The one who did Mia's."

"Maybe we should wait until the adoption's complete," Tak suggested. He caught a glimpse of her glower and returned to his paper.

"Or . . . maybe not."

Deena stood a moment longer, nostrils flaring, before she turned back to her dress. Tak's gaze shifted just slightly, from an amazing backside to the boy at the door.

"Tony, *knock*. Remember?"

"I did. It wasn't closed. Just kinda floated open."

"All right." Tak patted the stretch of bed next to him, and the gangly preteen leaped onto the bed.

"What's up?" Tak asked.

"Well, I'm not really asking for anything, you know. For my birthday—"

Tak raised a skeptical brow.

"It's just—I don't know if you had anything planned, and if we're doing anything, that's okay. But if we are—"

"I'm not taking you and Wendy on a date," Tak said.

"What!" Tony cried. "That loud mouth."

Tak shrugged. "A man likes what he likes."

"I wanna do paintball for my birthday. Just the guys. Me, you, John. He seems pretty cool."

"I'll be sure to pass the compliment," Tak said. "Just be careful that you don't find him cooler than me."

Tony nodded and slipped out the door.

Tak grinned. He was getting comfortable enough to ask for things. It was progress.

CHAPTER FIFTY

Another night of loneliness in Kenji Tanaka's house. The dinner she'd prepared, an unintentionally charbroiled chicken and canned green beans, sat on the table, uneaten. From a nearby entertainment center tantalizingly promising love songs wafted through the air. Lizzie couldn't recall turning it on, though she couldn't recall Kenji doing so, either.

She wondered if it bothered him the way it bothered her; if his spirit felt tormented by others singing about a love that seemed beyond their grasp. Or was it her? Was love her dream? If so, when had she first begun it?

Lizzie sat up. She'd inadvertently used the 'l' word. She hadn't meant it. Or had she?

"What?" Kenji said softly, guitar in his hands.

Already, she felt the color rushing to her cheeks. No explanation would come to her mind for the sudden start, no explanation, that is, except the truth.

Lizzie swallowed.

"I—I wanted to dance," she said.

She couldn't read his expression. Horror? Anxiety? Discomfort?

He turned back to the guitar. "I don't think that's a good idea," he said, fingers gently stroking strings without plucking.

She wondered if he meant more than the dance.

But didn't dare ask.

CHAPTER FIFTY-ONE

Two-week suspension over, Deena returned to work feeling renewed from her time at home and the notion that the saga of adoption would soon be over. Waiting on her desk were a stack of manila folders she knew hadn't been there the day she departed. Curious, Deena snatched them up.

Orders. Half a dozen of them, all requests for homes. She hadn't done a single family home in years, though they'd been her mainstay in the early days. Why had they come to her? She could think of three other architects who were desperate for this sort of work. Deena tossed them to her desk with a glare. It was only then that a handwritten note slid to the floor, formerly amidst the stack. She recognized her father-in-law's flourishing script immediately.

Daughter,

These projects are to remind you of why you became an architect. Devote to them the spirit and energy you would give a much more prestigious project. The reward will be great.

Daichi

Deena trashed the note with a scowl and slumped into her chair. Immediately, she went into the database to return her mediocre projects to the workload and grab something more prestigious. There was nothing.

Open assignments were available on a hierarchy at the firm. The newest architects had access only to the lowest pool, where Deena suspected the house orders had come from. Those were the firm's most basic projects. In many cases, there were requests for bringing a building up to code instead of designing one at all. Midlevel architects had access to remotely better endeavors—shopping plazas and midsize public facilities in addition to the lower level work. Only senior level architects could access the mouth-salivating enterprises—million-dollar projects limited to only those who were partners, unless, of course, your name was Kenji Tanaka. He was allowed nowhere near such monumental work.

Again, Deena scowled at the database. Though the icon next to her name still clearly indicated she was a senior level exec, dozens of better projects were grayed out and unavailable, leaving her only with her pile of homes or another.

She picked up her desk phone and punched in Daichi's direct line.

"Deena, do as you're told. We'll talk later." He hung up the phone, and she hurled it at the wall.

Deena left work soon after, stoking fury in a flurry of curse words that hardly helped the situation, driving at top speed. She knew why she wanted to be an architect and didn't need some self-righteous old man reminding her. What was it to him if she built one thing or another, so long as it didn't hurt his bottom line? Wasn't that all he cared about, anyway?

Deena slowed. She knew that not to be true. Daichi Tanaka had offered her the first job she ever had, with the bonus of it being both close to home and more prestigious than any she rightly hoped for. Had he not, she never would've come back to Miami, or within a hundred miles of the family she despised. Hadn't it always been her hope to meet someone in college, or later, marry them, and draw a straight line from Miami to the point furthest but still within the United States? There was the place she'd intended to move.

But then she met Tak, Daichi's son, without her knowing it. Boy, had he stirred something in her—something dead, dying; perhaps never existing without him. And now, she had more than a poor black girl with a dead father and murdering mother could rightly deserve. She had everything.

Because of Daichi Tanaka.

Deena had another revelation shortly after that. Much of the Tanaka firm's policies and overall code of conduct were adopted from The American Institute of Architects' Code of Ethics and Professional Conduct. How much of it had she violated? There was a clause about obligation to disclose conflict of interest to the client, another about candor and truthfulness, a third about upholding human rights in all designs. Violation of these tenets could result in harsh disciplinary action. She could've lost her license for the price of retribution. Her father-in-law had known that all along.

Deena returned to work early the next day and set about designing the first of a series of houses. She pulled down books that, no doubt, had newer editions, and read over philosophies she'd long since

242

dismissed. She compared them to that of her dead idol, Frank Lloyd Wright, called her "dead" version because Tak insisted Daichi the living one. Passion stirred in Deena once again. How was it that everyone didn't see the necessity of harmony with humanity and nature in architecture? It seemed so plain. And yet, it was only then that Deena realized how far she'd flung herself from long cherished ideals when she sought to deprive her mother of these very things.

Deena sketched concepts by hand, researched the latest in cost-effective, energy-effective architecture, and implemented them in every single design. For weeks she worked, careful not to bring her projects home, no matter how much she longed to, but rising early to address the first of the many loves she now had.

A month and a half was her usual design time for a small-scale house; she was able to do the first in a month. After submission upstairs and then onward for client approval, Deena was called up to Daichi's office.

"Very nice," he said. "Your design just passed my desk. Usonian?"

Deena shrugged. "I guess."

She closed the door behind her, uncertain of why she felt embarrassed.

"One of the mainstays of the Usonian design is the emphasis on the main living area. Large enough to encourage congregation of the family in a central location."

Deena blushed, but said nothing.

"Did you enjoy your time off?" Daichi said.

She nodded head down.

"Good. I'm leaving for Sydney in a week. I'd like for you to join me."

"Are you serious?" she cried.

Daichi raised a hand. "You're only there in an advisory capacity.

Two weeks and you return. I expect to be there for a month."

Deena squealed. Sydney. Two weeks. Another Tanaka firm that she would have a hand in opening. If only her father could see her now.

She only hoped that Tak would be as overjoyed.

Chapter Fifty-Two

For weeks, Kenji's best friends had been e-mailing, text messaging, and social networking him to death about the upcoming Comic Con festival in Tampa. Through four years of high school as teammates, Kenji and Brandon Sweets had made attendance at the annual comic book festival a priority. When they got to the University of Miami and found like souls in Zachariah Palmer and Cody Holmes, they bonded just as swiftly as the moment college roommates George Charles and William Webber woke with a sudden fluency in Swahili in the graphic novel *Prelude*. Two friends became four in the transition from high school to college, with Kenji's group swelling to include Brandon's roommate, Zachariah, who they introduced to graphic novels, and Kenji's roommate, Cody, who was already acquainted. As athletes only roomed with athletes, all four were already members of the baseball team.

Before Lizzie, Kenji spent most of his free time with his favorite teammates. Now that he had her—though he felt certain he didn't even know what "having her" meant—he saw them less and less. Brandon, his oldest friend, had taken to complaining first.

And now Comic Con had arrived and suddenly Kenji was too busy even for that. Better still, he couldn't explain why.

It was one of those weird things, where two people seemed to be together, yet no one had the gall to utter it. Thinking of her with another pained him, yet he knew he couldn't truly claim her for himself. Still, it didn't stop him from wanting. In his waking hours, it was as it was in his dreams, when a large and loud man shrouded in shadows laughed at the thought of a prostitute being anything other than a prostitute.

Kenji scolded himself for allowing his mind to drift once again. He returned his thoughts to Comic Con. After all, the guys were pissed that he'd bailed at the last minute, indicating he couldn't go only once he realized they expected him to. And now, as he sped from office down the interstate, bursting with an idea, he realized he'd created a false dichotomy: go with the guys or don't go at all.

He made four phone calls. The first to the ABC Costume shop downtown. Second, to a hotel. Third, to Brandon, whose attitude laxed only when Kenji promised to meet up with them in Tampa. The fourth was to Lizzie.

Why shyness seized him so suddenly he'd never know. But by the time she picked up on the third ring, he was ready to call the whole thing off. With a burst of faux nerves, Kenji took a deep, unsettled breath and told her to pack a pair of weekend bags for both of them.

"But why?" Lizzie said. "Is something wrong?" Panic. "Is someone hurt?"

"No, it's—well, there's something I do every year. Usually with a couple of the guys I went to UM with. I just—thought you'd be game and want to get out of the house and, you know, all that. But it's kinda lame, goofy as far as stuff goes."

"Well, what is it?"

Kenji swerved to avoid a merging car and nearly missed his exit in the process.

"Comic Con. It's a comic book convention in Tampa. You go dressed up as your favorite superhero, and there are all these comic book and sci-fi legends there signing autographs. The big guys show up and unveil stuff that isn't even on the market yet. Dealers sell vintage Marvel Comics, DC Comics, everything. Network execs premiere prime-time pilots and ask for audience opinion. There's really nothing like it. Three years ago, my friend Sweets snagged a rare copy of *The Eagle* once." When she met him with silence, he added. "It's an old British comic."

Lizzie paused.

"I'm sorry, did you say 'dress up'?"

Kenji blushed. "Last year I was the Joker."

"Everybody goes out in broad daylight dressed up?"

Kenji scowled. If she had a mind to laugh, he wished she'd just get it over with.

"Yes."

Lizzie giggled.

"I dunno, Kenj. Sounds kinda . . . corny."

"Yeah. Well, it is," he snapped. "And immature and a bunch of other stuff I don't wanna say. But, I like it anyway. And I thought maybe that you . . ." He took a deep breath. "Never mind."

"Are you mad at me?" Lizzie said.

He was mad at himself. For assuming she'd want to do something so dumb. For making all those plans—

"I think it'd be nice to dress up," Lizzie said softly. "Pretend I'm someone else."

"Pack," Kenji said. "I'll be there in a minute."

He was there in fifteen. True to their agreement, she was ready; two hardback and hastily packed suitcases full of necessities were propped at the door. Kenji grabbed both and headed back down the elevator. The drive to Tampa took a full five hours from the beach and already it was 5 o'clock rush hour. Briefly, he cursed himself for not booking flights.

They crawled along the interstate. Why she wanted the top down on the Audi while parked amidst the smog of the city he'd never understand. Fingers drumming the dash, Wild Boyz on repeat, then Thrice Jacobs, an indie rock group that made Lizzie complain. How she preferred the whining of R&B to that, he couldn't figure. Still, he'd make time for it, as he'd done the other night, when she'd asked him to dance.

By Tampa, Kenji's eyelids drooped, while Lizzie still looked sunny and fresh, probably on account of sleeping from Naples north. They checked into the Hyatt Airport and headed for the top floor. And, of course, Murphy's Law dictated that he could no longer sleep.

There were two beds. Lizzie sat gingerly on the edge of one, ruby fingernails running along the stitches of a plush white blanket.

Kenji, who'd collapsed atop the bed while still wearing his canvas Ralph Lauren lace-ups, blinked at her wearily.

"You don't know what you want," Lizzie said softly.

There was no need of an explanation.

"And you do?" Kenji said.

She dropped her gaze.

"I don't . . . like to want things. It's better not to hope and hurt."
She stole a look at him. Kenji rolled onto his back and sighed.

"Did you bring your GED books with you?"

She recoiled.

"No."

"Well, you should have."

He was met with silence.

"You don't have to treat me this way," Lizzie said suddenly.
"I'm going to pay you back for everything you've done for me."

Kenji lifted his head.

"What?"

"The place to stay, the food, the help with schoolwork. I'll repay
you. You don't have to treat me like a child you've gotten stuck with."

Kenji rolled his eyes.

"Okay, now you're just being dramatic."

"I am not!"

"You're yelling," he pointed out.

"Because you're pissing me off."

"I'm just trying to get some sleep. You already got yours," Kenji
said.

"Fine. Get your fucking sleep."

She chucked a pillow at his head. Kenji knocked it to the floor
and turned on his side, so that his back faced her.

Too angry to sleep, he lay there, jaw clenched until the soft sound of sobs chastised him.

He was being a fool.

Even with the knowledge of that, he couldn't go to her; something prevented him. But whatever it was, Kenji knew it wasn't his heart.

Lizzie hated being treated like a child. Or worse: like a patient. Where Snow had been her cancer, Kenji had designated himself her chemo.

He fed her, clothed her, and helped her with schoolwork, careful to retrace their boundaries in thick chalk. Originally, for a moment, she had thought she repulsed him. But at least that was a real emotion. This, she knew, was far worse. She was his patient, and all that she clung to was but a mistake for him, a brief lapse in judgment. It wasn't passion for her that he felt, but pity, responsibility, she now realized. Their relationship was as sterilized as she was stupid.

Meaning completely.

"Kenji?" Lizzie said, her voice but a quiver.

He snored in response.

CHAPTER FIFITY-THREE

Kenji and Lizzie rose early enough for breakfast and dressed in their costumes. For Lizzie, it was her first time in one, since Grandpa Eddie, and, by proxy, Grandma Emma, believed Halloween was of the devil. But when Lizzie unraveled the stretch of black leather and a blonde wig slumped to the floor, she looked on in confusion. However, since Kenji had awakened complaining about missing the Preview Night and pre-kickoff festivities, she wasn't about to delay him any longer by questioning him about the getup.

Lizzie braided her hair into a series of quick and sloppy cornrows, slipped into a black leather jacket that wore like a corset with sleeves, pulled on the matching leather pants, and used the bedroom mirror to tuck her hair underneath the platinum synthetic wig. The bangs ran straight against her forehead, blunt like the ends at her shoulders. It was then she noticed the small box of contacts on the floor.

Kenji stepped out the bathroom with his hair mousse'd, sideburns applied, a wife beater on, and tight blue jeans. On his right hand was a claw the length of his forearm. Lizzie looked from it to the muscles of his chest. Not hulking and obnoxious, but as unassuming as him. She swallowed.

Sunday mornings he spent hours at a batting cage, sculpting what she saw before her. She always went with him. He was lean and sinewy, and it caused her to suddenly recall long, strong arms wrapping her, broad shoulders just above her, silk hair sweeping and smelling of . . .

"I should've brought my Louisville Slugger," Kenji said, "had I known you were gonna look like that. These claws won't be enough to keep 'em off you."

Lizzie looked down at herself. She must've gained ten pounds while living with Kenji, most of it in her thighs and backside. But the wet leather sculpted and molded her to beauty. And as always, she was grateful for the opportunity to wear long sleeves, thereby hiding her track marks.

"I don't know what I am," she admitted.

Kenji's lips parted in astonishment.

"When you get downstairs men will fall at your feet because you look so much like the real Storm. And you don't even know who that is."

"I take it she's black."

Kenji snorted.

A bang at the door interrupted him.

"Come on, come on! Let's see the Japanese Wolverine!" someone shouted through the door.

A chorus of laughter followed.

Lizzie looked at him wide eyed.

"The guys," he said breathlessly. "Sweets, Zachariah, Cody."

Kenji headed for the door and shot her a troubled look only once there. "You love this stuff, okay? They'll never understand why I brought you otherwise."

Lizzie nodded, though she didn't understand why he'd brought her either.

The door swung open.

There was a black guy in a leather suit and mask which seemed complementary to hers; a white guy with long, wavy greasy brown hair, a camel trench coat, black tee, blue jeans, metal boots, and a long silver stick; and behind them, a second white guy, tall and slim and donning a single, pale blue cat suit with a face spray painted to match, and hair, also the same icy blue and spiked to stand up on end.

The guy in the trench coat let out a low whistle. "And now we see where you were last night." He nudged the black guy who grinned stupidly.

Kenji shook it off.

"This is Lizzie Hammond. Lizzie, this is Brandon Sweets," he gestured to the black guy who matched her fashion, "Zachariah Palmer," the trench coat guy, "and Cody Holmes," the iced up one.

251

Kenji grabbed his room key and stuffed his wallet in his back jean pocket. With an impatient arm he swept aside the three guys, making room for Lizzie to exit.

"I see why you don't return phone calls," Brandon murmured, a hand over his mouth to hide a discreet conversation.

Kenji shot him a look. "Don't start, Sweets."

"Well, if he won't I will," Zachariah said, falling back to quietly join their whispers. "You kidding me? I mean, when were you gonna tell us about *this* one? Her ass is incredible."

"You'd like the ass of a hippo if they put her in heels," Cody said.

All four had eyes on Lizzie's backside, who led the way to the elevator. Kenji's temperature inched toward scalding.

"She's good looking. You gotta admit that. Even you, Cody, and you only do blondes," Sweets said.

In reality, Cody didn't do much of anything. His luck with the girls was about as erratic as Kenji's. It was Zachariah, tall, dark haired, athletic, and naturally good-looking in an Elizabethan sort of way, who got away with shit like calling a Jill a Jen in bed or forgetting a date altogether.

"Where are we going for breakfast?" Lizzie called, already at the elevator.

"Lobby!" Kenji yelled back.

"Man, I tell you, if you weren't my boy," Zachariah said quietly, gaze drifting from the swell of Lizzie's breasts southward.

Brandon looked from Zach to Kenji, whose mouth clenched.

"All right, Zach. Twenty-second rule is clearly in effect," he said.

"Is it really?" Zach said.

252

"Yeah," Kenji said. "It is."

Sweets, Zachariah, and Cody drank up Lizzie one last time before looking away in unison. That was the twenty-second rule. With it invoked, they'd been allowed one last sweeping look at her before she was considered off-limits forever. The implication was that things were serious between Kenji and Lizzie. They would treat them that way from there on out.

In the elevator, Sweets launched a formal complaint about all they'd missed already. "HBO, Showtime, ABC, and CW previewed pilots," he announced.

Sweets shot Kenji a look, knowing how much he prided himself on foreknowledge of the TV lineup.

"I'm sure it was lame," Kenji said unconvincingly.

They sailed down the elevator shaft.

"You wish," Sweets said, and Kenji groaned inwardly.

The group took a continental breakfast in the lobby before moving on to scheduled events. There were some morning Q&As on the schedule, an autograph session with one of the writers from *Mutation*, and an hour-long talk about the creativity process from game developers at Sony. Afterward, there was lunch, an appearance by indie phenomenon Gil Crutcher, and a panel discussion on the fate of comics on the silver screen. In between were photo shoots with surprise guests and enough autograph sessions to satisfy the neediest of fans.

Lizzie got double takes the moment they came downstairs. And requests for pics with other fans. One from a guy with a razor glove like Kenji's, another from a pair of bikini-clad girls in boots and capes. Even the group, a most impressive copycat of the X-Men with Lizzie at their side, got stopped faithfully for photo ops with attendees.

It was funny, but back in Overtown and Liberty City where she wore painted on minis with much ass hangage and would've blown every guy in a five-mile radius for twenty bucks or less, Lizzie thought they hardly fawned over her in such a way. Prostitutes were things, not people, and therefore, hardly worthy of acknowledgment beyond the pleasure immediately provided. Telling a prostitute she was beautiful after doing

253

her was like petting a toilet after taking a dump. Both were ridiculous.

Lizzie liked seeing Kenji out with the guys, even if she did get relegated to following them around like a puppy on a short leash. They had inside jokes, random bouts of wrestling, and insults to go around. Intermittently, one would fall back and talk to her, causing Lizzie to instantly bristle at the attention. She worried about how to handle advances from one, and then wondered why she'd even worried. She wasn't Kenji's girl. He'd had her; maybe he would pass her, first to Zachariah, then Sweets, the black guy. What would she do if they suggested it? She owed Kenji so much, and yet, the thought of him passing her along without thought caused as much nausea as her withdrawal from heroin had done.

But the moment never came. She didn't understand these guys, who'd stolen glances at her body to start with, but now seemed as harmless and playful as an old lab, tugging at her hair, making obscene jokes about a presumed nighttime itinerary with Kenji—"Oh, you guys'll be busy by nine; we'll cross *that* event off our list,"—and pushing her forward for pics with Kenji.

"Sexy, sexier," Zachariah would call, bidding her to pout her lips or flip her hair, encouraging Kenji to grip in some raunchy place or another, until she inevitably ruined the picture by threatening and chasing him till he behaved.

Oddest of all perhaps, were the questions they asked her. Instead of *if* she'd gone to college, it was *where* she'd gone to college. Instead of whether her parents had stuck around, it was what they did for a living, what she did and where she'd grown up. Every question brought an automatic glance at Kenji, who answered with neatly packaged responses. She'd thought about UM and a few other places but ultimately didn't go to college; her parents were deceased and she was about to start school again. Where, she still had no idea.

Zachariah caught Lizzie toward the tail end of a Q&A on the deteriorating artistic integrity of graphic art. Among the last few able to grab a seat, they occupied a back row, with Zach on her right and Kenji's empty seat on her left. He was in line to ask a question at the mic.

"This part isn't really for me," Zach explained quietly. "I'm more of a fan. I like the experience. Kenj and Sweets are into the experience behind the experience, how things are created, the inspiration, et cetera.

Just give me the finished product."

Lizzie gave him a small smile. She did her best to keep up when Kenji showed interest. Likewise, he blinked sleepily, but remained awake, whenever she insisted on watching R&B videos.

"How long have you and Kenj been, you know," he nudged her, "an item?"

She shot him a look.

"We're only friends."

Zach's gaze drifted after the backside of Wonder Woman.

"He know that?" he said, when turning back to Lizzie.

She snorted. "Know it? He makes sure of it."

Zach raised a single walnut brow. "I think you're confused," he said.

"I know you are."

The two glared at each other.

"Listen," Zach said, "Kenji's a good guy. The best."

"I know that."

Catwoman passed and once again, Zach's gaze followed her. Only once she sat did he turn back to Lizzie.

"Whatever he said, just, forgive him, okay? He blurts shit and—"

"Zach. Let me save you the trouble. Kenji doesn't want me, okay? He's just not interested. So drop it."

He stared at her in disbelief.

"I said drop it," Lizzie warned.

Zachariah sat up straight, facing forward again.

~*~

Dinner was at a nearby buffet. Twice while Lizzie was up refilling on crab legs, she could've sworn Zach and Kenji were trading whispers. When she returned to the table and Zach got up, Lizzie asked if everything was okay. Overly engrossed in their food no one seemed to hear her. When she asked again, Kenji looked pointedly at her.

Dinner done, the group returned to the Hyatt for a meet and greet with celebs Lizzie had never heard of. Kenji sat still for all of two minutes, however, before barging out the ballroom.

"Kenji!" Lizzie cried and shot a look of annoyed confusion at his friends before going after him.

She rushed out into a vacant hall. The meet and greet was apparently the biggest event of the festival. When Kenji turned on her with an unexpected fury, doubling back at an angry pace, she froze in uncertainty.

"Why'd you talk to Zach about us?"

Lizzie blinked. "What?"

"You heard me!"

She took a step back. "There is no 'us' as far as I know," she said. "So, I don't see how I could've talked about 'us' to anyone."

He glared at her. "Fine," he snapped, so close she could've touched his face.

Eyes tearing, she searched for something, anything in his gaze that wasn't rejection. When she couldn't find it, she looked away.

"I love you," she whispered and brushed a tear when it fell. "But I don't know what you want."

Realization dawned on Kenji, so unmistakable that even Lizzie couldn't miss it. He loved her, too.

Kenji backed away and hurried down the hall, moving with the steps of a man near panic. Quick, quicker still, he had to get away.

"What the hell are you afraid of?" Lizzie screamed.

He stopped, stood still in the hall, talons reaching for the floor.

He returned to her.

"Hurting you," Kenji said quietly. "Every man you've ever had in your life has only wanted one thing from you."

His gaze dropped to her body.

"By the time we get there again, you'll know I want more. Way more than that."

He turned, but this time she was ready, grabbing him by the hand and pulling him to her. Her kiss was soft, dampened by tears, but he intensified it instantly, pressing her to the wall and parting her mouth to deepen. Body flattening hers to the wall, she placed a hand at his waist as if to pull him closer than physically possible. Kenji crushed her, mouth reckless and promising before ripping away altogether. Down the hall he went, leaving her to pant and stare after him. Halfway to the elevator he paused, doubled back, snatched her by the hand, and tore for the hotel room upstairs.

CHAPTER FIFTY-FOUR

Winter was but a suggestion in Miami. Where those just three hours north pulled on coats lined with fur and deep boots to guard against the chill, Dade County fretted over finding a decent two-piece in November.

When Kenji and Lizzie weren't fretting over GED books, they were now out on the town, either by themselves, or with his buddies—all of which had taken to calling her "Liz-boo" as a mockery of her and Kenji's relationship. But there was little Sweets, Zach, and Cody could do to make Lizzie angry, or rather, stay angry. After all, it was only with their arrival that she realized two things—she'd never had friends before, real friends, and she didn't want to go back to that again.

They now spent Sundays at the batting cage, together. First Lizzie, then Kenji's former teammates, pestered him on giving baseball a second go. Brandon told stories of broken records in high school, Cody of scouts from the major leagues in college. Even Zach, never one to be outdone, admitted that Kenji was so fierce at bat that if you pitched a newborn baby to him, he'd knock it out the park without thought. Whenever these conversations came about, Kenji grew irritated, pointing to a torn rotator cuff as the source of his downfall, one that had long since healed, apparently. As if to irritate him further, Zachariah began to make offhand announcements about open tryouts for various teams. Kenji would always go deaf at these times.

Miami Dolphins and Heat games with and without the gang, concerts, spontaneous drives up the coast, rented sailboats, comedy clubs, and dinner at five-star restaurants were now all regular appointments on Lizzie's itinerary of life. For her birthday, Kenji rented a gondola on the bay. Under the light of a full moon they had sparking apple cider, strawberries dipped in white chocolate she loved, and a dinner of orange duck. Once back at the house, he pampered her, making love in slow and torturous fashion, alternating it with kisses, caresses, and whispers of love.

They couldn't go back to before if they wanted to.

CHAPTER FIFTY-FIVE

When Deena told Tak that his father had invited her to Sydney, he gave her a "good for you" that meant he already knew. Despite a departure she figured would put a strain on the house, the Tanaka brood behaved in quite the opposite fashion. Tony, who'd taken to planning his "Men Only" birthday outing with vigor, was beginning to show improvement, both in grades and attitude according to his teachers. Even Mr. Keplar remarked that Tony had raised his hand once to read in class. Tak and Deena credited the extra hours tutoring for that. Tak also pointed to the drum and guitar lessons, which he felt were beginning to give Tony a bit of confidence.

Shortly before Deena's departure, Mrs. Jimenez startled them by indicating her mother was ill and that she needed to return to Mexico. Tak purchased an open-ended ticket to Mexico City, giving her the option to return when she thought best. But the prospect of Mrs. Jimenez's departure sent the family into an uproar—much more so than Deena's did.

"If she's in Mexico and you're in Sydney, what'll we eat?" Tony cried.

Apparently, Bismarck seemed a long way off.

"C'mon," Tak said, "there's plenty of Spam in the cabinet. And I know tons of recipes. Spam sushi, Spam and eggs, Spam and rice. I've even got a friend in Hawaii that can make Spam eggrolls. I can call him for the recipe. It'll be great."

Tony gagged.

"I'm going to stay with Uncle John!" Mia cried, eyes pooling.

Tony shot her a look. "I think I will, too."

In the end, Grandma Emma volunteered to come over. When Deena expressed concern about her ailing health, the elderly woman recited a list of daily activities she took on that included cooking three meals a day, cleaning, and spanking children among them, going on until her granddaughter gave in, admitting that her résumé was formidable. After hanging up, she made a mental note to have a talk with Caroline about allowing the woman who'd been in need of round-the-clock nurse care, according to her own description, to do so much on a day-to-day basis.

~*~

Tony rose early Sunday morning, but he was too late to see Deena off. A five A.M. flight to Sydney meant arriving at Miami International by three, which, according to Deena's logic, included leaving the house by one. Under the guise of seeing her off, Tony's plan had been to stay up late. He could play his new *Pirates The Series* game, maybe even catch a glimpse of some late-night stuff. As if reading his mind, however, Tak told him his services wouldn't be needed.

Padding from his bedroom to the kitchen, Tony's mouth smacked sleepily with the thought of Cocoa Pebbles in milk. He stopped at the sight of an old and mountainous black woman.

"Well, good morning," she said, sounding surly.

He blinked.

"Who are you?"

She got up as if the question were beneath her. Often, Tony had heard people say that someone could look at them and make them feel naked. And while he'd never experienced that, he would've welcomed it instead of this woman's look, as if trying to determine his worth.

"Sit down. You ain't eatin' no cereal. I'll get to breakfast."

Tony took her in, a hand on the back of a dining-room chair. She wasn't all that tall really, not more than average height, with big grandma tits that sagged. Thick black brows made a "V" of scorn, her mouth a little "O" of meanness. She reminded him of the lunch ladies at the group home, mealy mouthed but cruel, telling him to eat but slapping his hand when he took too much.

A yawn from behind made Tony jump.

"How'd you get in here?" Tak demanded easily.

"Don't worry 'bout how I got here! I got here one goddamned step at a time, that's how."

Tak burst into laughter and rounded the dining-room table into the kitchen, where he wrapped arms around the old lady, even as she pretended to bat him away.

"You crazy ol' tomcat," she said. "Get away from me, is what you oughtta do." Even as she said it, she laughed, obviously enamored with his attention.

"Sit down," she commanded, "so I can get this breakfast going. Half the thangs in that fridge look crazy, but I'll do the best I can."

Tak grabbed a chair next to Tony.

"This is gonna be great," Tak said. "Wait till you see how she cooks. All the old stuff, eggs, bacon, possum—"

"Possum!" Tony cried.

"Boy, get away from round here telling lies! I ain't never fed you no possum!"

"Dad though," Tak said.

"Yo' daddy a surly man. He needed some to humble him."

Tak laughed.

"They go back and forth with this bizarre foods thing they do. Trying to figure out who's the toughest. Only rule is, it has to be from your culture."

"Possums from her culture?" Tony cried in disbelief.

Skillet in hand, Grandma Emma turned a hard look on Tony, who shrunk instinctively.

"It's part of *your* culture, boy, and don't you forget it."

And as the old woman cooked, she shared the story of necessity, of slaves who made do with what they had—discarded portions of meat and vegetables, and game like possum, squirrel, and raccoon for survival.

What she put before them for breakfast was a spread more

261

magnificent than any Tony thought possible. Giant pieces of fried catfish, fat and sweating sausages cooked so they split down the middle, salmon croquettes, cheese grits, hoecakes, and biscuits with gravy.

"Is it always so much?" Tony said.

"Try everything and see what you like. Old Tak here like everything so no matter what you leave behind he'll get to it 'fore the day out."

Tak grinned, back curved with the eagerness of eating. He licked fingers, grease-laden fingers, and returned to the catfish.

Tony didn't think he could eat with her staring so intently. Where was her plate?

"Eat," she barked.

Tony picked up his spoon and tried the grits. Though there'd been no grits in Bismarck, he'd lived in Louisville and Tulsa, where there'd been no shortage. After adding butter, salt, and a sprinkle of cheddar, he found they were as good as he remembered. They ate in silence.

"Boy, I tell ya, it's like holding a mirror up to yo' daddy, you favors him so much."

Tony sighed. He had but one picture of his dad, the one from the news clipping. It got him to thinking about how much he wanted to look like a murderer and drug dealer. Not much was the answer.

"Yeah, I know," he said.

Again, she gave him the frank look. "Yo daddy was a handsome boy, just as you are. I 'spect the long face then is cause he disappoints you."

Tak froze, fork to mouth. He looked from one to the other . . . waiting.

"I guess."

"No sense in saying you 'guess' when you know," she spat.

Tony tossed the fork.

"Jeez! You cook all this food, and then you won't let me eat! I don't know my dad! I'm never gonna know him! Okay?"

"Tony," Tak warned.

But the old woman held up a hand. "Now ain't nobody keeping that fork from your mouth but you. But maybe what you mean is that the conversation don't agree with you. And that's fine. But you gonna eat anyway since I went to the trouble of cooking."

She waited, glaring at Tony till he picked up the fork again.

"Now you listen here," she said. "Your parents is your parents. They makes you, but they not you. You decides who you gon' be and what you gon' be worth. Don't matter what you look like. But a handsome face like yours helps."

"Here, here," Tak said and shoved catfish in his mouth.

"Though I worries 'cause good looks and money goes to some folks' head." She nodded indiscreetly toward Tak. "Just don't let it go to yours."

Tony grinned. "I'll try."

Just then, the sound of silverware clattering noisily to plate filled the room. Somehow, Tak had finished a meal made for two, possibly three. He looked innocently from Tony to Grandma Emma, before getting up in search of more.

CHAPTER FIFTY-SIX

Deena settled in for a twenty-four hour flight with a single connection at LAX. Her father-in-law, seated next to her in subdued Armani grays, immediately took out his briefcase and retrieved his laptop and an assortment of papers. Deena looked down at her novel and blushed. She should've known better. On their flight to Shanghai, Daichi had scribbled and typed and scowled for most of the seventeen-hour flight. Later, he attributed it to an inability to sleep midair. Still, it made Deena ever conscious of her constant snoozing and leisure reading.

As usual, he was all business on departure. He declined the morning cocktail the stewardess offered and frowned at Deena's choice of a Mimosa with her breakfast.

"When you've finished vacationing, I've something for you to look over," Daichi said.

Even as she insisted she hadn't a coherent thought before breakfast, Daichi pulled out a bound stack of sheets. He handed them to her.

Theorizing Architecture, by Daichi Tanaka.

Deena flipped to the table of contents.

"My thoughts on a variety of subjects. Aesthetics. Theory. Urbanism. Ecology. Reactions to varying philosophies. Even a philosophy of my own, I suppose."

Deena gaped. A flip to the end showed better than six hundred pages.

"This is tremendous. I can't imagine when you would've done it all."

He shrugged—as if capable of being bashful.

"Years ago, when I worked without ceasing—I did a great deal of it. Afterward, I contributed to it when life permitted."

"You'll publish it," Deena said. "And it'll become standard text in every classroom in the country."

"I'd like you to review it," he said.

"You mean read it."

"I've a fair command of the English language, Deena."

She blushed. "I can't imagine what I'd contribute."

"You've contributed more than you know, already. Still, I'd like your input. Read it at your leisure."

Breakfast arrived and with it, Deena's Mimosa. She drank only a little before queasiness set in, causing her to send it back. For that much, at least, Daichi seemed pleased.

On arrival in Sydney, a driver transported them to the Four Seasons near Sydney Cove. After dinner at the hotel and some rest, they rose, still off-kilter from crossing the International Date Line, and took a trip to the temporary site for the new firm, a series of rented floors within a fifty-story bank in the central business district.

Anyone who traveled with Daichi soon found that every matter, no matter how small, was related to business. Dinner was taken with deans from the University of Melbourne, Sydney, lunch with prospects at competing firms. There were presentations at universities, talks of internships, and always, always, the offer of a visiting professor position or emeritus, should Daichi decide to retire.

They rose early, respecting neither time nor fatigue, and worked till Deena's back ached and her head pounded. Seven days at a stretch they went, and still unable to accept every invitation extended. Even with her daunting schedule, Deena made sure she spoke to Tak, Tony, and Mia each morning before she did anything else. Her seven A.M. phone call from Sydney translated into a five P.M. version back home. All talk was about Tony's birthday and a Laser Tag party that Mia hadn't been invited to. When Tak jumped on the line, it was to tell her about all the Spam dishes he'd made that no one else had wanted.

Deena was grateful for the trip's end, despite her ambitions, so anxious was she to get back to her family. When the time came for her to return, Daichi surprised her by taking the flight with her.

"I'll return in a few days," was all he'd give for explanation.

Just as their departure from Miami had been early, the one from Sydney departed at six. On the return, Deena ordered a Mimosa with her breakfast.

"That's not going to agree with you," Daichi predicted.

Sure enough, two sips later, nausea caused her stomach to lurch in contempt. She sent it away.

"You've been doing quite a bit of that lately," Daichi remarked.

Deena shrugged. "Australian food disagrees with me. While I'm glad to say that I've tried barramundi, I don't think I'll be revisiting that adventure again."

"There were other things that disagreed with you, too," Daichi said. "I shouldn't think French fries too exotic for your palate."

Deena scowled. But even as she did so, realization dawned. Vomiting she attributed to foreign food. Fatigue from jet lag. Backaches from standing. But there was one thing she couldn't blame on Australia.

Her period was overdue.

CHAPTER FIFTY-SEVEN

Grandma Emma was over at the stove, cooking again. And she said odd things when she dumped food before Tony, about needing black folk's food. Was it true? Could a race of people need a particular kind of food? He would ask Tak when she left.

Before him was dinner. On that day, he'd already eaten enough food to shame him into contacting a homeless shelter and confessing— but that was the norm with Grandma Emma. She was a damned good cook, flavoring food so skillfully that he watered at the thought of it, anticipating the moment it would dance on his tongue.

Wendy came by. First on the pretext of returning a magic marker she said she'd mistakenly taken from his room. Grandma Emma forced her to eat, though she protested at the idea of eating fried food. After the first day, she came back three more times, for more fried food and to watch M*A*S*H with Tony and Grandma Emma. No one could make him admit it'd been fun.

Tony sat at the table with a mound of fried chicken, mashed potatoes and succulent gravy, country biscuits, and collard greens, all on a Wednesday evening. As usual, Grandma Emma sat at his elbow, inspecting his plate, demanding he eat more and fatten up.

"It's good, ain't it?" she demanded.

"Of course," Tony said. He'd taken to smacking his lips like Tak when he ate her food. It came automatic.

Tak, who painted in the living room that evening because Deena wasn't there, cast sidelong glances at Tony's plate. He remained steadfast in his assertion that he would finish his work before eating.

"I needs to ask you something," Grandma Emma said and stole a glance at Tak out the corner of her eye.

The hushed tone was so at odds with her usual bellow that Tony paused.

She leaned forward, arms on the table. "Why you tell these folks yo momma died in a car accident?"

Horror singed Tony. He turned to his plate with vigor.

"She did," he mumbled.

"Regina Sanders ain't die in no car accident! Regina Sanders—"

"I know how she died!"

Grandma Emma glanced over at Tak, and Tony's gaze followed. He continued to paint.

"If you knows, why you ain't tell the truth?"

Tony's nostrils flared. "Cause she's not my mother. She's nothing. Only mother I knew—"

"Is your aunt Pam."

Tony scowled.

"If you know so much," he demanded, "why you didn't know to come get me?"

Emma shrugged. "Anthony says you wasn't his. Who was I to say different?"

Tony stabbed at his drumstick with a fork.

"My mother killed herself. You think I want somebody to know that? My dad killed people, and my mom killed herself. Who wants a kid like that?"

Grandma Emma snorted. "Let me tell you something. And I hope it shows you how far and how much in life you still got to learn." She tilted her head toward Tak.

"You see that man over there? He's a good man. Good as they come. He loves hard. Him and Deena."

He believed her. Somehow, he believed her.

Tony found Tak the next afternoon on his feet and before the

TV, scowling. His first thought was to come back later. He shook it off.

"Tak?"

Tak glanced up at him, the frown still etched on his face.

"Can I talk to you?" Tony said.

In old cartoons, little mischievous boys always dug a toe in the dirt when they were under scrutiny. There was no dirt here, only Deena's ten thousand-dollar carpet that Tak had covered with tarp the day before. Tony dug his toe in that, instead.

Tak turned off the TV.

"Of course. What is it?"

"I told you a lie when I got here. About my mom."

Tak waited.

"My real mom . . . didn't die in a car accident. She killed herself after I was born. They said it was post partial or something. I don't know what that means. But it was my aunt, Pam, that raised me till I was seven. She's the one that died in the car accident."

Tak looked thoughtful. "Why didn't you tell us before?"

Tony shrugged. "My dad killed people, and my mom killed herself. I didn't want you to think I was a nut job."

Tak nodded as if conceding the point.

"I should be honest, too," he said. "Since you gave me a secret, I should give you one."

"You have a secret?"

"I always wanted a son," Tak admitted. "But I didn't think he'd be four feet tall when we met."

Tony laughed, stupidly, a big guffaw that turned into a sob. He didn't know how. When Tak embraced him, he returned the favor.

"I love you," Tony said. "Is that okay?"

He couldn't tell the rules anymore, or if there were any at all.

Tak squeezed. "Of course, kiddo. I love you, too."

Was this what a father was? How a father made you feel? God help him, Tony couldn't be without one again.

He looked up, sniffling. "Should I call you 'dad'?"

"Only if you want."

"And what about Deena?"

Tak shook his head. "No. She wouldn't want to be called that."

Tony grinned.

"You're ridiculous."

But he soon turned serious with the thought of calling Deena 'mom.' He'd never had a father before, didn't know what they were like. But mothers—mothers left him. They killed themselves, died in cars, or changed their minds about being a mother altogether.

"I don't think I could take another mom leaving me," Tony said.

Tak hugged him again. "Neither one of us would ever willingly leave you. You're our son. And you owe us money."

Tony wrestled away from his embrace, declaring that he would never pay Tak, only to be tackled amid a fit of tickles that made him writhe and near pee. In the end, he agreed to pay.

CHAPTER FIFTY-EIGHT

When Lizzie woke, it was to the sight of a blackened room, silenced like a sinkhole at night. Next to her, Kenji slept with an arm across his eyes and a smile on his face, naked beneath the sheets.

Her heart pounded. It was the pound of a marathoner's run to exertion, pain, collapse. Sweat prickled her face, cool on clammy skin. She smacked chapped, stiffened, and fat lips as muscles yawned and creaked with the slightest of motions; though she supposed that could've been from so much sex with Kenji.

She looked back at him regretfully and stood.

It came all at once, a flood, an avalanche, a drowning so complete that even Kenji disappeared. She needed something. Something coursing through veins, ascending her up and out, showering her with pleasures so intense: so thrillingly intense that sight, sound, and touch magnified in a euphoric mania.

She couldn't wait. There was too much time between that top-level condo and the streets of Overtown; she needed a fix, a buzz, a taste, a high—she'd die without it. Panic detonated and Lizzie shot like a rocket, out of the room and to the only place that promised relief.

She pitched into the bathroom with a fit, tore open the medicine cabinet and hurled Band-Aids, dental floss, cotton swabs, aftershave, rubbing alcohol, and various bottles over her shoulder. She dropped to her knees and dove into the under-sink cabinet swiping out great swaths of goods. And then she saw it. The tiniest bottle of Tylenol: unassuming in the shadows. She snatched it and stood, hurrying to unscrew the top.

Four.

Four goddamned pills.

He kept no alcohol in the house. No beer, no wine, no vodka, no alcohol.

Or so it seemed.

Lizzie lunged for the bottle of rubbing alcohol and was snatched midair. Kenji's arm swept her in a single motion, heaving her out the door.

Lizzie howled as they struggled down the hall. She clawed at him, through him, for the fix she'd been promised. No matter how she struck, how she tore at his flesh, he held to her—firmer and stronger than she ever thought possible, muscles flexing as they moved from bathroom to bedroom, where he tossed her onto the bed.

Lizzie shrieked and bolted for him, talons bared, but he snatched her into in an embrace, blunting her blows.

He wouldn't let her go this time as he bear-hugged her in a side shuffle back to the bed, arms so tightly bound that she could only snort and pant her fury.

They dropped onto the mattress together, her beneath him, straining and beating in vain.

"Forever," Kenji blurted. "That's how long I'll hold on to you, if it means keeping you from hurting yourself. So you might as well calm down."

She continued to strain.

"We'll grow old together, Lizzie, right here in this bed before I let you do what you're thinking. Try me if you don't believe me."

Lizzie thumped against him, shuffling and shifting for an inch, no more. He'd meant what he said. He'd not let her go.

Only when she began to cry did Kenji loosen his hold.

The sudden tenderness of his touch deflated her, seeping out fury and panic, until only shame and fatigue remained. A scratch above Kenji's brow stood fiery red while the boxers he wore hung torn and limp. Lizzie looked away.

"It's okay," he said.

But it wasn't. She'd hurt him. The only person who'd looked at her and seen more. More than a hell-bound whore and discarded drug addict, more than there was, perhaps.

"One mountain a day," he promised and kissed her forehead. "One mountain a day."

~*~

Kenji rang the doorbell to Tak's house and waited, grateful for the midday and absence of kids. He couldn't go into work with a gash on his forehead, not to the company where the marquee bore his name. Deena would be looking for him, no doubt to weigh him down with one speech or another about the burden and honor of being a Tanaka in architecture, but as far as he was concerned, she could have that mantle, gladly.

Mrs. Jimenez opened the door.

"I need to see Tak," he said, cutting off her concern.

With a scowl of disapproval, she led him to the gym.

Red faced and with puffed cheeks, Tak lay on his back, heaving a barbell weighted with iron in swift, even strokes. Kenji waited by the door.

"Come spot me, you bastard," Tak gasped, weights slowing.

Kenji rushed over and stood overhead, peering down at his older brother.

When the weights sailed up, Kenji grabbed hold and returned them to the machine.

His brother sat up. "What happened to your face?"

Kenji hesitated. He'd come to talk about Lizzie, but the wound wasn't where he'd planned on starting.

His brother stood, a half head taller, scowling, disapproving, already knowing. Kenji looked away.

"So, she hits you now."

He went for a towel. In Tak's voice was distaste, disappointment, disgust. And Kenji couldn't bear it.

"It's not like that."

Tak dabbed his face with the towel and tossed it to a corner. "Don't," he warned and went for the water cooler opposite him.

Kenji followed him, wanting to let the conversation go, but unable to.

"You think she's bad for me."

Tak filled a paper cup and tossed the water back in a go. Then he crushed it in a fist and dropped it in a nearby waste bin.

"Don't ask me obvious questions."

"But she—"

Kenji halted at the squeak in his voice, appalled. Why was it always this way? Demoted to childhood in the presence of his brother, compelled to whine at his slightest disapproval. Where was the man he'd been last night; strong when Lizzie was weak? Could his brother know what it was to love an addict? To find doubt, turmoil, fear, and hope every day? Those were his realities; that was the proof of his strength. And it was high time Tak knew it.

"I know what I'm doing," Kenji blurted. "And I don't need you to approve of it any more than you needed Dad to approve of you and Deena."

Tak headed for the leg press.

"Deena wasn't on drugs," he said and dropped low into the seat of the machine.

"And neither is Lizzie. She's been off for months now. I know it because I see her every day."

Tak grunted before shoving his machine's metal plate with his legs so that his seat sailed backward to the hilt.

"Do you have any idea what the statistics are on drug relapse? Fifty to ninety percent, Kenj, depending upon the severity of addiction, drugs involved, and length of treatment."

Tak's knees rose and fell as he pushed against weights, the muscles of his calves straining.

"It means you're biding your time," he continued. "And from the looks of things, your biding's just about up."

Kenji's jaw clenched. "She had a setback. That's all. And she's past it."

Tak said nothing.

"We will!" Kenji cried.

Tak glided to a halt and climbed off. Kenji, the inadvertent little brother, took a step back, uncertain of what was to follow.

"Kenj, I'm not trying to upset or hurt you in any way. I just know that you've been sheltered—"

"And you haven't?"

"Listen. It's obvious you care about her. I'm not making light of that."

"Yes, you are."

Tak sighed. "Fine. Be emotional."

Again, Kenji's jaw clenched.

"You *are* making light of it! And you did it right from the start. When I told you I'd been seeing her, you asked me how much it ran me an hour."

"She's a prostitute!"

Kenji's fist smashed into the wall.

"She *was*! I told you she quit!" Chest heaving, nostrils flared, he stared at his older brother with a foreign sort of fury.

Tak looked at the stretch of rustic wood grain he'd pummeled,

275

none of which had given way, before glancing down at Kenji's hand.

"You okay? That's probably—"

"I'm okay!" Kenji yelled. Meanwhile, he ignored the dull throb of his hand.

Tak stared at him, as if expecting some other truth to be revealed. When it didn't come, he sighed.

"Listen, kiddo. I—"

"I'm not a kid, Tak! Now, I'm warning you! If you can't talk to me like a man—"

"Hey! Calm down, already. What is all this? I'm just worried about you, that's all. I'm not," he gave Kenji a once-over, "questioning your manhood."

A smile tickled at the edges of Tak's mouth, forcing Kenji's to do the same, until he looked away, cursing his brother for making him laugh.

"All right, come on. Talk to me. What's going on?" Tak said and took a seat on a sculpted oak grain bench.

"I was gonna kick your ass," Kenji said and sat down next to him.

"Yeah, okay. Don't get carried away."

Kenji grinned.

"I thought the wall would break when I punched it."

"Reinforced for hurricanes."

Deena. Of course.

Tak frowned at him. "So, it's serious, huh?" he said.

"Very."

Tak pondered this, gaze on his black Nikes.

"What's she like sober?"

"Smart. Funny. A little bit of a smart aleck. Sweet. Sensitive, sometimes."

Tak stole a glance at him. "And the guys . . .?"

Kenji sighed.

"It's a lot sometimes. She tells me stuff, and I listen, but I only listen because I'm supposed to. There were guys in her life that I think I would murder if I ever met them, and some of the things done to her that don't make for decent conversation. But the other stuff, the stuff she willingly did for drugs or money," he shook his head. "It's hard not to be jealous. Or to not think that someday, some guy's gonna see us out and offer her ten bucks for a blow job. He wouldn't even understand why I'm choking the shit out of him."

"And you've been tested? You and her?"

"When I sent her to rehab they did a full physical. But yeah, we're clean, and we use protection. Who doesn't these days?"

"Me and Deena didn't. If we did, it was, like, once."

Kenji stared. His older brother, content to be his role model, and Deena—the bastion of decorum and responsibility?

"You guys never had to . . . you know . . . did you?"

"No." Tak paused. "Can I ask you something?"

Kenji hesitated.

"Do you love her?" Tak said.

Kenji opened his mouth, but denial wasn't possible. "Yeah."

"Then leave the past to memories. She's not some prize to possess or be angry about when someone else seems to have possessed it. She's a human being, with her own wants and emotions, however right or

277

wrong they might've been."

Tak gave him a sideways look.

"Got it?"

Kenji nodded.

"Good. Now go ice your hand."

Relief washed over Kenji. It had been throbbing like hell.

CHAPTR FIFTY-NINE

Two home pregnancy tests and a doctor's confirmation later, Deena sat at the breakfast table chewing on toast and considering. She ate toast all day, as she'd done with Mia. It wouldn't be long before Tak noticed.

They had never considered the possibility of three children. When their love was still new, they'd joke of having a dozen, all wild haired with the smug smirk of a Tanaka. But with Mia, life had changed more dramatically than either had suspected. Early on, Deena had been loathed to be without her, keeping her cradle in the bedroom for the nursings that took place every two-and-a-half-hours round-the-clock. Even when Tak gave her breaks with breast milk in a bottle, Deena slept fitfully, waking to check on her newborn.

It was a standing complaint with Tak that family life somehow meddled in his art. Certainly, his stagnation was proof. Before marrying, he'd been a rogue; now, he drove around with a booster seat and juice box, just in case. Deena couldn't predict how he'd respond to another child.

Tak strolled into the dining area, whipped a kitchen chair around so that the back faced Deena, and sat, eyes level with hers.

"Toast," he observed.

"Toast," she confirmed. "It helps."

He jumped to his feet. "You're pregnant? Definitely pregnant?"

Deena nodded.

His mouth parted, unnerving her with her inability to distinguish whether he was thrilled or horrified.

Then suddenly Tak let out a whoop and snatched her into his arms.

"And you're okay with this?" Deena cried.

"Okay? I'm about to hire one of those New Orleans brass bands to just follow my ass around!" He grinned at her. "You want one, too?"

"Tak!"

He squeezed her again, so tight her toast threatened an encore.

"Damn, I love you, Dee! I love you so much." He gave a derisive little laugh and got down on one knee.

"And you too, little guy."

He covered her belly with a hand. When Deena looked up, she caught a snatch of brown hair fleeing.

Tony.

Tak cursed and darted after him with Deena right behind.

Tears already streamed down Tony's face before he hurled the door shut with a grunt.

A baby.

Of course.

Why had he thought them any different? All married people wanted a baby. Not a twelve-year-old liar and thief.

His gaze swept the room, desperate for luggage. There was an oversized duffle bag in his closet; he'd used it on the trip to Disney.

Tony snatched it from the shelf and tossed it to the floor. Over his shoulder went whatever he could find—shirts, jeans—designer mostly—all destined for the bag and the streets.

They would have their son.

A little boy who looked like mother and father, instead of just a relative of mother's. They would take him to the playground and the park, and all the other places parents took new babies. Tony could only guess. He'd never had such an experience.

Tak had said he wanted a son. How long had they been trying? With the adoption underway, they'd resigned themselves to a stupid misfit of a kid who stumbled over big words and got into fistfights, too. How often had they wished they could have a baby instead of him? Always, he imagined—always.

"Tony, open the door!" Tak yelled.

Tak was a good guy, the best Tony had ever met. He would miss him being his father.

"Tony!" Deena shrieked. She banged on the door, rattling it. "What are you doing, Tony?" she cried.

He was her brother's kid, not hers. She felt responsible for him. He would free her of that now. It had been wrong of him to come there, insert himself in their lives, their perfect lives, pretending to be the son they wanted.

"Please open the door," Deena said. "Talk to me at least."

"I'm leaving," Tony announced. "Don't stop me."

He jammed shirts in the bag, a handful of Polos, and followed them with jeans. He hadn't the money he'd stolen, but he felt good about that, not bad.

"Why are you leaving?" Tak said. "Because of the baby?"

Tony didn't answer. He didn't want them forced into saying things they didn't mean, things from some script of parenting that were worthless in the face of truth. They had their son. They had their baby. It was time for Tony to move on.

He shoved Jordans in his bag and snatched his console from the TV. It was heavy. It would slow him down, but he wouldn't leave it unless they made him.

"Tony!" Tak cried.

"You have your son now!" Tony roared. "You don't need me!"

He was too furious to cry, too furious at himself for being naïve,

281

and at the world, for being shitty.

Silence followed, and he supposed they agreed.

The thought proved too much. His body racked with a gut-wrenching sob so strong he keeled over with it, with the realization that he was nothing and had nothing—not mother, not father, not even a sister anymore. It was more than he could bear.

"Tony."

He whirled in horror.

Tak sat in his now-open window. Deena, standing just outside, was at eye level with Tony.

"Come here," Tak said.

"No! I don't want to hear—"

Deena clamored into the window with the help of Tak, and automatically, Tony scrambled over, so worried was he that she might fall and hurt herself or the baby they'd been trying for.

"You're not leaving," Deena said. "The day you walk out of here will be the day you board a plane for college. You're a boy. Our boy. I don't care how many miles you've hitchhiked or how that makes you feel like a man. We're your parents and while we believe in giving you choices, the ability to walk out of this house isn't one of them. Now if this house is truly where you don't want to be, then you'll have the chance to tell the judge that at your Final Hearing on Thursday."

"I do want you to be my parents," Tony said pitifully.

"And yet you're packing," Deena said.

"I thought you didn't want . . ." he trailed in shame.

"The only thing I don't want is you ever trying this again," Deena said.

Her face crumpled, just a tad. When Tak reached to touch her back, Tony felt shame. She was about to cry. He was about to make her

282

cry.

"You're my son. My brother's son. And I can't go back to before you were here. Okay?"

She brought him to her harshly, pressing his wet face to her softened belly. Tony closed his eyes to the warmth.

"Okay?" she said, firmer still.

Tony nodded.

She released him and strode for the door, stopping only once to look at him before exiting.

"You know, Tony," Tak said, the moment she was gone. He began picking up clothes and hanging them in the closet.

"There's no rule saying I'm allowed just one son. China's one-child limit doesn't extend to Dade County."

Tony blushed. It sounded so obvious now. People had two children. Four. Ten. God knew they could afford it. Suddenly, he felt like a Looney Tunes character with a stupid stamp from Acme on his forehead.

Tak hurled a shirt at him. "Pick this stuff up," he said. "I don't work for you." And with a grin, he was gone.

Tony began to work, slowly, methodically, placing clothes back in their rightful place, reattaching the console to its station beneath the flat screen. As he worked, one word throbbed in his mind like the thump of his heart:

Thursday.

Thursday, and his adoption would be final.

CHAPTER SIXTY

For the whole of summer and fall, Florida escaped the wrath of Mother Nature. But according to weather reports, that was about to change.

With Thanksgiving at their backs and Christmas on the horizon, bright and multicolored lights were being strung, both in the city and in the Tanaka home. Though Tak was Buddhist, he remained festive about the holiday season, so festive, in fact, that it confused Tony.

"But Christmas is Christian, right?" he said as they hung lights about an eight-foot tree.

"Christians invented Christmas," Tak said. "But even people who don't believe in God celebrate it. Because it's the spirit of it that resonates with everyone."

Satisfied for the moment, Tony continued decorating. But as was always the case, more questions would follow.

"The government of the Cayman Islands has issued a tropical storm warning in conjunction with Tropical Storm Lucille. Tropical storm conditions are expected on the island within the next twenty-four hours," an urgent voice warned from the television.

Collectively, the family turned at the ominous interruption to *The Grinch,* and saw an illustration of the storm's probable path. It teetered toward the Caribbean, swallowing South Florida.

"It's coming here!" Tony shrieked.

"Hurricanes come every year. They bring rain, which is good," Deena said calmly.

Tak messed Tony's hair with an oversized hand, leaving glitter in his wake. "They're only guessing this early. No cause to worry," he said.

Days passed and the tropical storm became a meandering hurricane, simmering in the warm waters of the Caribbean, content on gaining strength. It caused flooding in San Juan, mudslides in Puerto Rico, the Dominican Republic, and Haiti, drownings in Cuba. It caused a handful of deaths, promising more. Each day it grew closer was another spent convincing Tony that death wasn't imminent.

They prepared for evacuation even as Christmas drew near. Each year, the Tanakas spent the holiday season at Daichi's California estate though Daichi didn't technically celebrate Christmas.

With the hurricane coming, they decided to head for California early. Deena hired a handful of contractors to commence with securing the house, leaving them to board windows as she packed important documents for safekeeping. Tony paced amid the constant movement, restless as if supervising, needing reminders that he too had to pack.

"Why did you build the house on the water?" Tony demanded.

"Because the water's exquisite," Deena said. She retrieved a stack of papers from a hallway safe, hidden just behind a painting.

"The hurricane is strong. Twelve people have died already. It's sweeping away houses all over the Caribbean. It'll take this one, too."

"This house isn't going anywhere. I designed it myself. The windows have a thick inner membrane, are impact-resistant, exceed all International Building Code Standards, are able to withstand small and large missile projectiles launched at over two hundred miles per hour. The siding of the house is two hundred forty percent stronger than cement. It can withstand winds of over two hundred miles per hour. The roofing has asphalt and a second shield to maintain a watertight roofing system."

"Then why are we leaving?"

"Because leaving is the safest thing to do. But the house will be here when we return."

"What if it's not here? What if it just sweeps the house away?"

"It won't."

"The Titanic was unsinkable, too!"

Deena punched in an intricate code on the wall safe and the door suctioned closed. She swung an abstract painting back over it.

"We can always rebuild," she said.

285

Tony just couldn't understand this family notion that expensive things were actually worthless.

"Did you get the proof of insurance?" Tony asked. "Andrea Gonzalez from Channel 7 News says you'll need it."

Since the storm's announcement, news was the only thing he'd watch.

"Yes. And the utilities will be shut off and the property will be landscaped to ensure that dead tree limbs and foliage are removed, thereby negating damage to the house."

"Okay," he breathed. "Okay."

Deena knelt down. "Never mind the storm. It's Christmastime. You're going to spend tons of time with family, eat till you grow fat, and have a beach right in the backyard."

But of all she said, Tony only heard the one word:

Family.

CHAPTER SIXTY-ONE

Lizzie rolled over and paused to unravel her body from a tangle of sheets. Next to her, Kenji flipped through the channels restlessly, eyes on the TV mounted high.

"What's wrong?" Lizzie said.

"Everything's about the hurricane! I had *Contenders* set to record. I go to watch it and get an hour of how to stock up on water and can goods. What's to know? Go to the store, put them in your cart, pay the money. The end."

Lizzie, naked on her belly, propped up on her elbows.

"They're saying it'll come."

"They always say that. How often are they wrong? It's all guesswork. And they're always ruining my shows for it."

"So, you're not evacuating with your dad?" Her gaze strayed to the window. "We're pretty high up, you know."

It was a sticky subject. As of yet, only Tak knew about their relationship. Evacuating with her meant revealing it at the worst possible time. Evacuating alone meant abandoning her.

"No need to leave," he said.

Kenji's way of dealing was not dealing.

"You let these people work you up because they're trying to sell wood, water, and potted meat. Don't be a sucker, Lizzie."

He continued to flip channels with a scowl. Lizzie waited.

"Sorry." He hadn't meant to call her a name.

Kenji leaned forward, tilted her chin up, and kissed her. "You know I get grumpy when they screw with my programming."

He pulled her so that she sat up. Another kiss, sweeter, nipping, and promising to deepen.

Their noses touched. She'd never kissed that way before him, nuzzling even when their lips didn't meet. Somehow, it seemed more intimate than anything she'd ever done. In a way, everything felt intimate with Kenji.

"You have to go to work," she reminded him.

"And you have to go down to Dade for registration," he said.

The community college. Next month, she'd begin a series of classes that would hopefully end in a GED. He read her thoughts just then.

"You can do it," he said and brought a hand to her hair. It was messed and matted from sleep, but he didn't care. He always acted as though it was beautiful.

"And you don't need me for it," he added.

Kenji kissed her again, lingering, before getting up with a groan.

"Work, work, work," he complained.

She got up as well, allowing sheets to fall away and expose her nakedness. When they were first together, the scars of her body humiliated her. Some had begun to fade, taking on another unexpected purpose. He'd bought scar cream for her and applied it as they talked, eventually coming to know the history of each mark. There were times when she thought he'd fling her away in disgust, but the moment never came.

"I hate this job," Kenji said, holding out two dress shirts and frowning at both. "It's boring as shit, for starters."

Lizzie picked out her clothes for the day.

"Go back to baseball," she said, thinking not only of his weekly devotion to the sport, but of all the things his former teammates said. "It's the only thing that makes you happy."

He came over and kissed her, a fat smack on the lips that made her smile like a fool.

"Don't need baseball. Just fine, right here with you."

He went back to the closet and Lizzie frowned, knowing the kiss's true purpose had been her silence.

"Zach told me that in April you can try out for the minor leagues."

Kenji tossed work clothes on the bed, grabbed towels from the linen closet, and treaded to the master bathroom.

Door open, Lizzie could hear running water from the sink. The next moment, Kenji stuck his head out and a blue toothbrush jutted from his mouth.

"Iron that for me, will you?"

Rebuffed, Lizzie nodded and snatched the clothes up for ironing.

An hour and a half later, Lizzie punched the down button for the elevator and waited. Already, Kenji had left for work. Though he didn't believe the storm was coming, everyone else did, including her. After all, Lizzie just couldn't ignore the ferocious red swath on the radar running the width of Texas. She figured the least she could do was walk the few blocks to a convenience store and buy canned goods just in case.

Lizzie had no driver's license, which meant that Kenji caught a conniption at the thought of her driving his second car, a BMW that sat in the garage collecting dust. So, she walked most places, or rode the bus, till the time when they could work on her license. For the time being, however, she didn't think she had the brain power to study for the GED and for getting a license.

Walking quickly, Lizzie frowned upward at the steely gray sky. The storm was still a way's off, but people had begun to evacuate. Tourists first, residents second, bringing a hush to the whole of Miami Beach. It felt eerie.

There was something about the absence of people that had an ability to unnerve. The loneliness of it all, the implication of having no one felt cruel, cruelest perhaps, of all things humanly possible. She never wanted to be alone again.

Lizzie slipped into the convenience store, greeted the cashier by name, and grabbed a hand basket. She filled it what she could carry: Dinty Moore beef stew, chicken dumplings, ravioli. The cans were dusty but unexpired, and Kenji would eat just about anything, anyway. Once back at the house, she would set about bottling the tap water. There was a recycle bin on the second floor of the building, always loaded with empty jugs. She'd use those, plus the can goods to ensure that they were okay. Lizzie paid for her purchases and took up a brisk pace back to the condo.

It was odd, the difference that time could bring. Last year, she'd been a whore, addicted to heroin and crack, and would've let a room full of men half kill her for the promise of either at the end. In fact, she'd done just such a thing on countless occasions. Once, in high school, she'd worked a party at a rundown motel on Biscayne. She was alone and yet, in a room with so many men that she could scarcely see the wall. All of them had fucked her.

How broken and alone she'd been back then no one could know.

But only Kenji had tried to understand.

Kenji.

Her cheeks colored at even the thought of his name.

She'd first seen him at Tak and Deena's wedding, an unimpressive thing, awkward and blushing, as if too conscious of himself to stand it. She'd snorted at the sight of him, thinking him an obvious virgin. By that time, at seventeen, she'd already dropped out of high school, left her grandmother's house, and abused three sorts of drugs on a regular basis. Hell, she'd been high at the wedding.

Looking back, Lizzie couldn't help but wonder what her life might have been like had she not been so dismissive of him.

He had a smile like a hug, a kiss like a blush, and a touch like a blessing. He didn't see a whore when he looked at her. He saw Lizzie. Just Lizzie.

School had been Kenji's idea. The GED, and then onward, to whatever else she aspired. Already she had plans to get a cosmetology license. He would invest in her, like a business, and she would open a shop on the beach. Hers. A hairdresser on South Beach! She could hardly stand the glamour of it.

She didn't deserve him—his sweet smile—the one he thought too big—or his gentle heart—the one that made him apologize four breaths after a single angry thought—or his tenderness. She melted under him, melted to him, weakened by his touch, so conscious was she of passion, emotion, worship even, in his every touch. Her eyes watered at the thought. She could never go back to anything less.

"Get in the car."

A voice sliced through her soul, cutting with its coldness.

Snow.

Lizzie turned to face a burgundy Monte Carlo.

God, no. Please.

"Get in the fucking car before I head down to 5 South Pointe Drive and shoot the first Asian motherfucker I see!"

Lizzie dropped her groceries to ground and fumbled with the handle of the Monte Carlo before climbing inside.

Immediately, he peeled off. From the right-side window, Lizzie watched as a half-dozen cans rolled aimlessly along the sidewalk. They raced onward, and quickly, her groceries disappeared from sight.

"You look good," Snow said.

He slammed the brakes at a red light, just before a multitude of gleaming high-rises—homes to the beautiful people.

"Real good," he added.

He reached over and touched bare thigh, sun-bronzed hazel skin that Kenji called candy.

Lizzie stiffened.

Snow grinned.

"You got some money for me?" he asked brightly.

She said nothing.

He continued to drive. Toward the highway. Further from South Beach and the groceries on the ground. Further from her life with Kenji. He would kill her. She didn't need him to tell her that.

A stretch of interstate later and they where in Overtown. But they didn't drive toward the apartment she once knew. Southeast he went, never speaking, until he came along a stretch she knew too well. Underneath and near the Metrorail Station women walked, clothes clinging and even absent, filthy even in some cases. It was the place most diametrically opposed to where she'd just come from; it was where lawlessness and hopelessness prevailed, and where people like Snow ruled supreme.

"You'll get on the stroll by tomorrow," he promised. "Back out here making money."

Briefly, Lizzie thought of another man, any man who wasn't Kenji Tanaka, touching her, stroking her, on top and thrusting, groaning, abusing. One word came to mind.

"No."

Snow laughed. Long, hard, and cruel. He put a hand on her thigh and moved up, till he found the crotch of her shorts. Lizzie grabbed his wrist in vain.

"I own that. And I own you. You gonna learn that tonight. And when I'm done, you'll be begging for a piece of the stroll, if only to ease your workload."

They pulled up to a single jut of dust-white building, offensive in comparison to the gluttony she'd come from. Snow parked the Monte Carlo and yanked Lizzie by her hair from the car.

She knew this place but could hardly believe the audacity of it all.

It was to family that Snow had taken her.

Up six floors they went on foot before he jammed a key in a simple brown door. It swung open, and he flung her inside. Lizzie stumbled and righted herself. This was Aunt Caroline's old home. Only Keisha lived there now.

"I need the house tonight," Snow announced. "For a party."

To the left of the door was an immediate kitchen counter. Keisha stood at it chopping onions. She scowled at the sight of Lizzie.

"You can't have a party tonight. The girls are coming, remember?"

Snow's face hardened; his jaw clenched, and for a moment, Lizzie felt certain he'd hit her. After all, she'd known them to fistfight and knew the look he took on before pummeling her.

But then, his face softened.

"All right then," he said and released Lizzie's arm.

Snow disappeared toward the back.

Lizzie surveyed her surroundings. Not much had changed since the time when Aunt Caroline lived there. Same sagging, rot-brown couch, same coffee table with wood chippings, brand-new TV mounted on the wall. Portions of the wall below it were stained yellow.

She should've felt safer with Keisha there, her cousin. She should've been able to run to her, and together they'd plot an escape. But what she felt was fear magnified even more. Keisha watched her, gaze guarded and fixed, never bothering to speak. Their history of hostility was long, born and nurtured by Snow.

He reappeared.

"You look clean," he said. "How long you been clean?"

Lizzie looked down. "A few months now."

"Hmph," Keisha said.

293

"Your cousin helped me find you." He nodded toward Keisha. "Kit's description of the Asian knight in shining armor was enough for her to figure it out. I went to his job and followed him home one day," Snow explained. "Came back today and found you."

It didn't surprise Lizzie. Not at all.

"Where's Kit?" she demanded instead.

While she and Keisha had been openly declared enemies, Kit was supposedly her friend. She would answer for betraying Lizzie.

"Dead," Snow said brightly. "They found her in the trunk of a car. She'd been beaten to death. Surprised you didn't hear about it."

Their gazes met. And Lizzie said nothing, suddenly understanding why it had taken him so long to find her. Kit hadn't been forthcoming at first. He'd bludgeon the information out of her, and then killed her for withholding.

But there'd be no arrest, no prosecution, no public outcry for a whore found dead.

There never was.

Slowly, Snow's mouth spread into a smile.

"Got a lot of new girls. Needed you around to show 'em the ropes. Had you stuck it out, been faithful, you would've been out the game by now."

Lizzie said nothing. It was clear that there was only one way out the game, and Kit had just taken it.

Snow dropped onto the couch and dug weed from his pocket. Keisha went to a drawer in the kitchen and withdrew a package of cigars without question. She brought them to him and retreated to chop more onions.

"How many new girls?" Lizzie said, asking and not wanting to know.

"Seven," Snow said and pulled a Swiss Army knife from his

294

sock. He flicked it open and cut a cigar down the middle.

"Let me tell you how I got 'em. Shit's genius," he said. "I get a young dude looking to come up. Pour a little money into him, take good care of him, and the girls flock to him, you know? Eventually, he steps to one. A shy one, not that good looking, looks like she comes from a real holy-type home like you. He asks her out. You know, movie, dinner, some bullshit that makes her feel pretty. She agrees; he picks her up in a nice-ass car. Then he takes her here or some other private spot I like to use. Tells her he needs to stop and pick up more cash. Invites her inside. Gets up in here and handles business, you know? Take that shit no matter what she says."

Snow lit the blunt, its spark like the hot anger in Lizzie's belly.

"But here's where the shit gets ingenious."

Snow took a deep tote.

"I've got fellas staked out, taking pictures while he's fucking her. Dozens of these shits. So, she leaves, all fucked up in the head from getting the shit fucked outta her and a few days later he approaches her, tells her he wants to see her again. When she says 'no,' he shows her the pictures. Now what's she gonna do? Dude is telling her that her mom, dad, preacher, hell, the whole fucking school, is about to see her with her pussy out like a freak, with her mouth gobbling dick. So, what's she gonna do? Whatever the fuck we tell her. And that's how she gets pimped. Right now, I'm using your little cousin T3, or Baby Tariq, to help me out. Dude's a natural. You should see him."

Lizzie stared. Once, she talked to Kenji about how dirty she now felt about being a whore and how stupid she'd been. He'd told her that girls like her, from certain families, were preyed on and manipulated by men. She hadn't believed it. But as she stood there, listening, she realized that every moment of her life, every thrust she'd taken, every ounce of crack and heroin, had been orchestrated by this man or another.

She stole a glance at Keisha, who stood motionless, thoughts far from the room. What could she be thinking? Lizzie's aunt Caroline and Keisha had always prided themselves on Snow's ability to "take care of business." Well, here was the business transaction. And there were absolutely no refunds.

This time, when Snow went into the back, Lizzie made for the kitchen.

"How many girls are you gonna let him do this to?" Lizzie hissed. "How many girls does he have to hurt?"

There was no denying the sickness on her face. Keisha was disgusted. Finally.

But then she quickly shook it away.

"They want it," she said simply and went back to chopping. "Just like you did. They could stop at any time."

"I was a child!" Lizzie cried. "A child."

Keisha chopped harder. When a toilet flushed, Lizzie knew Snow was about to return.

"Do something," she hissed and walked to the opposite side of the room.

~*~

Afternoon passed to evening and Lizzie didn't dare pull out her cell phone. Though she knew Kenji had to be sick with worry, she also realized that Snow hadn't thought to take it from her. She would bide her time, only to make an escape, somehow, though she couldn't say how. No one talked of evacuating for the hurricane. No one left her alone. And with each hour that she remained there in that house, Lizzie crept an hour closer to her death.

Keisha's daughters arrived that evening. There were three in all, each from a different father. The oldest, Treasure, was 16; the middle girl, Temple, 15; and the baby, Moondisha, called Mooney for short, had turned 12 just a few days ago. Eventually, all three were supposed to move in, but for the time being, Treasure lived with her father's mother, while Temple and Mooney lived with Aunt Caroline.

That evening, the family watched a movie. Something bootleg and grainy called *Firestorm*. The girls sat on the floor, a pizza between them, with Mooney text messaging nonstop. Snow sat next to Lizzie on the couch, whispering things that only she could hear.

"You let another man come between us, Lizzie, after all this time. After all this that's been between us."

She swallowed.

"What he give you that I ain't give you? Money? You don't need that shit. I took care of you. Made sure nothing happened to your ass."

She looked down at the faded scars of her body, the ones that called him "Liar."

"He can't protect you. I've seen him. What you want with him? What he do for you?"

She didn't trust herself to speak. If Snow knew the real depth of her emotion, than he would harm Kenji instead. That way, he could keep his product and make his point at the same time.

The easiest thing to do would've been to deny him, to say that she'd used him in the greatest hustle of her life, but Lizzie knew her mouth wouldn't form the words.

"I know you," Snow said. "He don't know you like I do. I've seen you in action."

She looked at him and saw in his smile every dirty thing she'd ever done. Every hole filled as a line of men waited, and her, enthusiastic, desperate, disgusting.

She looked away.

Snow laughed.

It was the longest night of her life.

One by one they went to bed, Keisha first, inviting Snow to join her. He snorted in response. Treasure went next, with an exaggerated yawn that told Lizzie she'd be up and sneaking out soon. Temple and Mooney left at the same time, heading for the smallest room with bunk beds. But Snow remained on the couch with Lizzie. Soon, she began to feign sleepiness in the hopes of encouraging the same with him. Nothing good ever came from being alone with Snow.

He was constantly on the phone, text messaging, text messaging, always. He flipped channels, blinking sleepily, and only occasionally glanced back at Lizzie.

"You got a cell phone with you?" Snow asked suddenly.

Lizzie bristled.

"No."

He pursed his lips in disbelief.

"Now if I make your ass strip down naked and happen to find a cell phone, I'm a kick your fuckin' head in. Now one last time. Do you have a cell phone?"

Lizzie didn't care what he said. Her cell phone was the only connection to Kenji.

"Search me if you want. I forgot it at home," she said.

He opened his mouth, but his own phone interrupted him. He looked down at it and put it away.

"Kit left the family Wednesday night," Snow said. "Told me she'd had enough. Friday morning, the police were towing away a 1995 Toyota Camry with her body in the trunk."

He stood.

"There's a lot of cars around here. Old cars. Junk cars that nobody pays attention to. You feel me?"

Lizzie nodded, sickly.

"Good."

She watched him head down the hall.

How long she stared behind him after he turned the corner she didn't know. Her heart pounded. Her mouth went dry. How long should she wait? A half hour? An hour? She could run out the door, but that would do no good. Months ago, when she'd first gone missing, Snow had

298

placed a bounty on her head. Such was the way of pimps. Every two-bit hustler from Overtown to Liberty City would look to bash Lizzie over the head and drag her back for the respect of an OG and a couple twenties in their pocket.

Lizzie stretched out on the couch. An hour. Snow had seemed sleepy. An hour would be long enough to ensure her safety. Then she would text Kenji and take her chances. That was the only way. Police were nothing in places like this. A cop would show up, take a statement, and leave her right where she stood, never even bothering to offer her a ride.

A sound in the hall made her strain to hear. A door opened. Or maybe closed. She'd been so embroiled in her thoughts that she couldn't tell which. Lizzie squeezed her eyes shut and pretended to sleep. She squinted just in time to watch Treasure tiptoe out the door.

More time passed. How much, she didn't know. Her heart beat too fast. The house was so silent she likened it to a tomb.

It was time to make her move.

Lizzie sat up, ears perked, and tiptoed to the hall. If she was stopped there, she would tell them she had to use the bathroom. Anywhere else in the house and her motives were suspect.

Still, she careened her head around the corner, darkness engulfing her completely.

Keisha surprised her, stock-still in the hall, motionless, arm extended, her face shadowed from view.

Something was wrong.

Curiosity bade Lizzie forward.

Her cousin eased into view like a slow-moving panorama. Keisha. Keisha's arm. A gun. Pointed into the open room. And then . . . the reason why.

Snow, in the bottom bunk, moving, groaning, grinding atop the smallest figure.

Mooney.

Above them, Temple still slept.

She wasn't crying as Lizzie had been, when Snow had her the same way at about the same age. In fact, she was the opposite, arms around his neck; soft mewls muffled by the grunts of a middle-aged man. Lizzie looked away, sickened.

Mooney screamed.

"What the—" Snow yelped and scurried away. Keisha's arm swept from where he'd been to where he ran at the foot of the bed. Cock jutting like a dagger, he eyed her steady, jeans and boxers at his feet on the floor.

"You filthy motherfucker," Keisha spat.

Mooney gathered up the covers to shield her slight body.

"You better get that gun outta my face," Snow said. "Baby momma or not, you know the rule. You pull a gun on me, you get put in the dirt."

Keisha's eyes watered. They were in a standoff, each staring at the other. Slowly, her gun began to lower. Snow smirked in response.

"Come on," he said. "You gonna shoot your fiancé?"

She lifted the gun again.

"You fucking my twelve-year-old, Snow? You fucking my baby, and you got the nerve to be smiling?"

He went for the boxers, pulled them on first, and followed them with the jeans. He could've been dressing to get the mail; he seemed so relaxed.

"Yeah. I am." Snow stood. "I fucked all three of 'em, matter of fact. And a couple of them nieces and cousins, too. But you knew all that already."

He took a step closer and instinctively, Lizzie, behind both Keisha and the gun, took one back.

"Now get that gun out my face," Snow said.

Keisha cocked it instead.

Snow stepped forward so that barrel pressed his chest.

"You ain't got it. And you ain't never had it. You ain't shit but a piece of dirty ass. What the fuck you gonna do to me?"

He held her gaze, steady, confident, and Keisha's arm slackened under it.

Suddenly, he turned his back on her.

"Fucking Hammond pulling a gun on me," he snarled. "Y'all ain't learn your lesson, yet? Last one to try that got unloaded on. Take that to your motherfuckin' nightmares."

"You!" Lizzie cried. "*You* killed Tony?"

"Yeah, I killed that motherfucker. And I'm 'bout to—"

Keisha fired.

One bullet into his back and he catapulted like a cannon into the bed frame. She stepped forward, steadied her arm, and pointed downward to where he'd slumped, partway on the bottom bunk, knees on the floor. He was groaning. She shot again, and it silenced him. Temple, now bolt upright, began to scream. Mooney joined her. Keisha pulled the trigger again. And again. And again, until the gun clicked empty and Steven Curtis Evans was silenced forever.

~*~

Kenji ripped through the streets of Miami, tires squealing in the night. He had no idea what had happened to Lizzie, or could've been happening at that moment. She called him, told him where to come and that Snow was dead. It was all he knew.

Kenji called Tak and told him what was happening. His brother, naturally, begged him not to go. When that didn't work, Tak insisted on following. Kenji gave him the address only after he promised not to come. Two children and one on the way meant this was Kenji's journey alone.

Tak had too much to lose.

Kenji pulled up at a high-rise behind a handful of squad cars. Were they taking Lizzie away? Had she given Snow what he deserved? If so, he'd have her out on bail in an hour with the best damned lawyer on her side.

The police, he thought with a sneer. They *would* be there to take Lizzie away. Never to stop the abuse, only there to tidy what remained of the mess.

Kenji jumped from his Audi, pushed past the growing crowd of bystanders, and burst into the building.

"Lizzie!" he roared, desperation boiling as he tore up the stairs. "Lizzie! Tell me you're all right!"

He couldn't bear to hear any different. *God, please. She has to be all right.*

A crowd of officers milled around on the sixth floor. Just as he reached them, Lizzie burst through and flung herself into Kenji.

Thank you.

He didn't know what had happened yet, or who had caused it, but still his heart pounded in relief. She was okay. There, in his arms. *They* would be okay.

Never had he thought himself a selfish person. For most of his life, he'd had everything. He gave to the poor and thought that enough, better than enough, in fact. But it occurred to him, in that dank hall, holding the woman he loved, that he had never been thankful for all he had. That he had never even understood thankfulness until that moment.

"Keisha killed him," she said. "They're reading her, her rights now. My God. She killed him."

Keisha.

He hugged her again.

CHAPTER SIXTY-TWO

The National Hurricane Center issued a hurricane warning for the Florida Keys at three P.M. Tak and Deena heard it just as they ushered luggage from the living room to the back of a waiting taxi. They were scheduled to meet the rest of the family at the Opa Locka airport for a private flight from Miami to California in just over an hour. Harsh, choppy winds, already whipping and threatening, made them move a little faster, still.

Tony dragged an oversized duffle bag that included too many games and too few clothes. A second bag, packed by Deena while he slept, ensured he had the things he really needed.

The drive up I-95 North was slow and threatening. Angry midday skies swelled as the first of torrential rain began to fall. Soon the city would be engulfed. As was the case with every storm that arrived, Deena prayed for those too poor to evacuate.

They met Daichi, his wife, Hatsumi, and John and Allison on the tarmac. There was no sign of Kenji yet.

"He'll be along," Daichi said. "I spoke to him but a moment ago. He had a stop he needed to make."

Tak opened his mouth but shut it with a snap. Deena shot him a questioning look.

Tak, Daichi, and John loaded the plane with luggage as Grandma Emma pulled up in a taxi. Tony rushed up to help her with luggage and Tak took her hand, easing the way on slick pavement.

At eighty-four, Grandma Emma was experiencing firsts. The first time she'd ride a plane. The first time she'd evacuate, and the first time she'd be away from her family at Christmas. Deena prayed for synergy with her and the Tanakas.

In the time they spent on the runway loading luggage, the sky went from silvery gray to gunmetal fierce. Deena squinted up at it, then back toward the tiny, private airport terminal. Kenji emerged. But he wasn't alone.

Hair like her own, wild but darker, framed the face of the figure next to him. Hand in hand they ran, each with a bag in tow.

Deena blinked in disbelief.

"Sorry," Kenji said breathlessly. "These last few days have been crazy and, well, we didn't know if we were gonna evacuate at all."

Four people stood: Daichi, Deena, Grandma Emma, and Tak, three with a look of astonishment.

"Judging by your faces, you all remember Lizzie," Kenji said.

He took her bag and headed for the rear of the plane, where the pilot helped him load. Daichi followed.

"Son, listen to me. I can see how you may have happened upon her and thought bringing her was the right thing to do. But you must understand—"

Kenji turned on his father.

"She's my girlfriend, Dad. It's not up for discussion."

Kenji brushed past him and boarded the plane.

Grandma Emma laughed.

"Well, well, Big Time! Guess he told you."

Daichi shot her a look. "Get on the plane, Emma."

With a simper of satisfaction, she ambled up the ramp. Only once at the top did she stop to look back.

"Hey, Daichi. I reckon I'm 'bout out of granddaughters, but call me when your nephews come to town . . . now that I know what you Tanakas like."

She threw back her head and whooped. Daichi warned her to shut it before they left her on the tarmac. He then followed her onto the plane.

Tak ushered the kids on board, followed by his mother, Hatsumi. Only once boarding himself did he look back, worry marring his features. His face told Deena what he hadn't: that not only did he know about Lizzie, but that he knew about her coming to California, too.

Deena turned to Lizzie.

She's sober.

"How long this time?" Deena asked.

"Four months. Almost five."

Rain began to fall.

"You look happy," Deena said.

"It's Kenji," Lizzie said. "I feel—I don't know. Whole."

Lizzie looked up at the sky, threatening like smoke.

"We should get on the plane," she said. It occurred to Deena that Lizzie had only ridden a plane once, when she and Tak threw her on it for rehab. How harsh had that been, to not go with her? In the end, she supposed, they'd been cursory, robotic in their efforts to help Lizzie. Giving up in spirit before emulating the deed.

"I should've done more," Deena said. "I should've tried harder."

But Lizzie shook her head.

"You're my sister, not my mother. You never could keep that straight." Lizzie smiled lopsidedly. It reminded Deena of Kenji.

Their pilot shouted that it was time to go. Indeed, the sky looked malicious. South and east of them, a Category 4 hurricane barreled in their direction.

"I love you," Lizzie blurted. "So much." She shook her head. "I can say that now. Can you believe it?"

Deena laughed.

"No."

But she swept her in her arms nonetheless.

EPILOGUE

Hurricane Lucille made landfall the following afternoon and exacted close to a quarter of a billion dollars in damage to the Southeast. Neither Deena, nor anyone in her family, suffered more than a few thousand dollars' loss though.

Just after the storm, Keisha was formally charged with murder in the second degree. Faced with the possibility of life imprisonment, she took a plea and was sentenced to twenty years.

In the spring, Kenji tried out for the minor leagues and earned a position as an outfielder for the Jacksonville Suns. When he moved, Lizzie went with him. They returned days later, when Deena gave birth to a son, Noah.

Lizzie sat for her GED just days before the following Christmas and began work on her cosmetology license soon after. It took a year to complete. No sooner had she done so than did the parent team of Jacksonville Suns, the Miami Marlins, offer Kenji a spot on the team.

Kenji and Lizzie opened her shop on Miami Beach. The following year, she and Kenji got married.

Daichi's magnum opus was released over the following summer, strengthened by a series of edits from Deena and a foreword written by her. For reasons unknown to them, it went on to become a *New York Times* Bestseller, giving her an in-field recognition she could've never anticipated otherwise.

On the day that Noah turned one, Deena received a letter in the mail from her mother. Upon opening it, a single sheet of paper slipped out and on it were three words:

We loved you.

Deena stood with the note a long time before tucking it into her purse. She kept it for the better part of a year, pulling it out and looking at it without really knowing what she felt. Never would her father come back, and never could she have a mother again. But it didn't mean she couldn't go on. Over the years, she'd learned that she and Tony had so much in common, more, in fact, than he and his dad. He dealt with anger over what his mother had done and what his father had been and realized in his own time that wholeness required he let go. Slowly, she'd learned the same.

So, with this thought, Deena took her mother's letter out and wrote one of her own, nearly equal in brevity and response. It was all she could manage before sealing the envelope and sending it on its way. But somehow she knew it enough. A single sentence and a single stamp bridged a chasm between one decade and the next.

A single sentence, yet truth no less.

I know.

Truth, no less.

Available From
Delphine Publications

Kisses Don't Lie By Tamika Newhouse
Who Do I Run To Now? By Anna Black
Her Sweetest Revenge By Saundra
And more…

CPSIA information can be obtained at www.ICGtesting.co.n
Printed in the USA
LVOW11s1543100214

373092LV00002B/433/P